# SONG OF THE WHEATFIELDS

# SONG OF THE WHEATFIELDS

*by*

FERENC MÓRA

Translated from the Hungarian by
GEORGE HALASZ

BREWER & WARREN, INC.

NEW YORK : : 1930

# SONG OF THE WHEATFIELDS

# SONG OF THE WHEATFIELDS

MOTHER turned the contents of the pot upon the threshold, and carefully scraped out everything that had stuck to it. Then she grabbed the tin ladle as if it had been a whip.

"Boisi! Boisi!" she called into the darkness.

A faint scratching of feet was heard from the direction of the willow fence and a black ball rolled out of the dark recesses of the night. It stopped near the mulberry tree, and a heavy panting indicated that the black ball answering in the name of Boisi had sunk into deep meditation.

"Come, Boisi dear, come and eat your supper."

Boisi cautiously stole forward. At the threshold he stopped again and looked up. From a wilderness of hair, two little glow-worms shone at Mother.

"The devil take you; don't be so finicky. Do you want me to beg you to eat?" And Mother lifted the ladle high.

No, Boisi had never thought of making Mother beg him. He came from a race that was not unduly proud, but at the same time he knew the law and respected its ceremonies. And it was written that Boisi should accept the invitation only when Mother had served him hard words by way of appetizer and threatened him with the ladle.

At that Boisi would wag his tail and step into the pot with both of his front paws.

"Hey, you, you fresh little pup!" The ladle descended sharply on the puppy's nose. "Can't you see that your supper is on the threshold?"

Boisi knew very well where his supper was dished out for him. Indeed, he was already lapping up the barley and potatoes eagerly, loudly, with his feet a-straddle. But five years of experience had fastened in Boisi a belief that he had no right to the grub unless he first stuck his paws into the pot. For if this were not the law why did Mother hold the pot in front of his nose? Obviously, the pot had been created solely for this purpose.

Which of them was at fault now? The puppy, or the woman? Or the pot? Indeed as Mother lifted it up from the floor to take it inside, she thought for a moment that she saw the light of the candle on the chair flickering through a hole in the bottom, so she took it to the candle and began to examine it, turning it upside down, and this way and that way. But she could find neither hole nor crack.

"I was afraid it had gone out of order too," she said as she set the pot upon the bench. "Well, it has served us for quite a long time. You bought it when I was your bride."

This to Mátyás, who was preoccupied with something that allowed him no consideration for anything else in the world. In short, his pipe stem. He had coaxed it, puffed it, twitched it with goose quills, wooed it with slips of paper, tried to regulate it with wire, but the accursed stem remained obdurate.

Then he tried to breathe life into it, his bushy white eyebrows concentrated into knots like reefs of canvas over his eyes.

Finally came the last resort of despair. He tore a sturdy twig out of the broom and cautiously worked it into the stem. This is a very delicate operation because the twigs of a broom have a nasty way of sticking in the stem so that there is no way of either pushing them in or pulling them out. In that case there is nothing for it but to take out the holiday pipe, and Mátyás had no mind to do that just then. First, because it was in its rightful place, high up on

the cross-beam, and secondly, because there was no sense
in using the machine-turned Sunday pipe when no one
was there to see it. Ah, thank God, the twig was coming
gently through the stem, at last.

"Done," said Mátyás with infinite content. It is a great
joy for a real man to make someone or something obey him,
be it horse, or woman, or pipe stem.

"Yes, done is right," echoed Mother, but her voice was
less satisfied than the old man's. "It's gone to pieces."

Mother simply could not believe that her eyes had played
tricks on her and she turned the pot round and round
until the hole was discovered.

.."Now what are we going to do with it?" She shook her
head. "Etel told me just this morning that the potter's
gypsy ran away. He's been drafted. The gendarmes are
after him now."

"They'll catch him," yawned Mátyás and took his sheepskin coat off the hook.

"Are you going?"

"Yes."

"Out?"

"Out."

He stopped and turned on the threshold:

"If you'd only let 'em, those bandits would steal one's
eyes out."

This was only a figure of speech because it would have
been very difficult to steal Mátyás's eyes out, even if anybody were to try. And then again, where in the world was
there a bandit who would have any use for those little
black porcupine's eyes hidden beneath huge tufts of white
hair? No. The bandits in question threatened Mátyás's estate on another point: they were stealing his water. From
which it follows that most of the bandits belonged to the
skirt-wearing sex, the female branch of humankind.

Women became quite used to Mátyás's well during the

war. To be accurate, the well had always been famous, even
before the war, for it gave water so excellent that one
wanted to drink more and more of it insatiably, which
was indeed a rarity in the village. There were plenty of
wells, but precious little water fit to drink. There were
wells everywhere, it was not even necessary to dig very
deep for them. That was just the trouble; even the pits
where potatoes were stored for the winter turned easily
into wells. The water in the bowels of the earth ran high;
the fourth or, at the most, the fifth spade-throw brought it
out. But this water was no good for man or beast; it was
either nauseatingly sweet or brackish; so bitter that not
even a horse wanted to drink it, if it was a thoroughbred
and knew what it wanted. It was good only for cooking
and lately not even for that. It was so muddy that the soup
got full of grit and cracked between your teeth. Since the
men had gone to war, there was nobody to clean the wells
and the water in all of them had become pulpy. The
women, of course, did most of the men's chores; they
plowed, sowed, hoed, and harvested; they attended to the
cabbages, even killed the pigs, but none of them ever tried
to clean wells. Maybe they were afraid of frogs, or maybe
of something else; God alone knows of what. Once a
young woman tried it and she was taken to jail for it.
True, she cleaned out the well all right, taking all the
rusty pots and broken pans out of it, but then she forgot
a new-born infant in it that had not been in the well before.

So that was why the women had grown used to Mátyás's well. The water in it was always as clear as crystal
and, even during the dog days, as cold as ice. They cranked
the handle all day long and bestowed profound thanks
upon Mátyás for every bucket of water.

"God pay you for it! I hope He will give it back to you
a thousand fold!"

God must have listened very attentively to all this for He did give Mátyás a thousand times as much for every bucketful. But He committed the mistake of giving it back all in one lot and that in the Spring, so that the little marshy lakes in the hollow of the land crept into the fields, and there were times when Mátyás's little property only showed in particles. Then Mátyás resolved that he would stop letting the Heavenly Administration attend to the payments. Whoever took a bucketful would pay for it herself, and at once, too: twenty *korona* for every bucket. That was no money for one who needed it, and whoever did not like the idea of paying could go down to the lake. There he might drink as much as he wanted to; with a couple of tadpoles to boot, if he was lucky.

Well, the folks knew what was what; they said nothing against Mátyás's law. Everybody can do as he pleases and Mátyás would be crazy to give away something for nothing if he could get money for it. But equally crazy would be all those who would pay twenty *korona* for something they could get for nothing.

Mátyás based his law on the theory of "large turnover, small profit," and he figured that during the Summer alone the well could bring in enough money to last. But greater politicians than Mátyás have been known to fail in their calculations. The village folk avoided Mátyás's farm during the day like the devil frankincense, but, at night, they drew every drop out of the well so that when Mother went out in the morning, the first bucket came up full of mud.

Consequently Mátyás, who was irritated not only by the lost profit but also by the damage actually suffered, decided that he would turn well-guard for the night. He spread out his coat on the grass, leaned his head against the rim, laid a staff next to him on the ground, and, quietly smoking his pipe, waited for the water-thieves.

"Well, Boisi, we will chew a little hair off their scalps,

eh? But keep your ears open," he encouraged the pup who confidently curled up at his feet.

The pup's demeanor was irreproachable. Stretching out his chin on the ground, he surrendered himself wholly to his job. But his master, lost in the contemplation of deep and weighty worries, would forget every now and then why he was there.

For Mátyás had sold the new wheat to the Jew that very morning and it occurred to him now that the Jew had most probably cheated him—what with these new-fangled bank-notes. Hell and damnation upon all inventions of new kinds of money! Of course, he told the Jew that he would accept only old money, but the Jew laughed in his face. Why, the old money was no longer good, and, from next week on those who still had it would be punished. Very well, but what about those who had silver *korona*? Great heavens, that was even worse! The silver would not only be taken from them, they would be jailed, too. Don't you know, the Jew asked, that all metals have been requisitioned in the city? Yes, yes, but not silver! Why not, of course, silver too, silver most of all, that's just what they need now for ammunitions, because the Italians have a new invention; ordinary steel bullets don't harm them at all, only silver bullets. No, he has never heard of that, one hears so very little on the farm, one may as well be deaf. Tse, tse, tse. Well, what's the matter with you now? Oh, nothing much, but I also have a few, oh, about one or two, silver *korona* in the bag. How many? Oh, something like three hundred or so. I'll tell you something, said the Jew now, I'll do you the favor of exchanging them all, I go quite often to Vienna, I might, I say, I *might* get rid of them there. Yes, and how much would you give me for them? Said the Jew, their full worth and value, three hundred *korona*. No, answered Mátyás, don't make fun of me, I'd rather take them to the county-seat and hand them in at headquarters. Then the Jew went up to four hundred, then even higher, finally the Jew offered him ten thousand. Mátyás took that.

And now Mátyás, as he lay on the ground, began, mentally to sort out the banknotes the Jew had given him. He put them in separate piles according to their color and size. But just when he had finished with the first pile, the dog yelped and Mátyás grabbed the rod at his side.

"Catch 'im, Boisi!"

There was nothing the matter with the puppy now either. Off he went like a shot, gave an angry grunt on his way, and leaped through the fence to the line where his authority ended. This authority was strictly limited to Mátyás's land; across the fence, in the neighbor's garden, the imperium belonged to another pup. Many a thing comes to pass in this world, sometimes a Mátyás plows away a slice from another Mátyás's field, sometimes a country plows away the frontiers of another country, but no such deliberate and flagrant border-incidents ever occur in canine society. It does occur that, giving way to certain internal emotions, even the Boisis cross the line, but that is another story. That is mere love-life in nature, an individual reaction, not the misuse of official authority and power.

The pup, therefore, returned, running much slower now than when he had rushed out to the field of action, but panting exaggeratedly.

"Master," his panting was supposed to mean, "I did everything in my power in the interests of the moral order of the world, the fault must lie somewhere else."

The Charles' Wain had already turned its shaft to the earth when Mátyás at last realized what was the matter. One cannot catch sparrows with drums; neither can one catch young women bent on stealing water with barking and yelling.

Mátyás, realizing all this, kicked his fellow-guard in the side:

"Well, Boisi, you may as well go to hell!"

He even took the bell off the pup's neck, to show that his official service was over for the day. Upon which Boisi stretched himself, shook off the worries connected with his job, and as a private individual, devoted himself to things which were nobody's business.

Mátyás turned on his side and covered himself with his coat. The night was warm, but old bones need care, for the marrow in them is old too, and the morning dew touches it easily. He even pulled the wide collar of the coat over his head, so that neither the crowing of roosters nor any of the other noises of the night should disturb him in his counting up of the banknotes. This time he figured his losses to perfection. The Jew had cheated him with three five-thousand *korona* and twelve one-hundred *korona* notes. Mátyás grew a little angry with the Jew and with the banknote printer, and with everybody whose business it was to fleece the poor farmer. Fortunately, the poor farmer was not without brains either, and Mátyás felt rather satisfied when he remembered that there had been twelve old twenty-five *krajcar* coins among the three-hundred silver *korona,* and that the Jew had not noticed that there had been nine hundred-weights of old, mouldy grain, buried since last year, ever since the requisitioners had been around, mixed up in the sixty-five hundred-weights of new wheat he had bought.

The window in the little house was lighted up three times during the time Mátyás was completing his balance sheet. Most probably Etel, his daughter-in-law, had troubles with the little child laid up with a sore throat. Well, well, Etel did whatever she wanted; she tilled her own land, and speculated with her money the way she pleased; nevertheless, Mátyás decided to tell her the very next morning that she had better dip her own candles; there was no sense in her showing off like city-folks, poor people didn't use kerosene nowadays, pretty soon it was going to be more expensive than brandy.

With this thought, Mátyás fell asleep, and woke only when someone stepped on his hand.

"Hey!" he came to with a start and blindly thrust out his hand. He caught something that felt like a piece of garment. But it seemed to him that it was pants and not a skirt.

"I've got you, you gallowsbird!" mumbled Mátyás, getting on his legs but never for a second relinquishing his hold on the thief.

But the thief leaped forward so that Mátyás fell on his nose, and the culprit escaped toward the shed.

"Stop, hey, stop! I won't harm you!" Mátyás yelled after him.

The window in the little house was lighted up again and now Mátyás recognized the canvas-clothed man as he stood in the door of the shed. It was the Russian from the neighboring farm, Piros's prisoner-of-war.

"Come here, Russky, come here, I won't eat you," said Mátyás, lighting a match and holding it up to his face so that the Russian could see the kind intentions in his eyes.

But the man in the canvas uniform did not move from the shed. All he did was to lift his hand to his cap.

Now it occurred to Mátyás that a man from a foreign country might not understand what he said. That, however, was nothing to worry about; Mátyás spoke a foreign tongue also.

"*Komm her,* Russky, drink water. I'll give you leave," he said in a friendly voice and shook the chain of the bucket.

The Russian was at the well in two leaps and lifted the bucket to his mouth with one hand.

"Drink as much as you want to," Mátyás encouraged him, and while he lighted his pipe—no mean job, in the rising breeze—he examined the Russian. He had seen him quite often since the beginning of Summer, but he had never had time enough to look him over thoroughly.

He was a handsome enough man, big, well-built and muscular, with broad burly shoulders. Very much like his own soldier-boy, Rokus. But of course, Rokus was more of a man because he was brown. This fellow here had a head like a piece of pot-cheese, so pale he was. But who could tell what the boy looked like now. God alone knew, and perhaps He was not sure. The black bull must have run through him too, during all these four years. Perhaps he was drinking now from some Russian well, lifting the bucket to his mouth with one hand. God grant it be so.

"No *voda* in here," said the Russian, pulling his head out of the bucket.

"There's plenty in the well," Mátyás suggested, pointing at it with the stem of his pipe.

The Russian grabbed the sweep with both hands but let go of it at once with a groan. The swinging bucket hit Mátyás in the chest.

"Hey, you!" Mátyás snarled. "Aren't there any wells in your country?"

"Arm hurts," the Russian explained humbly. "*Kosta* grown together bad. *Kosta*—that's Russian. Bone!"

"So you've missed the word only," said Mátyás in a pacified voice and pushed his guest aside. "Wait a minute, I'll draw water for you."

According to custom, he spilled the water from the first bucket into the trough. But as soon as the Russian heard the splashing he leaped at it.

"Oh, much good *voda*," and he began to lap up the water.

Mátyás could hardly pull him away from the trough.

"You're a man yourself, too, after all, even though you're a Russian. Calm yourself a while. Don't lap up that stale water, horses drink from there."

The Russian drank a bucket and a half of water and stopped only when Mátyás began to scold him.

"That'll be enough for today, Russky. Take a rest now."

The Russian leaned against the well.

"Thank you, mister. Hungarians good men. Russians good men also."

"Why, yes," Mátyás remarked a little superciliously.

The Russian pulled out some paper from his pocket, fussed with it for a second or two, then spoke up:

"Here you are, mister. Cigarette."

"I don't use that stuff. Smoke it yourself, Russky, if you like it."

The Russian lighted it. He had an automatic lighter made out of a cartridge. Mátyás nearly lost his eye looking at it.

"That's handsome! Where did you get it?"

"Made it."

"Who made it? Yourself?"

"Me. Many. For mister officers also."

"A handy man you are, Russky. What's your business at home?"

"No business. My father is peasant. Me peasant also."

"What's your name, Russky?"

The Russian told him: Pavel Antonovitch Spiridinov.

"Well, sit down, Spirituto."

Spirituto sat down. For a while, both kept silent. Then a faint muffled sound was heard from the direction of the mulberry tree.

"The devil take that red tomcat, he's always around," grunted Mátyás and took aim at the invisible tramp with a clump of earth. "How big is your land, Spirituto?"

"Much big land. Hundred and fifty acres."

"Sand?"

"No! Black soil. Like grease."

"Wheat?"

"Half wheat, half corn."

It's the same in Russia as it is here, thought Mátyás. But: a hundred and fifty acres! His land was twelve in a wet year, and nine in a dry one.

"What's the price of the wheat over there?"

Spirituto could not answer that question. All he knew was that everything was very dear. And anyway, what was the good of having so much land and nobody to till it, to sow, to reap? They had taken away the horses, and the men. Two of his brothers had been killed in the war, everything was going to the dogs, his father was an old man, he might even have died since he was home.

Mátyás had never before thought of such things and now the discovery that the world was the same everywhere surprised him greatly. He asked how old Spirituto senior was? The Russky counted it on his fingers: sixty-three.

"He has white moustache, like you, mister."

"That's possible," Mátyás answered, and tried to figure out whether he was sixty-two or sixty-three.

Spirituto sighed, looked up at the slowly paling sky, and was about to attack the bucket once more.

But Mátyás took him by the arm.

"Come on, *son,* light that fancy match of yours."

And Mátyás sauntered over to the barn with the Russky, offered him a seat on a bench, and picked up a bottle.

"This is going to make you warmer than the water," he said, and began to draw wine from a keg. "Drink it, Spirituto."

Mátyás's wine was horribly bad. It was of the kind that people called "three men's wine," because two men had to hold the one who was offered a drink lest he run away. On the other hand, Mátyás was not in the habit of inviting anybody to drink of his wine. Indeed, he might not have kept any had it not been for the secret hope that Rokus might come home one day.

Spirituto gulped it down with a slight shudder and promised Mátyás that if he should ever find himself in his country he would be treated to wine as fine as Christ's blood.

"I doubt that," the old man shook his head, "I don't think I'll ever be a prisoner of war in my remaining years."

The Russky laughed a bit merrier now that he had tasted the wine. He assured Mátyás that he had not meant it that way. Not as a prisoner, of course not, but as a guest. He had been told down at the war-prisoners' office that the war would soon be over; there was a revolution at home, the Czar had been killed.

"What the devil!" Mátyás said, amazed. "Now what do you know about that! So they have killed him. They should have done it before—er—Spirituto."

By the time they left the barn it was already light. Pigeons were cooing on the roof and Csillag and Szikra in the stable neighed; they smelled men around.

"How many horses have you, Spirituto?"

"Oh, seventy."

He showed the number on his fingers.

Mátyás's face expressed honest astonishment.

"And cows?"

"Big cows forty-two, little cows many hundred. I don't know name in Hungarian. I don't see little cow here on farms."

"Little cows? You mean calves, don't you? Eh? Moo-oo-oo."

"No," the Russky said shaking his head. "Mek-mek-mek."

"Oh, I know: goats."

"Yes, goats," the Russian said happily. "Hundred, two hundred, many hundred."

Mátyás became a little low-hearted now.

No, these Russians were not perfect men after all. A low kind they were. If he had a hundred acres he wouldn't ugly his land with goats.

But he accompanied Spirituto to the fence just the same and shook hands with him in a friendly manner when they parted. He had already walked back a few steps when suddenly something occurred to him. He stopped and yelled after the Russian:

"Hey, my regards to Piros."

He did not say this out of mockery but because it behooved him to do so. After all, Piros was his kin by marriage.

## II

IN the resplendent glory of the morning of the Nativity of the Blessed Virgin the swallows chattered merrily under the eaves. The young birds were being reviewed by the older ones to see whether they were fit to undertake the long journey southward. There was one chicken on the ground that had been found too weak for the trip. His mother was jumping about him wailing loudly. She smoothed down his ruffled feathers with her wing, and then suddenly hopped over to a distinguished old swallow. (He must have been at least a surgeon-general among swallow for he hopped about very angrily and had a bald spot on the top of his head.)

"Has anybody ever seen a stronger chick from a late hatch?" she cried.

"Chivitt-chuvitt! Chivitt-chuvitt!" chirruped the champions of various opinions in the great melée.

"The swallows are going," Etel said glancing up as she combed her daughter's hair.

For a second, she stood there gazing at the noisy birds, then turned again to the child who was tickling the cat with her apron string as it lay purring at her feet.

"Don't you hear what I say? Do you think I waste my breath for nothing?" she chided her.

And Etel warned Marika for the third time that unless she held her head straight, she would bring out the big sheep-shears and cut off her hair to the scalp, like a gyspy girl and a little bit of her head too.

Nevertheless, Marika did not run away in a fright. If

a poor man's child took seriously all such threats as:
"I'll stick a knife into you," or "I'll run you through with
the big pitchfork," or "I'll clip your nose with a pair of
pincers," or "I'll split your head with an axe," or, finally,
"I'll push you into the hot oven on a bread-baking shovel,"
then the poor man's child would do nothing from morning
to night but run around cackling like a chased hen. But
behind Marika's narrow back there was not only an angry
mother but also four long years; consequently Marika, bas-
ing her attitude on factual experience, stood her ground,
as solidly as the situation required. Besides Marika knew
full well that it would be rather difficult to get hold of
the sheep-shears because they had happened to fall into
the lake yesterday when she had been cutting parasols for
herself out of mullein leaves.

And so, as the sole owner of this secret, Marika felt herself justified in shaking her head once more, just for spite.

Whereupon her mother flew into a rage. She gathered
the child's strong, hard, black hair in her fist and pulled
it towards her.

"You frog, you! From whom did you get your restless
blood?"

But the moment she said it, she let go of the hair and,
with puckered lips, breathed upon the tender white skin
which had turned pink from the teeth of the comb.

The blue eyes became tender for a moment as the mother
bent her fair head over her child's darker one. Was it because the mother felt a holiday, or suddenly the spirit
of the feast, because the child could not notice it, as she
stood merely with her back to her mother:

"You're just like your father," she said, a smile playing
about the corner of her mouth as she answered her own
question.

Yet the question was purely rhetorical. It was one of
those the Reverend liked to ask, with much righteous

wrath in his voice, in his Sunday sermons: "Where are you now, Caiaphas?" It was lucky that Caiaphas never told him where he was. Of course, lucky not for him but for the Reverend. Because if Caiaphas had one day stepped down from the garret—he must have been up there, since every time the priest put the question to him he looked up there—the Reverend could not even have offered him a seat. When the German soldiers passed through the village last Winter they burned up everything, even the pews and benches of the church. They only spent one night there, the Riff-raff, yet how much roguery they did during that short time! They broke in the doors on women in about ten houses; in many places they let the wine run out of the casks and even knocked off the head of the statue of the Blessed Virgin Mary which stood in front of the parish house. Although some people claimed that the Germans were Christians too, the Reverend yelled at them from his window that they were worse than the Tartars of Crimea. This alone would not have caused any trouble because the Germans did not understand it, but the Reverend, not satisfied with curses, picked up his rifle with which he used to frighten away birds and aimed it at the Germans. This threw everything topsy-turvy; the German general-in-chief wanted to shoot the Reverend, and although he relented later—realizing no doubt that it would not be nice to shoot an old man—things turned from bad to worse. For the Germans then decided to burn down the farms. The Reverend had to go down on his knees; had to beg them, crawling in the dust, not to make so many innocent people unhappy. Thereupon the Germans became milder, they even gave some army bread to the poor. It might still be up in the church garret, for nobody had wanted it, and now they didn't know what to do with it. They could not feed it to the animals, because after all it was Christ's body, although nothing was baked into it but ground oat-stalks.

Ever since that time the Reverend was not what he used to be. In former days, he liked to talk to the women after mass, he calmed them and consoled them, saying that sooner or later their men would come home and that they were to pursue decent lives. He would draw maps in the sand, and show them where Siberia was, and Serbia, and God knows what else. But, this past year or so, he had grown grim and morose; he did not even return greetings. In his sermons, he no longer chastised Caiaphas but Holophernes and all sorts of other German kings from the Old Testament, people not very popular hereabouts, at least Etel had never yet heard of them. It was possible though, that they were nothing but a kind of proverbs, like the daughters of Jezebel, whom the Reverend had mentioned on the church-fair, pounding loudly the pulpit with his fists.

"Where are you, you God-forsaken Delilahs, you impertinent wives of Potiphar, you dishonest daughters of Jezebel? I ask you, do you know of a curtain in the whole wide world which the Lord's eyes cannot pierce?"

That was a very moving sermon, indeed, the old women all nodded assent with their shaky old heads; they said, "so it is, so it is," and shot murderous glances toward the war-widows—but the Delilahs, the wives of Potiphar, and the daughters of Jezebel did not bat an eyelid. Only the tips of their red slippers glistened in the sunshine, as if saying: "Look at the old man, my, how excited he is! And they say he is a holy man!"

Etel fell to wondering, while unsnarling the twisted strands of her daughter's stubborn hair, just what made her remember these old things? So vivid were her recollections that she seemed to hear the shuffle of the red slippers, and the Reverend's voice cackling in her ears. Why of course, it was because she had mentioned that restless blood.

She threw a glance across her shoulder back at the window and tossed her head, like a race-horse. She was not afraid, God could look through her window any time He pleased. More than four years had passed since that red slip of paper had been brought to Rokus, summoning him away at once; he could not even cut down all the alfalfa. She had been in bed, for all that had happened barely five days after the birth of this little brat here—and ever since that day, the curtain had never been down in her window, except once or twice, and then only on account of the flies. On the other hand, she did not often open the window either, except when the room was being white-washed, and only once this year, on Palm Sunday, when she had put out the three twigs of consecrated pussywillow. One, the smallest, for Marika, one for herself and the long-est for Rokus.

Then it happened that one of the war grass-widows, that brazen Modol Boca, laughed in her face:

"What's the good of putting out pussies for him, Etel?"

"For whom?" Etel asked, surprised.

"Why, for your Rokus, of course! As if you wouldn't know it yourself! Don't you know that he is warming a Russian woman's bed by now, or maybe more than one? Why do you guard his place so carefully when you are young and pretty and could live your own life? If I were you I would have asked for a Russky from the prison camp a long time ago! And I'd let him watch me so that nobody stole me! Am I right, girls?"

The women giggled. Modol certainly had a sharp tongue in her head.

"The devil needs them, not I!" Etel shrugged her shoul-ders. "I have other things to tend to than to watch a pris-oner that he shouldn't escape."

"Make him lie inside, you goose!"

The women laughed so loudly that every time Etel thought of it her face turned as red as if beaten with nettle. Not that Etel came from a family high up in the world or had been taught by the Sisters just when to blush! Etel was an orphan, somehow or other related to the Mátyáses, and they brought her up according to the ancient laws of peasant education. Etel's eyes were opened just as soon as those of other chickens. Indeed, as far as such things were concerned, she never felt the lack of a parental home. She saw what the other children saw, she heard what the other children heard, and she played what the other children played. She herded flocks of geese, learned how to throw and to mould pots, did various chores around the farm, weeded, gleaned, and bound sheaves. During harvest time, she often slept at the foot of stacks. No, Etel was not wholly ignorant of the ways of the world when the simple engagement took place. There was really no need of an elaborate ceremony; after all, the groom and the bride had been living under the same roof ever since their childhood. All Mátyás did was, one day during Advent, while Etel was washing, to slap her where she was roundest:

"I guess, girl, you are big enough now to stand the Blessed Mother's bed!"

Etel did not blush nor become angry, but, rising and holding her head high, faced Mátyás and laughed back at him:

"I suppose so myself."

"Shall we hold the wedding on Twelfthnight? What d'ye say?"

"If it suits Rokus!"

Etel never even imagined that she could be anybody's but Rokus's wife. True, no one else ever approached her with such intentions. Everybody knew and everybody agreed that Mátyás was bringing up Etel as his daughter-in-law. The orphan's little inheritance, five acres of land, all wheatfields, lay between Mátyás's fields like a wedge in a hole, and this alone, even if there had been no other reasons, was sufficient proof to the neighbors that the Almighty had created the two youngsters for each other. But there were many other reasons too. She was blond as the day and he was black as night, and both of them strong and husky. No one, of course, ever asked them whether they loved each other, for such talk was absurd between two people about to enter holy matrimony. It is another thing with boys and girls who play around beneath the pear trees, or at the foot of haystacks, in Summer; yes, then it is necessary, it goes with youth, as a sword does with a Hussar. But when two join hands for a lifetime, the only person who asks them about love is the priest and even he only at the altar.

Gyurka Messzi, who was such a wise old watchman that if he had been born in the city, he would have certainly become a lawyer, said such things about love at the wedding that the devil himself would have laughed at them. Etel laughed too, as she did often afterwards. For she was no more bashful nor more of a hypocrite than any other female. Yet, and God only knows how this happens, there are cats who can walk across the courtyard after the biggest rain without dirtying even the tips of their claws, and then there are others who, no matter how much they clean themselves, always look as if they had slept in ashes. It's just how they are born—whether cats, or women.

Yes, Etel heard a lot, and knew much, and she saw with her own eyes how the war had made fools of the men, but she would never have thought that her man could also lose his head. Until they were locked into the fort of Przemysl, he had been sending letters regularly to his father and mother, and never left out of the field postal card the sentence: "and furthermore I send kisses and greetings to Etel and remain faithful to her and furthermore I send kisses to my child." Then, all of a sudden, the little pink postal cards stopped coming; there were no more for her, or for Piros, either, or for Modol, and none for the entire countryside, because all the men had been taken prisoners. There was plenty of confused, helter-skelter talk going the rounds those days, people did not know what a prisoner of war was, they went by the fairy tales and ancient legends. There was an old woman, for instance, who began to cry: "Woe to the soldier but more woe to the prisoner, because he will be hired out to Tartar khans, and they will put a yoke on his neck, and use him in the fields, like oxen, and in the winter they will slaughter him, and eat him up." (Gyurka Messzi confirmed this; he said that when he had been taken a prisoner at Sadowa, in '66, he had had to plow a big tract of land, at least ten acres, all for millet. And just about when the first snow had fallen, they had taken him to the slaughter house, and God knows what would have happened to him, for the knives had already been honed, if peace hadn't been signed right then.) For a while, the village lived under a spell of terror, but then the wiser ones enlightened the women that the prisoner was very well off, he did not have to duck bullets any more, all he had to do was to eat and to drink and to smoke his pipe, until the time came to go home, and even then it would be the Emperor's business to pay for his board and lodging. It was silly to cry, indeed, they should be happy about it, because the prisoner was in a better place than the soldiers, and the more were taken prisoner the sooner the war would end.

Etel gave thanks to God that Rokus was so well taken care of, but she found it rather queer that he never as much as notified his family how life treated him, despite the fact that soon the authorities established mail with the prisoners in Russia. True there was not much to read in the first cards which arrived from Russia, it was very difficult to decipher the pencilled messages, they were smeared and blotched by the long journey. And the incredibly long and impossible Russian names baffled them. But, as time went by, they learned to pronounce the Russian cities, for more and more Russian prisoners came to work on the farms, and slowly the grass-widows grew accustomed to the foreign idiom.

"I need a translator," thus argued Piros, to hide her sin, when she took the big Russian into her house. "At least I have somebody who can write letters to Ferenc."

"It's your business, your worry—not mine," Etel returned curtly and shrugged her shoulders. And she went on harvesting, hoeing, mowing, cutting reed, going to the market; she did everything that Rokus had used to do, and her money in the savings bank grew from day to day. It was a year or so after the catastrophe of Przemysl that Piros came over to the Mátyáses one morning and said that she had news about Rokus. Here's the letter, Ferenc wrote it, and the Russky said that there was a name like Rokus in it, and that could be none other than Etel's husband.

Mátyás fished out his spectacles from behind the big looking-glass but he was so excited that he let them drop half a dozen times before he could put them on.

"That's him, so help me God," and his face brightened up. "He writes here, 'Neighbor Rokus is also here in this city and he's living'—— there is something else after this but my old eyes can't see it."

Etel was not very well versed in the sciences yet it was she who fared best with the letter. True, she read it with the eyes of a wife; on the other hand, Ferenc wrote as clear and legible letters as a schoolboy.

"'Living high,' that's what it says. 'Neighbor Rokus is also here in this city and he's living high.'"

"Blessed be the Lord," Mátyás said, rubbing his hands together while Mother rushed to the picture of the Radna

Virgin and made the sign of the cross.

Only Etel remained silent and she gazed at the letter in her hands, lost in thoughts. Living high—living high— how can a prisoner of war live high?

"Well, I've got to hurry home now, the Russky will soon be back from cutting beets, and he will be cold, I'm sure. I'll just have enough time to fix up a little hot, spiced wine for him," Piros said, and tied her shawl round her waist.

"So that is the way the prisoners live high?" Etel thought, looking after Piros, but said nothing.

Well, they would soon find it out. Now Rokus too would write, surely. But he did not write. Moreover Ferenc did not answer either, when they asked him for Rokus's address.

Then, all of a sudden, the gossip went around the farms that Etel's husband was living with a Tartar woman, an innkeeper, and had grown a big belly. It was possible that the Tartar khans ate up their prisoners, but the female khans apparently liked to keep them on roast chicken and cake. After all, that was the way of the world; women were more kindhearted everywhere.

Etel was ashamed to talk about this at home, but she spared no effort to hunt down the father of the gossip. She wanted to see the letter, she wouldn't believe anybody but her own two eyes. But no one could show her the letter. A soldier home on leave had told it first, but he had gone back to the front already. What was the number of his field post-office? She wanted to write to him. This and this. But it was no sense in writing him. He had also heard it somewhere. And why make so much fuss about it? There was a war going on, and such things did happen in war time. Etel went home a bit calmer. Gossip, hearsay. What donkeys some people are! When they see one rotten plum they think all plums are rotten.

She grew so much calmer that she even brought it up at home. The next time they were feeding the geese, she told the story to Mother. What do you say, Mother, how the world has changed!

Mother silently went on stirring the maize in the deep wooden dish.

"God knows, my child. It's possible that over there everything is the same as it is here. You can see it for yourself, just look at that Piros woman; she's been feeding that Russky of hers for almost two years now."

To Etel it seemed that the world had suddenly turned upside down.

"What do you know, Mother? Tell me!"

The old woman looked at her in surprise.

"What should I know, my child? But, you see, Rokus, too, is only Adam's son."

Etel squeezed the neck of the goose she was holding in her hands so tight and so fast that the poor bird did not even have time to breathe its last. Etel might even have burst into tears had not her father-in-law done something he had never done before in all his life. He was cutting tobacco on the threshold in his accustomed manner slowly and silently, because that was the way to do it. But as soon as he heard the old woman's last words, he leaped to his feet and lifting the big knife, pointed it at Mother's breast.

"Roza, you are going to die now!"

Etel screamed, but the old woman just stared at him, open-mouthed; she could not even shriek. Had he gone mad? In the fourth year of the war such things did happen, although mostly on the front. His eyes shone, like those of a mad dog, and his lips trembled.

"So you have confessed it at last, you old witch. So he *is* Adam's son! Roza, I'd have never thought that of you! If you'd only tell me which Adam is his father, that I should know whom to kill——!"

Whereupon they all broke into laughter, because the women saw at once that old Mátyás had just played a joke on them.

"And I thought the devil had gone into you," stammered Mother, wiping her eyes. "Lord, but you've frightened me, I can't even sigh."

Mátyás went out into the yard to separate the tobacco from the splinters that had gotten mixed up with it. He turned back for a second only.

"If a man couldn't even sigh, he might as well die," he said quietly.

"Have you ever seen the like of this?" Mother asked Etel.

No, never, Etel shook her head. She could not understand the old man. To be sure, he had not been in good humor for quite some time now, but ever since this morning, ever since he had come back from the store, he had not uttered one single syllable.

Several weeks passed before they learned that Mátyás's heart very nearly broke when he played about with the big knife, and it was a wonder that he did not shed any blood. Because Mátyás had met a soldier in the store, home on leave, who had been a prisoner of war in Russia.

"Say," said the soldier, "I see that your family has also picked up some fancy new notions."

"What do you mean?" Mátyás asked, casually, not interested in the soldier at all.

"What I mean is—since when do you bury without a priest?"

"There never was any point in burying the priest as well," Mátyás returned the jest, but, suspecting something bad, he held on to the counter.

"That's true," the soldier said, lazily, "but I don't think that your Rokus got even as much as a grave."

"What!" The pipe fell out of Mátyás's mouth but he caught it in midair.

"But that's the way it must have happened," the soldier went on, elaborating the details after these tender preliminaries. He had heard that Rokus and four others had escaped from a place called Bourmania, three of them had been immediately shot to death by the Russian guards; the two others had been lost in the forest, the poor fellows, where charcoal burners had later found their frozen bodies, and reported it to the authorities.

"Of course, I can't say all this for sure," the soldier said turning his palms inside out, as one who wants to express doubt, "but these are the circumstances I heard."

And that was why Mátyás ran amuck with the knife, in the first tormenting wrath of his paternal sorrow. But he managed to control himself, and when a couple of weeks later the gossip reached the women, too, Mátyás immediately denied it.

"He must have been drunk, the tramp. I heard it too and I asked the Reverend about it. It couldn't be true, he said, especially not if the soldier talked about the Boers. You see, the Boers live in Africa, he showed me their country on the map; Rokus could not have possibly got there. And then, there is no Boer war now; Rokus was a baby in arms when the Boers had their world war, I can remember it very well myself."

And that was the end of it. From that day on, they heard neither gossip nor news of Rokus. Mátyás went to the city several times, went from office to office, from counsellor to lawyer, but nothing came of it except that, one day, on the macadam road, Mátyás's horses ran wild when an automobile whizzed by, and they turned the wagon into the ditch. Mátyás broke his arm, and since trouble never comes alone, one of the horses broke its right front leg, and the harness broke, too.

As time went by, they gradually stopped talking about Rokus. There were times though, especially when requisitioners came to the village, when Etel suddenly pictured the big, strong man before her in her mind's eye. She remembered an incident when, one day, before she had become his wife, he grew so angry with a tax-collector who had insulted his father that—this happened in the Fall—he threw him into the big wine press.

"If only Rokus were here now!" she once said, quite involuntarily, when one of the requisitioners, a young whipper-snapper, made Mátyás squat and act as a stoop as he climbed up to the garret to look for maize.

Mátyás, on the other hand, mentioned the boy only when he sold something at a great profit in the city. Then, to celebrate the event, he came home a bit illuminated. At such times he stepped to the corner of the house, where one could look away into the far distance, and, with his pipe between his teeth, he explained to the women:

"You see, all this was once one estate: my land, and Etel's, and even Ferenc's, and what's beyond that. When I was a child I often heard that all this once belonged to the grandfather of my great-great-grandfather. Now, if God won't help Ferenc home, it seems to me Piros will squander away everything, even her land. I say to you, the time will come yet when all these lands will again belong to only one person. Remember, Etel, what I say now, Rokus will be a fortunate man one day——"

Then Mother began to cry and asked Mátyás why he liked to break her heart.

Time passed, and Mother's heart was broken less and less frequently. Just the other day, for instance, Mátyás was looking for something in the little shed behind Etel's house, and when he came out, he had Rokus's hat on his head. His withered little head was completely lost in it, together with the ears, but on the whole, the hat seemed to be rather new.

"It's good and comfortable," Mátyás said, and proudly he walked off with it to church.

Mother, no use denying it, looked at him a bit sadly, but all she said was that he might have waited a little while longer.

"Well, I might have if I could have," confessed Mátyás. "But Rokus will find it just the same, if he comes home, and I haven't got a Sunday hat now. The government takes away your son from you, but won't give you a new Sunday hat in his stead."

In this regard, Etel agreed with Mátyás. They could not very well have defined just what government was, but they knew that the requisitioners were government, and that the revenue agents were government, and the tax-collectors were government; in short, government was everything to whom one had to give money for nothing. And then there was, over and above all these governments, a government that took away the husbands from their wives, and the fathers from their children, and carried them away, no one knew why, no one knew whither.

"Yes, the government is responsible for everything," Etel said, and a shadow settled on her clear brow. With a nervous gesture, she grabbed the red ribbon she was holding between her teeth and began to wind it in the child's hair.

But with this she did not get far, for Boisi suddenly began to yelp so angrily at somebody or something behind the currant bushes that it was clear some new kind of doom was impending. The weight at the end of the rope to which the pup was tied banged loudly against the hard-trodden clay round the dog's house as Boisi leaped around; then, all of a sudden, the pup himself landed on the ground with a thud, and began to whine bitterly. This made Etel realize in which of its many forms the government was favoring them this time.

"The constable! Abel! Run along, my child, and tell your grand-daddy not to stay at home, tell him to go out to the corn-field."

For, after all, one could never tell what the constable wanted, and it was best at such times that no man should be around the house.

"Why, what brings you here, Abel?" Etel asked, and the red ribbon in her hands almost turned white of fright. Only yesterday she had plastered up the pit where they had hidden a little of the new grain, and it occurred to her that some busybody, or jealous neighbor, might have discovered her manipulations and denounced her.

"You may well ask!" Abel was twisting his black moustache. "Good morning, Etel. Am I going to get a nice kiss if I bring you something good?"

"Sure," Etel answered, slowly recovering herself. "Two, even, but little ones."

"That's fine! Well, here are both of my cheeks," and he pushed his face near hers.

"I don't like to buy cats in a bag," Etel chased the twisted moustache away, quite good-humoredly. She would not have been a woman had she not sat down right on top of the pit hiding the grain. "Tell me now, what's in your pocket."

"Why, this, look!" the constable answered, pulling forth a blue sheet of paper. "They have found your man. I mean, Rokus."

"Found?" breathed Etel, and she held fast with both hands to the brim of the pit-cover.

"Yes. That is to say, they have found out that he cannot be found. He is lost. Disappeared. That's what the army reports here officially, on paper."

It was as if a swallow had flown by, fast as lightning, before her eyes, back and forth, twice, only to stop just in front of her, in midair. But by that time, it was no longer a swallow, but just a black dot.

Abel pinched her cheek. He liked her fair face very much. There was no other like it in the whole country. And now it had turned especially pale.

"Well, what did I say, young woman? Isn't it good news, eh? Now you can get married before Lent. And, confidentially, I know of someone who might give you a little consolation until then!"

He dropped his hand on Etel's shoulder and began slowly to move it downward. Etel knew this gesture well, from the days when she had been a young girl. "I just want to see, little girl, whether you've been stung by a bee!" The white face turned as red as the ribbon in her hands and her strong five fingers cracked loudly on the constable's hand, like a whip.

"Very well, let's console each other!"

"Hey, damn your nails!" cursed the constable, rubbing his hand. Then he pulled his cap down over his eyes. "It's pretty hot today. Well, God bless you."

"God bless you too," Etel smiled.

Left alone, she tried to read the paper. But she could not see another word than "disappeared," and even that she could not understand. What do they mean? The government takes a grown-up man, a strong, big man, from his family, and when the time comes to return him, it says, he's disappeared. Like a lousy, little kitten, or a weak, defenseless chicken. Where has it put him, why didn't it take better care of him? When she was a gooseherd, a little goose, a stupid, senseless little thing, was lost once. Then Mother shook her so that all her bones creaked in their hinges and she tore out her hair by the fistful. Yes, and she deserved it too. Everybody deserves it who does not know how to take care of something he is entrusted with. But whom should she shake, whose hair should she tear out, whose eyes should she scratch out?

A hen, having laid an egg, cackled in the shed.

"Holy Virgin!" Etel leaped to her feet and hurried to the shed. It was only yesterday that the skunk had sucked out all the eggs forgotten in the shed.

In her hurry, she pushed aside an empty barrel. The barrel noisily started to roll and crashed against the wall of the barn. A piece of lumber dropped to the ground with a loud thud. The swallows rose and took to flight. The army of birds started on its journey. The weakly swallow chick fell to the earth. The cat jumped at it immediately and ran with it up the mulberry tree.

# III

MÁTYÁS went down to the lake to cut some reed, but there was not much he could do. There was no ice yet strong enough to carry a man.

"It'll be a hard winter," Mátyás thought. Then, just to test it, he swung his sickle into the bush. "The pith of the bulrush is rather punky."

He turned back in bad humor. Hard winter meant much snow, much snow meant much water, and much water meant that the lake would creep into the fields, and then they would harvest leeches instead of wheat.

He was so lost in his thoughts that he did not even notice that, instead of turning back to the path leading up to his farm, he had walked up to the high road. And all at once he found himself in front of the store.

"Look at it!" Now what kind of a newfangled invention is this?" he exclaimed, his gaze arrested by something in the window.

The goods in the window were the same as at any other time. That is to say, not quite the same, for there was no blue vitriol in it; blue vitriol had become very precious, they said, the Army needed that too. Although that sounded much like an excuse to pull some more skin off the backs of the poor. For what did the Army need blue vitriol for? Did they want to spray the enemy with it? Why not let him keep his phylloxera if he had it! Rather the enemy than the grapevine!

There was no blue vitriol in the window, only rock candy, "fish" candy, St. John's bread, and flypaper, the pleasant mixed with the useful. And there was a poster in it, printed in the national colors, red, white and green, with the legend, *"Under The Protection of The National Council."*

That was the newfangled invention Mátyás had never heard of before. He had heard of a council, yes, of the City Council, which leased out the fields, collected rent for the use of the pasture, built roads, that is to say, which was supposed to build them but did not, only collected tax for them. Why on earth they took it in their heads now to protect the nation when this had always been the business of the government, he could not figure out.

"The devil knows what's the matter with them again," Mátyás concluded, and was about to go on when the storekeeper stuck her head out. She wore a black kerchief on her head because her husband had also been killed in the war. Ever since that time she was carrying on the business herself; she was a great business woman.

"Do you like it, Uncle Mátyás?" she asked, very friendly.

"I'm trying to figure out what kind of goods it is."

The storekeeper did not know it either, she said, the innkeeper had brought it from the city. According to the innkeeper, there was a great rebellion in the city, all the stores and shops were having such things in their windows, some of them had four even, or five, so she had bought one for her too, because if everybody had one, the village shouldn't be without them either.

"Well, it's nice, sister, to one who knows what it's about," Mátyás declared and, being there anyway, he decided to visit the Club for a second, to pick up a little news.

The Club was in the same building as the store. That is to say, the inn was in the same building and the Club was in the inn. Between the two was the blacksmith's shop, but that had been closed these two years, because the blacksmith was also away in the war. In the old days, they used to discuss the ways and news of the world in the shop while the horses were being shod, or the harness repaired, but since the blacksmith had left they had met in the Club, whenever they had time on their hands.

When Mátyás entered, the diet was in full swing. There were at least four or five lambskin caps observable in the hazy smoke when Mátyás sauntered in.

His entry was acclaimed by a fire of curt greetings, and as he stepped nearer, and dissipated the smoke a bit with the fresh air he had brought in, he recognized the men belonging to the lambskin caps. They were all of his age, his kind; relatives, kinfolk. And now that they all knew who was who, they gave each other their full due:

"God give you a good day!"

"And to you, too!"

"Well, what's been settled so far?"

"Oh, we've just been figuring out this and that and that and this—that is to say, how it will be hereafter."

"The same as it always was," Mátyás said, spreading himself out on the bench. "The sheepskin coat will go on cutting the wood, and the ermine cloak warming itself by its fire!"

A little man with bristles like a burr where his moustache should have been nodded emphatically.

"Yes, sir, that's just what I say."

A tall, gaunt man, whose Adam's apple ran up and down his neck like the windpipe of a goose, shoved his elbow further in on the table.

"Now that's just it! They don't want to have it the same way, they want it differently. They say that not only the ermine will get warm but the sheepskin too."

Whereupon the little burr of a man again nodded assent; "yes, sir," that was just what he thought. And

Mátyás, throwing in a surprised "What the hell!" pushed his cap further up on his skull. Thus he managed to free his ear better to hear the news. Because he did not know anything at all in the whole wide world, it was only by chance that he had brought out that sentence about the sheepskin and the ermine.

"Well, what's the news, brother, say it."

They told him what they knew, and how they had heard it.

There had been a revolution in the city. The streets were swarming with people; there were as many of them as ants in a nest, and all had buttons in the national colors in their buttonholes. They said the king had abdicated, by now, he might even have taken out his passport. The war was over, all the nations on earth were brothers, the prisoners were to come home, ours would get their discharge too. Bands were playing everywhere and a gentleman with a ribbon round his arm announced in front of the City Hall that Hungarian liberty had been achieved, and that the fatherland was free and independent at last.

Mátyás pulled his cap back in its original place. This was no news, he had heard it all before. And quite often, too. Even before the war; every time there was an election. The deputy would come down from the city, and lots of candidates, and even the burgomaster himself, and then there was song and music and bands and speeches, and in the evening *bürge-paprikás* in the Club, and then the next day they all disappeared and the poor farmer did not see them again for years.

"Yes, sir. That's just what I say."

The fellow with the goose-windpipe begged Mátyás's pardon but it wasn't that way now, not exactly. Because yesterday, when he went to town to pay in the war-tax, the tax-collector, that little, brown man, who had always been a friendly sort of man, had said to him, "Go home, unc', take your money and drink on it a toast to Count Károlyi, because he's abolished the war-tax."

"God shall not help me home if I don't say the truth, Uncle Mátyás!"

"Yes, sir, of course, that's just what I say," added the burr enthusiastically.

Mátyás's heart within him suddenly missed a beat. Why, that certainly was different, if one no longer had to pay war-tax! Sure, he would go as if to pay it in tomorrow himself, but he would ask for a receipt, for a proof that they did not want to take the money from him. Because he did not believe anything, not unless the double-headed Viennese eagle itself warbled: "Long live the Spirit of Forty-eight!"

They all laughed. But then a reddish-faced man in the corner, whom Mátyás had not noticed so far, spoke up. He must have been an umbrella-maker, or some other similar kind of a gentleman, not of this neighborhood, that was sure. Mátyás could not remember ever having seen him.

"That's over now. 'Long live Forty-eight' is over and done with!"

Was the man mad? He must be to be sitting there beneath Father Kossuth's picture and belittling Forty-eight!

Mátyás called him sharply to order.

"So, and what's the great idea now, if you please!"

The reddish-faced man brought his fist down on the table with a bang:

"Why—long live communism!"

A silence followed. The burr ventured upon a loud, "Yes, sir," then quickly modified it by adding, "possibly."

The reddish-faced man got up. And they saw that one of his legs, from the knee down, was of wood. He limped over to the company.

"Will you permit me, comrades, to say something?"

Of course he was permitted. He looked like a gentleman. He was smoking a cigar.

"Do you know what communism is?" and he put both of his elbows on the table. "I'll tell you. It means that there's to be no more gentlemen and no more peasants, only comrades. Everybody who believes that all men are equal is a comrade."

"We are all equal before the face of God," somebody remarked.

The wooden-legged man picked up the word.

"God! He's an invention of the priests! We'll do away with him too!"

The men grumbled. The wooden-legged one continued in a lower voice. He turned to an old man with eyes like those of a carp.

"I don't want to hurt anybody's feelings, but tell me, comrade, where was God when they took your son to the front?"

The carp-eyed old man shook his head.

"They didn't take my son. And they never will."

"Oh, so he's exempt."

"Not that, but I haven't got a son. All I have is three daughters, but not even the soldiers want them."

They giggled quietly. Redface threw out his net again, for a better catch.

"Is it justice that one man should bathe in milk and honey and the next should live like a dog? Is it justice that one man has a hundred acres and becomes a councilman, and the next one works his whole life through with his nose to the grindstone, never gets anywhere, and stays a servant to the end of his days?"

By this time, the Club was filled with heavily smelling, ragged, furrowed-faced peasants. All of them murmured that that was no justice and even Mátyás acknowledged that the gentleman-like fellow was on the right track.

"Justice says that we should take away the property of those who have much and divide it up among those who have nothing."

"Yes, sir, that's justice!" the burr bellowed at the company. All repeated it, only Mátyás did not. He looked around. He saw that none of the men in the Club had more than five or six acres, that all of them were renters, tenants, some of them even in partnership. Of course, they would have liked to see the lands divided! Not that he wouldn't have gone where they were dividing up the hundred-acres! But he wouldn't give up a square-foot of his land, not to anybody! What did that umbrella-maker think anyway? Mátyás, however, was a wise man, said nothing. Why set oneself against so many when all was nothing but words, wind.

But even if he had wanted to say something, he wouldn't have been able to because Redface now threw his trump card on the table.

"Is it justice that I smoke cigars while you, honorable comrades, suck tobacco grown on trees? Justice says that I who have many should divide them among those who have none."

And with this he threw a big leather wallet on the table. It was full of cigars and banknotes. He took the banknotes out of it, put them back in his pocket, then shoved the cigars in the center of the table.

"Help yourselves, comrades. There's plenty of them still left where these came from."

Whether there were many more left where these had come from, one couldn't very well tell, but those on the table disappeared in no time. Mátyás too stuck one between his teeth, and right away he perked himself up, lifted up his head. It's funny the way a cigar makes one hold one's head high. A pipe pulls the head down, a cigar props it up.

"Go on, mister, go on!"

The gentleman went on. Loudly and determinedly, for he felt very much at home now.

"The communist has only one law, and that is that there's no law. We don't need no soldiers, no judges, no policemen, no tax-collectors, no customs officers."

"No priests neither!" someone yelled from the door.

"And no Jews!"

"Hey, men, not so fast! Hold your horses!" Mátyás lifted his arm. "The priest and the Jew ain't no government! There's only the government the gentleman mentioned. Well, then, if there is to be no more government, I'll take on that thing too, that whatchumaycallit—comomism!"

"Communism," the umbrella-maker corrected him. "But, you see, there will be a government even then, because communism is also a government, but a republic-government."

Mátyás thought the time had come to pour clean wine in the glass:

"Wait a minute! Who will be the king in that republic-government?"

"Who will be the king? Nobody! There's no king in a republic," the wooden-legged fellow laughed.

Mátyás rose. With the confidence of victory, he strutted to the communist.

"That's all fairytales, do you hear me? If there's no king, whose picture will be on the money? Eh?"

The umbrella-maker rose too. He was angrily gesticulating with both of his arms. He mentioned America. But nothing helped, the men slowly crept away from him. Mátyás had defeated Communism, but his triumph did not make him haughty. On his way out, he offered a friendly hand to the comrade he had felled in a battle of principles.

"Well, God give you good work."

The innkeeper was plucking a goose on the counter. She had no black kerchief on her head but a sort of bonnet, for she was a Jewess. The Jew himself had run into trouble early in the war down in Serbia. And that was a pity, because he was a mighty decent man, he never once cheated his patrons. It was he who founded the Club, so that the folks should grow more accustomed to the place. He even sat down with them whenever he had time—Jews always have time on their hands—and he loved to bet. And that was what finished him. He used to stick his head out over the trench when he was dared to. And he won money on it, too, until one day the Serbs mistook him for a bull's eye and hit him. There was more than a thousand *korona* in his box, he had won all of it on betting. They sent that home to his wife. She speculated wisely with it; as soon as she got the money she bought barrels, and she had barrels for sale even when every cooper in the city ran out of them.

Mátyás thought very highly of the clever Jewess and he never missed a chance to talk to her.

"When will you kill your pigs, neighbor? I'd like to come for the bladders already," he asked her.

The innkeeper kept her faith, she never ate bacon, but being an innkeeper, she had to keep meat in the house. So she fattened and butchered three pigs every winter and gave the lung-bladders—good material for tobacco pouches—to Mátyás.

"I don't know, Uncle Mátyás, not before the weather grows a little harder I guess," she said, drying her hand so that she might shake hands with Mátyás.

But Mátyás did not wait for that. He had noticed the Russky through the door pane as he passed by the house and he wanted to speak to him. He had an old, dry walnut tree in his garden which he wanted to dig up, because the cabinetmaker had offered a fine price for it. And he needed the Russky's help.

"Hey, Russky! Hey, Spirituto!"

The Russky turned around. He was still wearing his sandals and canvas pants, but there was a worn sheepskin jacket hanging on his shoulders. It did not cover his waist, it was too short and too tight. It must have belonged to Ferenc.

"Well, Spirituto, how many weeks are in the world?"

"Oh, Uncle Mátyás, don't ask me such things."

Mátyás looked at the Russky. He noticed only now that the Hungarian soldier's cap he was wearing was backwards on his head, with its shield in the back, and that his eyes were full of tears.

"What's happened to you? Are you sorry to leave Piros? I hear your year is up and you are going home now."

The Russky burst into tears, loudly, like a chastised child.

"Piros is dead."

"The hell you say!" Mátyás started. "What did you do to her? Why, I saw her only the day before yesterday. I even told her that she must have served the Kaiser faithfully, it seemed to me there was going to be a double-headed eagle in the cradle by the time Ferenc got home."

"Yes, that was the trouble," the Russky said wiping his eyes, "you got pretty good eye."

Piros might have borne twins if she had only waited for her time. But Ferenc wrote that he was on his way home and Piros became frightened. She wanted to hurry up the matter, to get it over with by the time Ferenc arrived, and she called in a midwife last night. The Russky did not know anything more. He was sent out into the yard with the little boy, Peter, all he was bid to do was to empty the bucket that was full of blood. He did it twice, his hands were still bloody. And then this morning the midwife and another old woman told him that Piros was dead, and told him to go to the doctor and report the death at the gendarmerie headquarters. As a matter of fact, the women said nothing about the latter to him, but he was a soldier, and he knew what regulations were, and, anyway, he had committed no crime. But there was no doctor around, he had been arrested some time before for freeing recruits, and there was nobody at headquarters either; all the gendarmes had run away, liberty had broken out and there were no more commands nor commanders.

"It's lucky for you that things've turned out the way they did, because this way you won't get into trouble. Still, you'd better keep your mouth shut," Mátyás advised the Russky.

But there was another trouble too. She needed a coffin and the Russky did not know whether Piros had any money and even if she had, he did not want to search for it. So he thought he would sell his gold coin and gold ring which he had kept hidden in his boots until now.

He did not dare to ask Mátyás to buy them, he merely jingled them before him in his hand. But Mátyás knew that one had to be careful about such things, and he did not want to get mixed up with the affair in any way. So he sent the Russky to see the Jewess and he himself directed his steps toward Ferenc's house. Mátyás was not of a curious nature, and he never liked to butt into other people's affairs, but poor Piros had been a neighbor after all, and not a bad neighbor at that; there never had been any trouble with her. It was a pity that she had fared so unfortunately.

And as Mátyás was crossing the withered fields, frightening up flocks of crows here and there, he made a budget in his head. True, Ferenc's house was worn, the walls were cracked, the paint had come off in blotches, the thatch on the roof was leaky in several places, but it didn't require much to fix up everything. And Spirituto had taken fairly good care of the fields, the Fall sowing had been attended to, the hundred or so rows of grapes were properly covered up. The Russky had even installed an apiary. Mátyás had never before cared for such a petty business, but honey was commanding a high price nowadays, the gingerbread makers were very much after it. He had even heard of a woman who had sold enough honey the other day to buy two cows. Etel might learn how to take care of it, if Ferenc cared to. Yes, Ferenc—because Mátyás now decided that Ferenc was to marry Etel. And then the fields that had always been one would at last be joined. Last Summer, when it seemed that Ferenc would never get back, Mátyás thought that he would buy the fields from Piros for Rokus, but if God in his wisdom wanted it all this way, one could do nothing but accept His command. His land, and Etel's five acres, and Ferenc's seven—all in all, it would make quite a handsome estate. And there were poor Piros' three acres too, why, he clean forgot about them. These, of course, would also belong to Ferenc now. True, they were on the other side of the lake and leased out on a fifty-fifty basis, but Ferenc might exchange them with somebody who had his land over there in one tract and just a few acres on this side. And if he couldn't, why, it wouldn't be so bad, even then there wouldn't be another farm in the neighborhood as large as theirs. And old Mátyás walked on the rustling sand, among the dream plants of his soul, as if rejuvenated. Then, all of a sudden, earsplitting screams came to him from the yard of Ferenc's farm.

"Peter!" Mátyás suddenly remembered. Look, he had forgotten that the boy existed! Why, of course, the Orphan's Court would take hold of Piros's land! And even Ferenc would have to give up a share of his land to his son. Ts-ts. But many a thing will happen until that day, children are mortal too. Just listen to him, he is seedy already, he will waste away in no time.

Peter could not have bellowed any louder even if he had known how his little life was being ground between the whirling millstones of Mátyás's brain. He was sitting on the threshold of the kitchen, tucked in a ragged little coat, and he protested with all the angry self-confidence of a three-year-old man that Etel had no right to harm his property rights to his little stub nose.

"You here?" asked Mátyás of his daughter-in-law and looked at the little boy who, between his big cap and little coat, showed nothing but his little red nose and his two big blue eyes. He looked at Mátyás like a kestrel, without a trace of tears in his eyes.

"I want to wipe the nose of this little spitfire," Etel remarked irritatedly, "but I'd rather not touch him or he might yell the dead back to life."

Marika, hanging on to her mother's skirt and staring with considerable sympathy at her little neighbor, now succeeded in tearing off one of the fringes of her shawl and, in order to exercise the virtues of mercy, bent nearer to the boy.

"Look, Peter, kitten's tail," and she tickled the boy's nose with it.

But Peter hated the female sex without distinction.

"I don' wan' it!" He pulled away and bumped his head against the door. He yelled for some Uncle Tali or Pali with all his might.

"Who is it the boy wants?" Mátyás asked.

"The Russky. He calls him Uncle Pali. The Russky's become great friends with him. When he went to plow, he carried the boy in a dosser on his back."

"Is Mother also here?"

"Yes. She is inside with the dead, praying."

The door was open, but Mátyás did not go into the little

room which smelled of pickled cabbage, ill-tended oven,
and heavy human sweat. Mátyás stayed outside. Not on
account of the odors, for he did not smell them, but because there were too many in the room anyway. And all
of them women. The older women were crying and la-
menting, but seemed visibly refreshed, the young ones
were pale and silent. Only Modol Boca was not moved,
but, of course, it was easy for her to hold her head up:
she had neither husband nor anybody else who might call
her to account, and it was impossible for her to be pale,
for she was painted even on weekdays.

"Will you look at her, Uncle Mátyás?" she asked and
lifted the shroud from the corpse.

The pale women bowed their heads even more, someone
screamed: "God in Heaven, look down upon us!"; a
young woman in the last stages of child-birth leaning
against the oven sobbed loudly, and Mother began to
shriek the All Saints' Litany. Mátyás dipped two of his
fingers into the chalice and shook his fingers toward the
bed. But the holy water did not reach it, its drops fell on
the chest of drawers, right on Ferenc's photo. There he
stood in his uniform, with his moustache haughtily waxed,
in the center of the pretty frame Spirituto had carved, with
hearts, tortoises, and kissing doves. The drops of water
rolled down the picture and it seemed as if Ferenc's smiling eyes were crying. But Piros no longer cared for those
tears, nobody noticed them anyway.

Mátyás hurried home because he had to cut some stalks
on the field, and he had to finish this job before the snow
came. And both the sky and his broken arm warned him
that there would be a snowfall soon. He did not go to
the funeral the next day either, partly because the work
was very urgent, and partly because the cemetery was far
away, they had put it far on account of the lake. He only
looked at the procession from his field, with his cap in his

hands, until the hearse disappeared, although there was a malicious wind blowing, and the cold sleet beat down hard on his bald skull. But, after all, one had to give the dead its due.

In the evening, at dinner, he asked Etel:

"And what's going to happen to the child now?"

"Which one?"

"Ferenc's. Peter."

"Why, the Russky says he will stay on because he doesn't want to leave the little orphan alone in the middle of the winter. I told him that we might take care of him until the Orphan's Court decided what should happen to him, but the Russky only embraced the boy and said that he would stay until he could give him into his father's hands."

Mother shuddered. For she was sure that this queer business would end in another death.

"We'll all see it if we live long enough."

"Possibly," remarked Mátyás. "But that fellow Spirituto is a very decent fellow. He's got a hundred and fifty acres at home, do you hear me?"

# IV

MÁTYÁS was right; Spirituto was a decent fellow, and if God ever helped Ferenc home, he certainly ought to frame him in gold. For Spirituto worked his hands off; he patched up and whitewashed the walls, painted blue and yellow stripes at their bottom as they did in his own country, thatched the roof—it was a miracle that it had not blown off earlier—and even inserted the date of the year onto it with lighter stalks of reed. No one had ever seen the like of it thereabouts, surely, and next year it was certain to be copied by all who could afford it. He fixed up the fence and constructed a door that was a veritable wonder. It had no lock, yet he could lock it by simply pressing something at the bottom of it with his foot. There must have been a fancy contraption down there, but what it was no one could find out. Neither could anybody find out where Spirituto had gotten the reed, and the lumber, and the wire, and all the rest of the things he used. But it was not fair to look for the why and wherefore of things when the man was not even working for himself. After all, where did the King get all his castles? He just got them. Well, the Russky did not do anything different either, he just got the things he needed. Something was lost on this farm, something on the other, but since nothing that was lost was worth much, no one reported his losses. There was not much sense in reporting one's troubles, anyway, for those were queer days, the authorities did not dare to do much. One day, for instance, one of the field-guards shot down a dog, for no reason at all, just because

50

the dog had barked at him, which, after all, was its office. The next day the field-guard was shot off his horse. Who did it, no one knew, but whoever it was he even went so far as to make fun of the guard by sticking a dog's tail into his mouth so that as he leaned dead against a willow tree, he looked as if he were smoking a pipe. At any other time, half of the men in the village would have been taken to the gendarmerie headquarters, from there to the city, and somebody might even have been strung up. But now— nobody did anything about it; the guard was quietly buried, not even a cock crowed. The law was simplified: "Watch out for yourself, and for what's yours." And that was the best law they had ever had, it fitted their world to a T. For houses were scattered around on the fields, each a castle and a fortress in itself, each living alone its lonely, introspective life.

But however things happened on other farms, it was a fact that nothing ever stuck to Spirituto's somewhat light fingers while he was at Mátyás's, although he went over there quite often. One day, he asked one of the women for a little milk, the next day the other one for an egg. Oh, not for himself, not at all, as far as he was concerned there was still some of last year's bacon left, chiefly because in the bygone days of plenty he had not much fancied it. And poor Piros had fed him so well that he could easily hibernate on his own fat. But he did want to improve the child's food, he just couldn't see the poor brat ruin his stomach on cabbage and potatoes. Nor did the Russky know as much about cooking as he did about fancy contraptions. Once, when he baked a pie for Peter, he very nearly burned it, and had to get it out of the pan with an axe. The Russky got so afraid that the shell-splinters would harm the glistening little teeth of the orphan that he chewed every bite of the hard dessert for him.

Yes, it was fantastic the way Spirituto treated the boy;

after all, he was nothing to him. The Mátyáses would sometimes look out from their window, when he was shoveling the snow, and at the sight of the ragged little child pottering around the big ragged man, they would burst into laughter. When the snow became harder, the Russky built tiny houses out of it, churches, steeples, castles, fortresses. Then he built a snow-man, as big as himself. He made two thin legs for him out of two sticks of wood, put a big belly on them, a bearded head on top of it all, and smudged soot over its face for eyes and a mouth. A whole red pepper was its nose, and it was a fine sight to see the red-nosed snow-man looking down at the little churches and castles squatting at its feet. Then the Russky placed a crown made out of the rind of a pumpkin on its head, so that even a fool could recognise the snow-man as representing none other but the Russian Emperor.

"Well, that's a good picture of him," said Mátyás, enjoying it all mightily, for he had always imagined that emperors looked like that. Of course, if he could have his own way, he would put him on horseback with an officer's uniform. "He must have had a mightly ugly-looking father; no wonder his folks got sick of him!"

The dethronement took place the following way: Spirituto ran toward the snow-emperor like a wild bull, that wanted to knock him down, but he always managed to miss him, and instead of the snow-man, it was always he who finally collapsed on the ground. Peter found this immensely entertaining, his frail little body shook with laughter. Then, at Spirituto's encouragement, he attacked the snow-giant himself. He rammed his head against its knee, which was as high as he could reach, and lo, Peter being much stronger than Uncle Pali, he succeeded in knocking the snow-emperor off his legs so that it collapsed, and buried beneath it all the little castles and steeples in its kingdom.

Mátyás did not like this, he thought it was a pity to waste all that work, and handsome work too, in such a way. Marika, on the other hand, enjoyed everything so heartily that her little nose nearly froze to the window pane. She longed to take a part in the destruction so much that her heart nearly broke. And when Spirituto pulled a sack over his head and went down on all his fours in the snow and walked round Peter like a bear! And when he got up again and danced like a dancing bear! Marika could not resist the devil's temptation any longer, she quietly slid down from the chair on which she was standing and, when her mother was not looking, sneaked out of the room, making about as much noise with her bare feet as a little mouse would.

But she met Mother in the pantry—she had been out in the shed to fetch some corn—and the mouse was caught.

"I'll teach you to play with the Russky, you little lizard!" Mother said, chasing Marika back into the room. "Don't you know he's cracked? Otherwise why should a grown man make a fool of himself like that."

This last sentence was addressed to Etel, although without any malice, for it had really made her angry to see how stupidly the Russky behaved for the sake of the child. Mother was old already; youth had become dim in her eyes, and she had half forgotten the time when Mátyás had been teaching Rokus how to throw somersaults on the lawn.

"Why is he cracked? Just because he likes the child?" Etel said to the old woman in an off-handish way.

"Just go ahead and defend your Russky," said Mother, pouring the corncobs from her apron onto the floor and kicking aside the cat which lay asleep at the foot of the bed, although it was absolutely not in her way.

No, the cat had never done her any harm, far less Etel.

But Mother was little and withered and shrunk up and covered by the cobweb of years like a plum tree that had lost its leaves. And Etel was big, strong, white-red, like a blooming apple tree in the sunlight. Furthermore, there had been only one good mother-in-law in the whole wide world so far, and even she had fallen a prey to the devil.

Etel's blue eyes turned to a shade of green, but she said nothing, and merely shrugged her round shoulders. She had never been a favorite with the old woman and it was against her nature to ingratiate herself with anybody, or to flatter anybody.

Although Mother did not notice the shrug of her shoulders, she remembered every word that Etel had said, and every word she had left unsaid. And whenever afterwards she noticed the Russky coming over for something, she always hid secretly to watch how Etel laughed with the fellow. Etel had never done such a thing before in all her life, but she suspected what Mother was after, and so she accepted it womanlike as a challenge! She always made a point of shaking hands with Russky, and one day Mother saw, from her hiding place behind the big cupboard, that Etel slapped him coquettishly on the back. She could not hear why, but she went to Mátyás just the same, and complained that Etel and the Russky understood each other very well. She added that she did not think there was anything between them, but that she would not like to see her daughter-in-law go on Piros's way.

"Certainly not! Take care that she shouldn't!" Mátyás said sternly and told Mother in great secret what his plans for Etel and Ferenc were.

Mother turned up her nose at them. She would have liked much better for Etel to keep on wearing the virgin-crown of widowhood, because she helped her a lot around the house. But Mother was not used to opposing Mátyás and so she consoled herself with the thought that hereafter she could order Etel about to her heart's content, since Mátyás was against the Russky too.

Not loudly, of course, or haughtily, because Mother liked peace. Her words did not wound but they pricked.

Etel was standing at the gate, meditating where to plant the vegetables this Spring, because the chickens had done much damage to the plants where they had been last year.

"Shan't I bring you your shawl, my child?" Mother asked her in a honeyed voice.

"What for?"

"This cold weather isn't very good for—peeping."

Etel quite calmly replied that as far as she could see Mother was peeping without any shawl at all, although the cold was more harmful to Mother's old bones than to hers.

Mother was hurt by the reply and did not so much as say even return "Good Morning" to Etel for the next three days. On the morning of the fourth, she asked her whether she knew where the black hen had laid her egg.

"I used it up."

"For your Peter perhaps?"

"For my Peter or not for my Peter—*my* hen laid it."

"But not for your Russky!"

Etel's eyes turned as green as those of a cat about to jump at a mouse.

"You seem to have much trouble with that Russky, Mother. Old as you are you are always thinking of men. I should be ashamed if I were you."

She enjoyed her cruelty greatly. She even licked her lips after it.

Mother went to Mátyás and with tears in her eyes, made a complaint against modern youth personified by Etel. If only *she* had dared to talk back to her mother-in-law, to Mátyás's mother! Yes, she had been a temperamental woman, God bless her ashes, not as calm and peace-loving

as Mother. No, she did not want Mátyás to talk to Etel,
she did not want to break with her for the little while
still left her on this earth but she had to open her heart to
somebody, it was filled to the brim with bitterness. And it
was Mátyás, after all, who best knew that she wanted nothing but good, and he himself had bid her take action in
the matter.

"It served you right. Why did you talk so much? You
got what you were looking for," he answered gruffly.

Words failed Mother. She pulled the little chair to the
window, took the Catechism off the shelf, opened it, and
from behind her spectacles poured tear after tear into the
pages of the book. She was not angry, but she felt, although she could not have put her feeling into words, that
all men were like Adam, ready to commit the first sin the
moment there was a woman at their side whom they could
blame for it.

And Mátyás was also right when he sided with Etel
against Mother. For Mátyás had gone and asked the
Russky whether he had already had a woman in Piros's
place. Of course, he did not ask it in so straightforward
a way, but in the form of a joke.

"Well, Spirituto, don't you think the bed is cold when
you've got to sleep in it alone?"

The Russky answered very seriously. No, he was sleeping with Peter. But Piros appeared in his dreams every
night wearing a black cloak just like the one the Holy
Virgin of Kazan in his country used to wear. She held two
sleeping Jesuses in her arms, one on each, only the crown
studded with red stones was missing from her head. But as
soon as there was a tombstone on her grave, she would
get her crown too, and then the eyes of the two little
Jesuses would open up.

The Russky wiped his eyes with the back of his fist and
asked Mátyás how much he would charge for that dry

old walnut tree.

"I don't know," Mátyás said. "You got any money?"

Cautiousness is always advisable. The Russky confessed that he had no money but promised that as soon as he got home he would send whatever Mátyás charged for it, at once. Whereupon Mátyás said that if he ever thought of cutting down the tree, he would certainly give all of it to Spirituto, but he was not thinking of cutting it down yet, it seemed to him there was still life in it, and he figured that there would be blossoms on it in the Spring.

A few days later, the Russky rolled a big vat over to Mátyás's, whereupon Mátyás remarked that now that the vat was there he might as well leave it, but it was not the vat he had needed but a carved chest, and if he could get one for him he did not mind if he cut down the walnut tree. Mátyás had cast an eye at the carved chest when he had visited Piros on her deathbed. It was a very handsome thing; the Russky had carved it for Piros.

The next day, the Russky took the chest over to Mátyás and the old man immediately went to the women to boast of the great bargain he had made. He even told them why the Russky wanted the tree, and this bit of gossip had a beneficent influence on the general state of affairs.

"So Etel's innocent," thought Mother, and asked her daughter-in-law whether she would like to have her black silk shawl, the one embroidered with the red roses. It was a little frayed along the creases but it was still very beautiful, and she could not wear it any more because it was too youthful for her age.

"Mother was right: the Russky is a little cracked," Etel thought, for she could never understand how anybody could love Piros, and she was positively shocked when she heard of the Holy Virgin visions. It was an impertinence for a mortal creature to mix up the Blessed Mother of God with his own petty business. And so she told Mother that she did not need to ask the neighbors about nuts for Christmas, she still had some in her garret, a little bagful or so, not all of them wormeaten yet.

And the Russky cut down the tree, chopped its branches off on the spot, sawed enough for a cross out of its trunk, rolled that piece home, and left the rest for Mátyás, who was once more strengthened in his firm conviction that it was never good to hurry because, if he had sold the tree to the cabinetmaker, he would have struck a far worse bargain.

Work on the cross progressed slowly, for Spirituto had neither shop nor tools. He worked in the big room, with only an axe and a knife, and every other minute he had to run to Peter lying ill in the corner. He had caught cold and his little body was as hot as fire. The Russky was brewing camomile tea for him, but there existed a natural antagonism between Peter and the camomile tea. They could be brought to terms only when Spirituto had recourse to doves, made out of bits of shavings and tied to strings, which flew and chirped and did several other wonderful tricks.

In a week, however, the outlines of the cross were roughly hewn out, and he was just about to start work on the details when his knife broke.

"*Bozshe moi, bozshe moi,*" he said in despair, looking sadly at the broken blade, when someone passed by the window.

He could not see who it was, because he was kneeling with his back to the window, all he saw was a shadow, yet he leaped to his feet and leaned pale as a ghost against the cross.

"A man," Peter announced, and sneered to express his misanthropy.

But by this time the man was already in the room. He closed the door quietly behind him and stopped on the threshold for a second. His eyes, blinded by the snow, had to accustom themselves to the dimness of the room. His hat, shoulders, and chest were covered with snow, and as the heat of the room penetrated it, a little pool formed at his feet.

He looked like an artisan; of medium height, with graying hair, big moustache, lean face, and weary eyes. He did not resemble His Majesty's dapper corporal who was standing "at attention" on the top of the chiffonier in a frame of hearts and kissing doves—yet Spirituto knew at once that the two eyes which penetrated him like a pitch-fork could have belonged to no one but Ferenc.

"Good day," the visitor spoke up, rather in a sort of what-do-I-care voice than angrily, and after rubbing his wet hand on the dry back of his coat, he reached into his pocket.

The Russky threw a desperate glance at the broken knife. Damn it, why did it break now! He was not a coward, and although he had considerably run to seed on his own cooking, he could still do some damage to Ferenc, if it came to that. He had been preparing himself for this meeting, for he had heard of *Magyarskis* who had stuck their knives into their faithless wives, and he knew that it was now his business to stand his ground, for Piros was waiting for the crown studded with red stones. The world was whirling round him. Yet he did not pick up the axe, he merely held on fast to the cross.

"Good day," the man said again and, stepping forward, pulled a little red candy whistle out of his pocket.

He blew it and the toy whistle shrieked and filled the room with merry jingling sound. The man then found his way to the corner.

"Look, Peter, what your father has brought you," so saying he gave the whistle to the child, but neither kissed him, nor even touched his flaxen hair. He immediately explained to the Russky why not. "I'm coming straight from the concentration camp. One can pick up all sorts of things there."

Peter, although still upholding his principles, accepted the whistle; he made desperate efforts to lick it, and was soon sucking it noisily. The wind hurled frozen snow flakes against the window pane, so that they tapped faintly against the glass. The Russky took a deep breath and stepped forward.

"So you are here," he said, in a very low tone.

"Yes," Ferenc nodded. "Have you got a bit of soap? I'd like to wash myself."

No, there was no soap—the Russky swallowed hard. He wanted to say that they had had no soap *since then*. Since there had been no woman in the house. He offered to run over to Mátyás, to Etel, for a piece of soap.

Ferenc tried to remember. "To Etel? Oh, yes, yes. No, don't go, you needn't, I'll go down to the store myself later. Why, if I had only thought of it, I could have brought it together with the whistle. But I did not know whether I had enough Hungarian money on me." He took out his purse. The Russky threw a stealthy glance at it; there were several elongated banknotes in it, which he had never seen the like of yet.

"American dollars," Ferenc explained, catching the Russky's glance. He had escaped in that direction, through Siberia and China. He had been working in mines, factories, and saved a little money.

Peter now interrupted the conversation, for he had discovered that one had to blow the whistle and not suck it. And the exhilaration of discovery dispersed even Peter's gloom.

"Speaks," he explained for the benefit of the ignorant.

Spirituto thought the moment propitious to reestablish the ties of blood. He patted the child on the head.

"You see what a good dad you have," and he looked at Ferenc.

"I don' wan' dad," Peter turned to the wall. "I wan' Uncle Pali."

The Russky became sad, but Ferenc only smiled. He stepped to the cross and slowly ran his hand over it.

"For Piros?"

"Yes," the Russky answered, and his lips trembled.

"I heard about her at headquarters. Poor soul. Pear tree?"

"Walnut."

"Yes, yes, that's what I meant to say."

Then Ferenc left. As he passed by the window, the Russky went out too, and looked after him until he was lost to sight. At first he was so happy that he wanted to turn somersaults in the snow, but afterwards he felt so sad and depressed that he would have liked to run out of the world altogether. Then he went back to the child, took him in his lap, put him to sleep with a lullaby, made the bed, and put the child in it, near the wall. He himself lay down on the sofa, fully dressed. He thought the day would pass quickest if he simulated sleep.

Ferenc came back, lighted a candle, went to the kitchen, and stayed out there for a long time; only the splashing of water was heard. The Russky would have liked to speak to him, but he did not dare to, although he was afraid that Ferenc would catch a cold. Then Ferenc returned to the room, sat down at the table, opposite the Russky, opened a package, and took bread, cheese, onions, salt, and paprika out of it. He ate and drank with gusto. The Russky watched him through his half-open eyes. He could not have been much older than himself, but seemed twice as old. His eyes were smiling, but there ran three deep wrinkles between his eyebrows. His hair was iron-gray, and when he put down the pitcher and wiped his heavy, yellowish-brown moustache, one could see that there were two long furrows in the corners of his mouth.

The Russky had time to watch him because Ferenc ate for a long time. When there were no more onions and cheese left, he cut the bread into small bits and dipped them in salt and paprika. But just as he was about to swallow the last bite, he suddenly turned very serious, and put the bread down. Then he stretched his arms, threw his purse and papers on the table, and looked around. He noticed two cigarettes on the chiffonier, took one of them, noticed his picture, looked at the frame, smiled, lighted his cigarette by the candle, and went out of the room.

The Russky opened his eyes. He noticed that an American banknote had fallen out of the purse and dropped to the floor. He made a move to pick it up, he was afraid it might get lost. But then he remembered that Ferenc could easily see him through the window, and so he did not move. He listened for quite some time how the snow creaked under his steps; Ferenc was walking up and down before the house in the night. Spirituto grew calmer, this was not the way to look for the axe.

Finally Ferenc came in and began to undress. He noticed the American banknote on the floor. He picked it up and threw it on the table, then he picked up the candle to look at the child, patted the quilt and pushed it between the child and the wall and finally blew out the candle, and, without looking at the Russky, went to bed.

But apparently he could not fall asleep, he kept turning round and round in the bed for a long time. Once or twice the Russky heard him sit up. Why? He had come a long way, buffeted by wind and snow, he must have been very tired. What was ailing him? Could it be that he was unable to sleep *in that bed*?

The Russky leaped to his feet and bumped into the table.

"What's the trouble?" Ferenc asked.

The Russky felt his way to the bed.

"Listen—I—I—I want to say something——"

He stammered and stuttered so that one could hardly hear him. Ferenc answered quietly:

"Don't say anything, brother. It was a human thing. You are not to blame. It could have happened to any of us."

"I am—I am—going away——" The Russky's voice broke.

"That's your business, brother. Now lie down and sleep. That's been settled already and that's the end of it. God give you a good night's rest!"

The Hungarian peasant's hand and the Russian peasant's found each other in the darkness and that was really the end of it. In a quarter of an hour, Spirituto was fast asleep. But Ferenc had not much rest; he spent the whole night covering up the child who was continually kicking down his quilt. And when the child left him alone, the Russky began to shout all sorts of foreign words.

"Russian cows' names," Ferenc thought, smiling. "He seems to be at home, too."

## V

ETEL was the first on the Mátyás farm to notice
Ferenc. The day after his arrival, Ferenc went out
with Spirituto to look over his fields. There was
not much to see, because the snow made one piece of land
look very much like the next one. Yet one's boot walks
quite differently on one's own land than on a stranger's.
On a stranger's, it merely stumbles and shuffles and
slouches, a little bored, unwillingly, wearily. But when the
boot feels its own soil under its sole, it squeaks merrily
and creaks joyfully, as if the bootmaker had put a special
cracker in it.

Although Ferenc was not wearing a pair of home-made
high boots, his factory-made American footwear learned
the law in no time, and trod the snow much harder than
the Russky's lazy sandals. That was just what aroused
Etel's curiosity.

"Look what a smart old man there is staggering around
there in the snow with the Russky."

Etel knew Ferenc, for they had been children together
until Ferenc had had an argument with his father—a
grouchy old soul who had once sunk his knife into his
wife—and Ferenc went to the city to become a driver or
what-not, and did not return to the farm until after the
death of his father. He was at home on Etel's wedding,
and was one of the groomsmen, but Etel never cared much
for him then, since he was a silent, close-tongued, awkward fellow who hardly dared to speak a word to the
girls. He married Piros during the Carnival after Etel's

wedding, but he did not ask for her hand, it was her grandmother who arranged the matter.

Ferenc had changed so much that not only did Etel not recognize him, but Mátyás, who went to the window now, did not either.

"Somebody from the city," he remarked, for the sake of saying something.

It was not till afterwards that it occurred to him that the weather was not especially fine for a businessman from the city to go a-visiting. Jews were not in the habit of marketing snow the way they did apricots and wine, although it would have been fine if they did because there was plenty of it. He was very curious, therefore, to find out what the Russky was up to this time, so curious in fact, that he began swiftly to look for his boots. He found one of them under the bed, but the other one was nowhere, although Mother went on stubbornly repeating that she had seen it somewhere while sweeping. By the time they discovered it—Mother herself having hung the boot on the clock as a weight—the Russky had disappeared with the city man, and the weather had turned so horrible that one would not have chased even a dog out of the house. On the contrary, they invited Boisi in from his own abode not merely into the house, but into the pantry. An ignorant person would not have found much logic in this particular practice of communism, because the snow did not fall into the dog-house but did drizzle into the pantry through the open chimney, but, on the other hand, together with the snow there dropped fat from the smoked sausages hanging in the chimney and dogs are not unique in preferring fat to ideals.

After all this they forgot all about the stranger and the window pane was so thoroughly covered wth frost that they could not look out anyway. It was only about three or four days later that they learned the news, through

Mátyás, who had been down to the Jewess to ask her about the raw-material for pouches.

"Ferenc has come home," he had said, stamping his feet to shake the snow off his boots.

"Home?" the women asked, looking up from their work—they were plucking feather down because the weather was just right for that sort of work—but not too hastily because plucked down does not particularly like rash gestures.

"Why, Etel," he went on, slapping his cap against the door, "that elderly man you saw the other day must have been Ferenc, you know."

Etel was surprised. Was that Ferenc? Well, war must be a pretty rotten business if it ruined men so terribly.

"They say that Ferenc was in America too, and he has so much money that it's a wonder to see that much in one pile. The storekeeper says he bought ten packs of matches and five pieces of soap at once. What in God's name does he need that many for?"

Mother cautiously covered the basket-full of down with her hands and turned her head aside. She was about to ask a question so exciting that it warranted all the precautions.

"And tell me, what's he done to the Russky? Knifed him?"

No, he did not knife him. On the contrary, he seemed to be rather friendly with him. Mother returned to her work; the rest was of no interest to her.

"They have even gone to town together, on a hired wagon. The Russky is preparing to go home, they are running after his papers. If Ferenc were home I'd go over to him right away."

Mátyás decided not to beat around the bush any longer. He bowed his head a bit as he uttered the bad news.

"The storekeeper asked Ferenc about the soldiers from

this neighborhood—Whom did he see—Did he hear of
anybody—in his journeys——  He saw Rokus——"

Both of the women leaped to their feet, screaming. The
plucked down whirled about in the room as if it had been
snowing inside too. Marika, silently playing with her dolls
in the corner, broke into happy shrieks and tried to catch
the flying flakes.

"He was the one who closed his eyes," Mátyás concluded.
And began to cough because the damned flakes stuck in
his throat. He went out of the room, to cough out the
cursed things, and stayed outside for quite a while.

Mother sobbed silently and the little girl overturned a
chair as she chased this new unmelting snow.

"Can't you be quiet," Etel cried at her, but she added,
"darling." Then she gathered together the down with a
feather-duster and asked the old woman:

"Would you like to have something for supper,
Mother?"

Mother shook her head, she could not eat. Mátyás remembered that there was a little wurst left over from
noon.

"I'll warm it up in a second."

"Never mind, Etel, it'll be all right the way it is. But
I wish you'd bring in a little wine for me."

Etel brought in the wine, listened to the child's prayer,
put her to bed, went to bed herself, did not even bid good
night to anybody.

But after a while she got up, went over to the old woman
who had nearly cried herself into sleep and was now dozing
on the little bench near the oven.

"Go lie down, Mother dear." She took off her kerchief,
her skirt, and virtually carried her to bed.

"And you, Dad?"

Mátyás's face was red by now and he winked at Etel
merrily.

"Don't worry about me, Etel. And don't you be afraid either, not as long as you see me. I'll fix up everything. Clever hogs dig up deep roots."

With this, he dropped his head on the table. It remained there until morning. But one shouldn't judge Mátyás for this. Quickly drunk wine often makes your head heavy and anybody who has ever found himself in a similar position knows that at such times wine just offers itself to you.

His head was muddled in the morning, too, but by the time he worked himself across the snow to Ferenc's, it had cleared up.

The two men were still busy with the cross. It was ready, but had to be polished yet, and they were at it with a piece of rag dipped in oil. They did make a fine job of it, anybody had to admit it, though it was trimmed a little too flashily. The entire Trinity was carved into it, and Piros's name in the center of a wreath of roses. And down below, where local cabinetmakers used to put the skull, Mátyás noticed a heart. There was some fancy lettering in that too which Mátyás could not read. The Russky must have carved it in his own language.

Mátyás did not plunge headlong into the business that had brought him over.

"Come here, Ferenc, and let me take a good look at you. I see that you've brought home quite a lot of snow on your head."

"They didn't charge anything for it," Ferenc nodded.

"And how is your health?"

"Wish it were better. I feel a pain in my chest sometimes. Not on account of the shot, because the doctors took the bullet out of me in the hospital. But I caught a cold in the Murman country, and I've been coughing since."

Mátyás waved this aside.

"One can cough only as long as one lives. But, wait,

where did you say you caught that cold of yours?"

"In the Murman country, on the coast of the Arctic Sea.
We were building railroads there for the Russians."

"Tse-tse. Why, isn't that Burman in Africa somewhere?
The Reverend says the Boers live in Africa."

"That's something different," Ferenc shook his head.
"It isn't Burman, its Murman. With an M."

"I know, I know," Mátyás said. "So that fellow must
have been telling the truth after all when he told me that
our Rokus was lost somewhere in those forests too."

"Well, not quite there, because there are no forests
there, only God damn' big swamps, and marshes. The
woods begin about three thousand versts from there."

"Kilometer," Spirituto threw in, to enlighten Mátyás.

"And did you see him? With your own eyes?"

"Why surely I did," answered Ferenc. "We escaped together, five of us, but only the two of us reached the woods,
because the *tovarisch* shot down the three others."

Spirituto again explained. He knew a thing or two about
the world and by that time even the gendarmerie headquarters flew the red flag.

"The comrades."

Yes, the comrades, they were much worse to the prisoners than the Czar's soldiers. They freed those who joined
them, but then sent them to the front, to Siberia, right
away. Ferenc and Rokus and three others did not want to
join up, they were fed up with war. There were no
*tovarisch* in the forest, but hardly anybody else, either.
Once in a great while they found a log hut, but they were
half a day's walk from each other. There they begged a
bite of bread from the *muzhiks*.

"Peasants," Spirituto interrupted.

Peasants, yes, but Mátyás shouldn't think that they are
like us. No, we all are counts compared to them. They
bake ground tree-roots into their bread. The first time

Ferenc and Rokus tasted them they spat it out again in disgust. Later on, they would have been grateful if they had had even that, for they lived on wild berries. Rokus could not stand it for long. One day they had fallen asleep beneath some big trees—and when the morning came, Ferenc tried to wake Rokus, but no matter how he shook him, he couldn't shake life into him. And later on he had closed his eyes and never opened them again.

Mátyás took the pipe out of his mouth. It was not burning anyway.

"Did you bury him?"

Ferenc did not, because the earth was frozen, and he had had no tool except a blunt old knife. But he had scraped together some moss and dry leaves and covered him up, so that at least the beasts of prey should not desecrate his body. There hadn't been anything in his pockets except his identification card, which he took and kept. It was here somewhere among his own papers.

Ferenc pulled out the top drawer of the chiffonier and gave Mátyás a folded-up piece of paper. Mátyás opened it and looked at the lines. There was not much writing to be seen on it, and if there had been it wouldn't have meant much to him because it was in Russian; but even if it had been written in the language of the angels, it wouldn't have called Rokus back to life.

Mátyás stuck the card in his pocket and rose.

"Thank you, Ferenc. And what are you going to do now?"

"What am I going to do?"

"Yes. What are your plans? Do you want to stay here, on the farm, or will you sell it?"

"Of course, I won't. I'd rather add a little more to it, if I could."

"I just mentioned it," said Mátyás and his face lighted up with content. Then he stuck his ears under his lambskin cap, as a man about to go would.

Ferenc remembered the rules of etiquette.

"My regards to Aunt Roza. Is she still around?"

He knew very well that she was; Spirituto had reported to him about everything. But it was a question he had to ask.

"Sure, she is, and fresh as ever. She also sends you her regards. And Etel, too."

"Oh, yes, Etel! I haven't forgot her either. My regards to her, too."

Mátyás shook hands with the Russky also.

"When are you going?"

The Russky took a paper out of his pocket. It was his passport. He was to start that afternoon.

"Well, then, farewell. My regards to old Spirituto."

The Russky's childlike face turned dark. God knew what had happened to old Spirituto. Ferenc said that the *tovarisch* had taken away all the lands, and those who wouldn't give in, were killed.

"What the hell, they wouldn't have done that!" Mátyás was highly indignant. "Why, they were the ones who killed the Czar!"

"They are all the same under the skin. Regards to the family."

Mátyás ambled away, and the two men returned to their work. By noon, the cross was beautifully polished, and they sat down for a bite of bacon. That is to say, it was only Ferenc who ate, for the Russky just couldn't push the food down his throat. He tried to cram it into Peter, but the boy turned away from him and was urging his father:

"Dad, gimme eat!"

From the moment the child had awoke at his father's side and discovered that it was much cozier to hang on to his mop of a moustache than to the bristles with which the Russky tried to make himself look like a man, Peter found the new roommate quite bearable. And since petty gifts strengthen friendships, and since the candy whistle was soon followed by chunks of rock candy and "fish" candy, Ferenc was now wholly in Peter's good graces. Spirituto did make a last attempt to reinstate himself as Peter's friend but the struggle ended in a complete fiasco. One day Ferenc sent Spirituto down to the store to buy nails and while the storekeeper was looking for them under the counter, Spirituto stole a fig from above the counter. God will certainly leave this out of His calculations on Judgment Day, because Spirituto appropriated the foreign property solely in order to reconquer Peter. The intention was noble, but the execution turned out rather badly. The fig stuck to Peter's teeth, the child began to howl, and while the Russky tried to get the fig loose, the unfaithful friend bit the finger of his former ally and thus definitely broke off all diplomatic relations with him.

Such a thing had happened already to powers with far more moustaches to their credit, nevertheless, Spirituto took it very much to heart, and he stared at the little blond boy with tears in his eyes.

"Well, let's go," Ferenc closed his knife and tying up the left-over bread and bacon in a bag, he gave it to the protesting Russky. "Put it away, it'll come in handy on your way, you can never tell when you will get something to eat."

They were to take the cross to the cemetery together. From there, the Russky was to go straight to the gendarmerie headquarters, to start on his way home.

"Let's see whether we can carry it?"

The two men lifted it and carried it into the yard. The weather was terrible; the wind bellowed, swept the frozen snow off the roof; the prickly crystals filled their eyes, ears, noses, mouths.

"Buran," trembled the Russky, and the bells of *troikas* on

the snow-covered steppes of the Don tinkled in his ears.

"Yes," answered Ferenc and withdrew beneath the eaves. "Guess it'd be better if we stayed at home in this blizzard."

But the Russky insisted. He could not wait and the weather might turn worse by tomorrow, it might even block the road completely. And, he added courageously, both of them had already experienced worse weather than this.

"That's true," nodded Ferenc. "Well, then, I'll bring the spade. But where is the spade now?"

The Russky seemed to remember that the last time he had used it he had leaned it against the door of the sty.

And while Ferenc went to look for the spade, the Russky rushed into the house, lifted his little friend, and no matter how he cried—he squealed like a suckling pig—kissed him where he could; his shiny hair, his shiny eyes, his shiny nose. Then he suddenly put down the child, picked up Piros's mother-of-pearl rosary that hung from the brim of the holy water vessel, slid it under his shirt, and hurried out of the house.

"Let's go!" Ferenc said, shoving his shoulder under the right side of the cross beam.

"It's heavy," moaned the Russky under the left tip of the cross beam.

"At least we won't be cold."

And that was the last they said until they reached the cemetery. They couldn't have spoken anyway, even if they had known what to. For in whatever direction they turned they found themselves face to face with the wind. Neither house nor tree showed above the blanket of snow, no dog barked, no bird chirped, there was no living creature anywhere. Only two little black beetles of men crawled forward, slowly and laboriously, in the infinite whiteness beneath the infinite grayness.

The Russky knew his way about in the cemetery.

"There she is, near that ditch. At that forked acacia."

They leaned the cross against the tree. The Russky searched out the grave with his hands. His arm sank in the snow up to his shoulders. He scraped it towards himself like a dog does the earth when he is digging for a mole.

"I got it. Here is the end."

Ferenc had the spade in his hands, he began to dig. But the earth was frozen and the blade penetrated it only slowly.

"It'll be softer lower down," he said, wiping his brow.

After awhile, the Russky took the spade from Ferenc. Now it sank in the soft sand like a knife into butter.

"That'll do, it's deep enough," Ferenc remarked.

They put the cross in the hole and Ferenc held it straight, while Spirituto threw the earth back into the pit.

"It's fast all right," he said; then let go of the cross and went to help Spirituto to stamp down the earth. By the time they had finished their work, a nice little snow-cap had settled on the top of the cross. Ferenc tried to shake it off but the cross wouldn't even tremble.

"It's as fast as a rock."

Spirituto did not answer. He was praying, with bowed head. Ferenc was staring at the heart with the Russian letters.

Spirituto made the sign of the cross, first over the grave, then over Ferenc, finally over his own heart, and offered his red, frost-bitten hand to Ferenc. For the first time in his life, he offered his hand to Ferenc.

"God bless you, brother."

He said this also for the first time in his life. But he said it clearly, bravely, free from constraint. Ferenc answered in the same way.

"God bless you too, brother."

Then the Russky jumped over the ditch and Ferenc started toward the cemetery gate. After a few steps, the

Russky yelled after him:

"Hey, wait a second!"

Ferenc turned back.

"Catch it! For Uncle Mátyás. To remember me by," the Russky cried and hurled something toward him.

Ferenc put the palms of his hands together and caught the souvenir. It was the automatic lighter made out of a cartridge.

# VI

IT WAS about a week later that Ferenc remembered
the lighter. And then only because it happened to be
in his pocket and knocked against the table. He put it
on the chiffonier, but it occurred to him that he might
forget about it again, or the child might pick it up and
lose it. So he decided that it would be best to take it over
right away.

When he arrived Boisi must have suspected him of having something to do with the government, for he attacked
him angrily. Ferenc began by paying no attention to him
and simply pushed him aside with his foot but when the
pup insisted on finding out whether there was any flesh on
his calf, he retaliated with spirit.

The dog bounced back like a ball, but it was evident
from his growling that his retreat was merely tactical.
Ferenc however did not kick him again, but just looked
at him, and instantly the dog withdrew to his house whin-
ing as if he had been whipped. There are looks which
make even so fearless and courageous a pup as Boisi tremble with fright and Ferenc could muster up such a look
when he felt the necessity for it.

Having been received thus cordially, Ferenc hesitated in
the yard for a second, uncertain whether his neighbors
were living in the small house or in the big house. The
chimney of the big house was smoking, to be sure, but it
seemed to him that he heard a door creak in the small one.

And indeed, who should step out of it all of a sudden
but Etel. She had been over there to fetch corn for the

chickens.

"Well look who's here! Ferenc! I recognized you right away," she greeted him in a friendly voice.

Ferenc looked at her somewhat curiously, but his voice was not unfriendly.

"And I almost didn't recognize you! Etel—aren't you? You have become quite Russian."

"Really?"

"Yes. That's the country where the women are so fair and blonde."

Etel blushed. So Ferenc was not so awkward after all. He dared look a woman in the eye. And Etel by no means felt like rejecting his attention.

"Well, at least you will come more often to us, whenever you want to remember the Russian women. You must have grown accustomed to them."

"And tired of them too," Ferenc answered, sincerely.

Etel did not grow angry with him for his sincerity. She asked him to step into the house.

Ferenc did not want to hold up Etel in her work. He had only brought something for Uncle Mátyás. But Mátyás was up in the garret with Mother, they were hanging up the smoked hams and bacon. Ferenc asked her to give it to Mátyás for him, it was just a trifle, the Russky had sent it, to remember him by.

"Don't be in such a hurry! Why, nobody is waiting for you at home?"

"No? And the child?"

Etel was so annoyed with herself that she nearly dropped the bucketful of corn. Suppose Ferenc were to think that she had never cared for the orphan at all. How in heaven's name could she have made such a mistake! Quickly recovering himself, she said:

"I said it because I was wondering where you put Peter? You should have brought him over, he could have played away the time nicely with my Marika."

They went into the room. In the doorway, Ferenc took off his hat, and put it on the top of the bed. Yes, there were actually people who took off their hats when they entered a room, and had to be invited to put them back on again. But Etel somehow felt that she could not very well ask Ferenc to do this, he was so different, so strange, as if he had not been a peasant at all. He did not sit on the edge of the chair, or spread himself out with feet and hands outstretched as if they did not belong to him; he sat straight, yet comfortably. His hair was combed nicely too, and parted on one side, although it was a weekday. And, when one took a good look at him, he did not seem old at all, his graying hair suited his black eyes nicely, it was only a matter of growing accustomed to it.

"So you are living with your father-in-law, Etel?" he said and looked around the room.

"Only in wintertime. So that we shouldn't have to heat and light two places."

"That's the way to do it," said Ferenc, and his glance fell upon Rokus's picture as it stood on the chiffonier. It showed him in uniform, and it stood there just like his own picture at home, only that this one had no frame, and stood against a green glass. A wide-faced, strong-necked, big man, a little greenish-yellow now from the reflected light of the glass.

Ferenc stared at the picture without saying a word. Etel hurried into the alcove, to pull herself together, because she had noticed that her underskirt was hanging out from below her skirt. When she came out—it took hardly a minute, although she had re-tied her shawl, too, and exchanged her creaking working slippers for her Sunday ones—Ferenc rose to go. He said he had to knead bread before noon.

"My!" said Etel, "that bread certainly *will* smell of pipe

tobacco."

Not at all, Ferenc assured her, because he smoked cigarettes, and touched pipes only when forced to. And he could cook anything in the world: paprika potatoes, potato soup, potato *tarhonya,* sour potatoes, potato mush.

"And how would all these potatoes get along with a little smoked wurst, or bacon perhaps," Etel said slyly and offered to give him some since they had quite a quantity, some from last year in fact, which they were afraid would get rancid sooner or later.

Ferenc was grateful for her kindness, but he figured that since he was going to the city the next day to the county fair, he could buy enough of everything to last until he didn't know how long. Etel did not want to force the issue. She did not want Ferenc to get ideas into his head. The man was still unborn for whose sake she would make as much as one step out of her way. She lifted her head high, as all these thoughts ran through her head, and drew herself up, her bosom swelling and her eyes challenging. She had merely taken pity on him, like a good neighbor—but she was careful to say all this to herself only. Aloud she encouraged Ferenc to come over whenever he found some womanish work too difficult, or was missing something. Either she or Mother would always be glad to help him out.

"Why, even that poor Russky came over here like our very own son. Don't you be any more of a stranger." Etel shook hands with him, and added, "Until you know just how things will turn out."

When Ferenc left, she looked after him from the window, but noticed only after a good five minutes that she was looking after him at all. Etel could not understand why she did it, but she had no time to ponder over it, she had to hurry and feed the chickens. Etel dashed out far more briskly and spryly than at any other time, but she did not notice this either, nor did she realize that on her way to the coop she broke an icicle off the eaves and whirled it in the sunshine like a child.

But during the ensuing weeks, Etel had to realize that a change had taken place within her and that this change had all begun the minute she had first noticed what shiny black eyes Ferenc had. She blushed when this thought flashed through her mind, and, facing herself in the looking glass, she reproached herself for it. But since the looking glass reflected a rather pretty, heartshaped, smooth, fair face, with very fitting slender brows, a small snub nose, and spirited red lips, she changed her mind and decided to forgive herself. True, she would have liked it better if her face had been more sunburnt and her hair a shade more chestnut colored and less blonde. Then she wondered why she thought of all this now for the first time in her life, why it had never occurred to her before!

"Baa-aa, you Russian woman!" and she mockingly stuck out her tongue at herself—another thing she had never done before in all her life. Yes, women do stick out their tongues occasionally, but not at themselves, nor in front of the glass, and certainly not at eleven in the morning.

"What are you doing there before the glass?" asked Mother as she entered, and Etel thought she would die on the spot—Mother had so much surprised her.

"There must be a blister on my tongue," she said, and withdrew it, although now was the time to stick it out.

Mother knew a very good remedy for blisters on the tongue and told Etel its recipe at once. She was rather surprised therefore when Etel began to spoon her steaming hot soup at noon as if nothing had been the matter with her at all.

"Isn't your tongue hurting you any more?"

"My tongue?" Etel looked at her in amazement. "Why should it? Never in my life did my tongue hurt me!"

If Mother had been more curious, she could have found out more things about her daughter-in-law to be surprised at. Usually so calm, and cautious, she had suddenly become rash and heedless. She broke a plate, for example, then a glass, or she forgot to shut up the chicken coop, or hid the scissors so thoroughly that no one could find them. Formerly, when Mother chid her for something, she had become depressed, or pressed her lips together and remained as silent as a fish for a whole day. Now, however, the louder Mother scolded her, the louder Etel laughed, and when Mother grew angry at that, Etel either observed loudly that Mother's hens were of a finer strain than hers, or suddenly found a few ounces of coffee in her chest, or expressed her fear that by the time she grew as old as Mother was she would not even be able to chew porridge, whereas Mother's teeth were still so strong that she could crack nuts with them—all of which remarks were not calculated to prolong Mother's anger.

Mother might well have pondered another fact too, namely, that her daughter-in-law was now constantly finding things to sew. She even dug up Mátyás's old torn shirts. It was curious too that she took her sewing to the north window—and perhaps that was the chief reason why her work didn't progress. And if Mother had seen this, and had accused Etel of sitting in the window for no other reason than that it offered a good view of Ferenc's farm— as she had some weeks before when the Russky was still around—why, then Mother would have been even more disappointed. For if Etel did sit in the north window in order to look out for Ferenc, then why on earth did she always hide when she noticed him coming over?

But Mother did not notice anything at all though Mátyás once brought up the matter. They were at the supper table when he spoke up:

"Say, you, since when do you think you're driving the

Charles' Wain?"

Etel was amazed.

"You mean me?"

"Of course I mean you. Who did you think, the Reverend? Now what have you against Ferenc?"

"I? Nothing in the world! I don't care for him one way or the other."

"That's just it. Instead of treating him with chicken and cake, you act as if he were just dirt under your feet."

Etel's face turned flaming red.

"Do you expect me to flatter him? Who do you think I am, father?"

"Look here, my child, you have only two holes in your nose yourself, just like the poor man's pig."

The woman who will not react to such a beautiful proverb must have a heart of stone. Etel's was not. She did not say a word, just rose from the table, without even finishing her supper, picked the sleeping Marika out of bed and began to wrap her up in her shawl.

Mátyás looked at Mother. He raised his eyebrows so high that they seemed to be lost in his cap. This movement was what he called a wink. It meant: "Go on, woman, pacify this other fool." Mátyás could not very well do it himself; after all, he had to think of his manly dignity.

Mother, as always in her life, obeyed, though she would have preferred to hurl the dish, together with the braised cabbage, at the young woman's head.

"What do you mean to do, my child?" she asked her, taking her by the arm.

"I'm going home," Etel answered.

"Home? Why, isn't this your home? Would you have the heart to take the innocent little soul out into the bitter cold?"

Etel put the child down. Mother was right. And anyway it is always satisfaction to be apologized to by one's mother-in-law. Of course, it came gratuitously from Mother since it wasn't she who hurt her.

"Your father doesn't want to harm you, my child!"

"Then why does he say such things to me," said Etel, with a curl of her lips, and sat down on the bench near the oven, turning her back on the table and the lamp.

Mátyás had been a little shocked by Etel's outbreak, and now to make the matter worse whatever way he thrust his knife into the dish, he could find no meat in it, only cabbage. But suddenly the knife knocked against the jawbone of the pig, and his appetite returned. It's good when a woman is silent, but when she is too silent, the devil is somewhere around. But Etel had spoken, and Mátyás knew that her resentment was gone.

"Now, come, what did I say to you? Look, here is the jawbone, break it yourself, if you like the marrow. My grandmother, God bless her, always used to say that it makes a woman want to kill."

Mátyás had never heard anything like this from his grandmother, chiefly because he had never known her, and if he accused her of such naughty thoughts it was merely because he wanted to keep the conversation in the right channel.

And indeed, Etel did turn her face a little toward the light.

"Father always says things to me as if I were Modol Boca. I am not anybody's hussy!"

"Blast any man who dares to say any such thing about you! No, my child, God forfend, but you're a widow, and not the last of them either, and Ferenc is a widower, and one of the finest, so you are just fit for each other. Now I've said it."

The busy white brows again disappeared beneath the cap.

"You say something too, Mother."

Mother also said something. She even took her lower lip between her thumb and forefinger, as always when she wanted to say something particularly important.

"Yes, my child, that's true. You fit each other to a T. You and Ferenc would make a very nice couple."

Etel burst into tears, although she was not a cry baby.

"I don't want to get married! Why do you want me to do something I don't feel like doing? Am I such a bad daughter to you that you have to get rid of me by all means? You don't need to stuff me down anybody's throat! I can live on my own; I neither dance away, nor spend what I have."

She spoke sadly rather than angrily. The old folks tried to pacify her with gentle words. They respected her, they said, they liked her, she had always been a good daughter to them. They wouldn't want to have her separated from them for the world. That was just why they would like to see her marry Ferenc. For then they all could stay together. And there would be a man in the family again, a man who could take a goodly part of the worries off the old folks' shoulders, a man to whom Etel could cling if anything were to happen to them. For they were old sparrows already, both of them, even dawn was sunset to them. And Ferenc was a decent, honest man; anybody with whom he took up could thank God for it.

"You watch out, my child! Some day somebody else will start to bake pies for him. Because Ferenc is the kind of candy every fly wants to lick, and it's possible that when he looks around more, his eyes will land on a rose blossom and not on a ripe pear."

Mother said this partly because she was a wise woman of the world, and partly because she was so perfect a mother-in-law that she wanted to prick her daughter-in-law even when she soothed her. And Etel—she couldn't do anything else—wiped her eyes, curled up her lips, and answered with her arms akimbo:

"Well, Mother, if Ferenc won't eat pie until I cook him one, he may as well rent out his teeth now, and for life."

"So you don't want to marry him?"

"Not even if he could make a silk purse out of a sow's ear! Not I!"

"No one wants to force you, my child," Mother said gently, but her old eyes were shining with joy. For if Mother had thought that the young woman was very much after Ferenc, she would not have blocked her way, because Mátyás was for it, but she wouldn't have helped her either. In that case, Mother would have viewed the amorous warfare with enforced neutrality. But the minute Etel showed that she was not interested in Ferenc, she was for him. She did not very well know what ailed the young woman; as a matter of fact, she did not very much try to find it out, because Mother was experienced enough to know that for things like this there was no explanation, but just the same, she immediately decided that, whatever happened, Etel would marry Ferenc.

Yes, when God created the female He planted queer ideas in her head. He must have found that one rib insufficient, and thrown in a little of most other beasts too. She has somewhat of the hen in her indubitably, because women like to cackle; she gets her querulousness from the crab, and (by a slight stretch of the analogy) her elusiveness from the dragon-fly. There it is, sitting on a reed stalk, basking calmly in the sun, not even suspecting that there is a man behind it, and you reach out for it, close your fist, you feel the dragon-fly in your hand already, you cry out: "I've got you!"—and then you notice it hanging nonchalantly on the sweep of the well, with head down. And the female of the species is just as perplexing and elusive —although there are times when you can catch even the dragon-fly, especially when the dew falls on its wings, or better still, when it gets sleepy.

Mátyás was thinking these things in bed, sucking his pipe in the dark, and any man who uses his head knows that Mátyás was right. They are all so queer, and so different, these members of the opposite sex, whether Rozas or Etels, whether dried prunes or red, juicy, ripe apples. Look at Etel, for instance. She behaved like the beautiful Princess Ilona, madly in love with Prince Árgyélus and yet just pining away in the Black Castle. When women of the city acted like that, women in silks who learnt their emotions from books, and who learnt them because they had nothing else to do all day long but to chase one sensation after another—well and good, they were born to it. But Mátyás had heard from the storekeeper, who was a woman well versed in the ways of the world, that nowadays even the Princess Ilonas of the city had grown wiser, and no longer hid themselves from the handsome young Árgyéluses; in fact, they went out to meet them, and showed them their legs, so that they could be noticed more easily. Mátyás could testify to the truth of this himself, he had seen with his own eyes how the city women disported themselves, displaying their calves. True, he was an old man, and was not supposed to notice such things, but then again, there was no sense in gouging out his eyes for so trivial a reason, and so see them he did. Well, then, why did Etel make so much fuss? After all, no matter how white a face she had and no matter how fair she was, she had been created for no different purpose than all other female animals. Mátyás, to be sure, had never caught his daughter-in-law doing anything immoral, and it was possible that she was cold-lipped and her blood was just so much buttermilk—there were even such creatures among hens, although, according to Mátyás, it depended very much on the rooster and not only on the hen. And Ferenc was a handsome rooster, not to be despised by any hen. A man with seven acres was worth a little running after nowadays, and she could have moved over to Ferenc's a long while ago, if she had only had as much brains as himself. It would be the best solution for both of them, and best for Mátyás too.

Yes, that was what should have been done, but maybe it would all come right in the end. Perhaps it wasn't so bad that they had to wait; after all, even the proverb said that rash dogs whelped blind pups. The law of life, figured Mátyás, would take care of itself sooner or later. But, for the time being, the law seemed to achieve nothing. Etel just threw herself hither and thither on her bed, the dried corn hair with which the mattress was filled rustled under her, and the more she pulled the quilt over her the colder she felt, and the more she pushed it off the hotter she grew.

There was no moonlight, yet the room was not quite dark. The whitewashed oven inside and the snow outside spread a faint shimmer.

Etel slid off the bed, and Mátyás saw a white shadow flutter in the dusk across the room, her naked sole hardly touching the naked floor.

"Anything troubling you, Etel?" he asked her quietly.

"I'm looking for the pitcher," she answered, feeling about on the chiffonier but facing the northern window. "My throat is parched, it's too hot in the room."

"Even the kernels of corn pop open on the fire," thought Mátyás, and with this pleasing thought he fell asleep. But Etel could not sleep for a long time; she saw that the neighbor's window was dark, but there were just as many sorts of darkness as there were kinds of light.

# VII

IT WAS a beautiful clear day and the snow was beginning to melt here and there. Among the bald branches of the mulberry tree, yellow buntings displayed their gold. Mother was looking over some things and came upon a pair of Marika's old shoes. Anybody could see they were not worth much but it occurred to Mother that they might still be good enough for Peter. They wouldn't bring in anything at the fair, the toes had no shape whatever, the heels were woefully run down, and one could only guess where the soles had been—God alone knows what these children of today do to their boots! They are spoiled, that's what's the matter with them, they aren't anywhere near what Mother used to be in her childhood days. She never wore boots on her feet until she became a bride, nothing but slippers until her wedding day, and when it rained or snowed she pulled them off and took them under her arm. Etel was nigh ten years old too when she got her first pair of boots, and she got them merely because Mátyás had sold two bushels of wheat to the cobbler and he couldn't pay for them, so Mátyás gathered up all the boots he found in his shop and took them home. And now look, Etel pulled boots on the feet of this little snubnose here when she was hardly three, because she didn't want her to run around in the snow barefooted! As if she couldn't have put on Mátyás's slippers! Morals aren't what they used to be, thought Mother, and if we live long enough we'll see the midwives bathing newborn infants in shoes!

"Look here, Etel, what d'ye think, shall I send this over

to Ferenc for his son?"

Etel was shocked.

"But Mother, it would look like a joke. Those shoes aren't good enough even for the dunghill!"

"They are good enough to give away. The brat may use them walking on the stubble."

Etel was no longer angry, she merely laughed.

"Stubble indeed! Why, we haven't even sown yet."

"Old women see far!" replied Mother, mysteriously, wiping the mold from the little boots with her apron. "Go and look after your own business and don't butt into mine."

Mother indeed saw far. She sent Marika to Ferenc with the gift, and the child forgot herself over there playing with Peter; Ferenc brought her back home in the evening. He carried her home all the way in his arms, pressing her to his chest under his *suba*.

Mother had not only foreseen this, but had actually taken it for granted, so that the moment Ferenc arrived she was already cooking *heröce* for supper. Etel suggested to Mother that she would help her, but Mother refused her right in front of Ferenc.

"Just look at that, Ferenc, these young people who grudge their elders a place by the fire!"

There was nothing to do about it; Etel had to stay inside with Ferenc. Mátyás arrived from the mill, they could hear him stamping around in the kitchen shaking the snow off his boots, but he did not step inside. Mother reported to him the situation whereupon Mátyás retired to the shed to draw some wine, a most advisable occupation when you feel cold.

The *heröce* sizzled in the fat for a long time and Mátyás surrendered himself so heartily to his business that in a few minutes he began to look cross-eyed. The young people had had time enough to reach the "until death do us part" twice over but they sat in the room as if they had been married ten years. Etel was sewing, and though she could hardly make the thread go through the needle's eye, and she missed it four times running, this happened only because lately they had been mixing the kerosene with water, or with something equally bad, and it burned so badly it was quite unbearable. Ferenc was talking to her about America, where even the stables were lighted with electricity and even hired hands owned automobiles. Ferenc spoke in a low voice, quietly, without gesticulating much. He rolled a terrible lot of cigarettes, and threw the little cigarette butts which stuck to his lips all in one place, behind the door.

"I don't think I'd ever be able to settle down in that America," remarked Etel, biting off the end of the thread. She had a shirt on her knees. Two years before she said she had bought a couple of ells of linen, but it wasn't good at all, all the shirts went to pieces in no time.

"Linen substitute," said Ferenc, fingering the shirt, and told her the name of an American city where he had been working in a textile factory for two months. They were making good honest goods there.

"You seem to have fallen pretty much in love with that America of yours," Etel reproached him jokingly.

"Yes, it's a different world over there." Ferenc could not say that he did not like it for a while, but, at the end, his heart drew him home.

"Your home is where your family is," said Etel.

Yes, true, but it was not only that. The soil was different here, and the wheat, and everything. While abroad, Ferenc had dreamed much about life at home, but now that he got home he realized that many things ought to be changed, not everything was quite right the way it was.

"Maybe you are also one of these who want to divide up the lands?" Etel looked up from her sewing. "Father told us there's a new faith now but I don't know what they call them."

No, Ferenc was not a Communist. It was possible that they wanted to do good but they went about it in the wrong way.

Ferenc had a curious voice, Etel had never heard the like of it. She could not describe it. It was not a sing-song voice, yet it reminded her of the church. Of the organ, maybe, before they had requisitioned the pipes. But whatever Ferenc's voice was like, Etel would have gladly listened to it until morning.

Mother had not been so thoroughly at peace with the world for a long time. She listened a little at the door, then went out into the yard, peeped through the window, and was happy to hear Etel laugh. But all she could see was that Ferenc put his hands together, and wiggled his fingers, so as to throw funny shadows on the wall, moving shadows of rabbits, and pigeons, and goats. The goat was so well made that it could even move its whiskers. Ferenc invented all this for Marika's amusement but Etel laughed too, and even Mother smiled at this foolishness. Although, come to think of it, two youngsters alone in a room amused themselves differently in her time.

"Let's go in." Mother urged Mátyás to stop his manipulations with the wine. "They think they are gentlefolks, the next time I'll draw the curtain on them."

But Mother was wrong this time. The curtain had nothing to do with it.

The minute the supper was over, in the course of which Mátyás drank a toast to Ferenc and wished him "wine, wheat, peace, and a beautiful wife"—Ferenc replied with only a "strength and health"—and rose suggesting that they should retire till the morrow.

"Accompany Ferenc to the gate, Etel, my child," said Mother gently. Etel obeyed her, although she would have done it without being bidden, because she knew the etiquette.

And now it was proved that Mother was quite wrong about the curtain. The curtain of the night was drawn in the yard, yet Etel returned almost at once, and her face was not a scrap redder than usual. On the contrary, her teeth were chattering and she was rubbing her hands together:

"My, but the weather certainly is biting cold, it almost froze the soul out of me!"

Time passed, the snow slowly withdrew from the fields, lying only here and there in the hollows like white spots on a black cloak. As Ferenc came over more often Peter also grew accustomed to the neighbor's house, and sometimes the children nearly brought down the roof. But as far as Ferenc and Etel were concerned, neither had budged an inch. This in spite of the old people who did everything in their power to make one couple out of the two fools.

When, for instance, Ferenc came over in the evening for his son, Mother whirled about him like a top.

"Why don't you leave that child be? Let them sleep together, they are so fond of each other! Like sister and brother!"

"Can't do it!" Ferenc jested. "Who will take care of me at night?"

"And I won't let you have him," Mother stubbornly replied. "I'll keep him here in pawn."

Whereupon, if Ferenc had only had sense enough, he should have answered that, in that case, Mother should keep him too. But Ferenc merely smiled, as was his custom, and gathered the little fellow in his arms. Peter's emotional life had undergone a decided change since he had begun to come a-visiting to the Mátyás's, and he showed more inclination toward the weaker sex than did his father. This change, of course, was due not only to spiritual causes, but also to such material goods as, for instance, dried sour cherries, or "owl's lungs." This fantastic name designated certain worm-eaten apples which, cut into two and dried by the sun on the roof of the shed, passed for fancy tropical fruits. It was Mother's custom to place these luxuries on the market around Christmas, but this year she refrained from putting them to commercial use.

At another time, Mother suddenly discovered that Ferenc's shirts were washed with chlorine.

"I don't think so," Ferenc smiled. Etel liked to see him smile, not only because a smile suited him well but because he had two nice, healthy rows of teeth.

"I do," Mother argued, "I know these laundries in the city. Why do you do that? Etel would gladly wash your little linen for you! Just look at Etel's washing. It's like virgin snow, even if I have to say so myself."

Ferenc looked at it, because the top button of Etel's bodice was open and the edge of her shirt showed. Etel felt ashamed of herself. Not because of her shirt, there was indeed no reason to be ashamed for that, but because she knew she blushed.

She had no reason to blush, though, because Ferenc smiled just as calmly as he had before he had seen this practical proof of Etel's dexterity. It would be queer, anyway, if a grown-up man lost his head the moment he saw a woman's linen.

"I take all the responsibility for the person who washes for me," said Ferenc.

"Really?"

"Yes. I wash everything myself. I had plenty of time to learn how."

Etel burst into laughter. It seemed to Mother that the laughter was addressed to her. Well, Mother, with all your tricks and knowledge, you've flunked!

Mother held council with Mátyás. Etel was a fool, and Ferenc a nincompoop. What did Mátyás think, was there ever anything to come of it? Mátyás answered there was, because it had to. He always carried out what he planned. The fields would be joined, even if the devil must eat his own tail, said Mátyás. He knew women, and knew that even the wildest beasts grow humble when they get hungry. Let Ferenc kiss her but once, and then she'd realize what she was missing. One had to be careful about Ferenc, though, because one couldn't tell what was in him. But he was a man just like all the others! Maybe he had somebody, Mátyás speculated, perhaps that was the reason he went to town so often. It was possible that he considered Etel below him, maybe he thought she was too much of a peasant for him. For he had certainly picked up some queer notions abroad! He brought home a newspaper every time he went to town, and even Mother must have noticed that his curses lacked spice. He didn't spit and he drank water with his wine. True, Mátyás's water wouldn't ruin any wine, but only gentlemen mix their wine with water. Mátyás now confided to Mother an even queerer thing about Ferenc, one he had observed. But, God, don't ever mention it to Etel! The other day, he went over to Ferenc early in the morning, and he nearly turned into a pillar of salt! There he was, standing at the well stripped to the waist, washing himself with snow! I am an old man; but tell me, Mother, have you ever seen my back or my chest naked in your life? No, nobody has, not since his mother taught him how to put on and how to take off a shirt, and nobody will ever look at them either, not until they wash him before putting him in his coffin. And it won't be his fault if he doesn't feel properly ashamed of himself then. He wouldn't mind, however, if it were only this; after all, Ferenc was a soldier, and in the army, in Siberia, they learned to be shameless. But he even washed his teeth! With a brush! Mátyás saw him do it with his own eyes; he wanted to ask him who did he think he was? A doctor or something? Because even among gentlefolk, only doctors do things like that, and only the young doctors, at that, because even doctors acquire sense as they grow old. Then he decided not to say a word about it, he was afraid Ferenc might turn up his nose. For he was sure Ferenc did it only during these lazy days. When they begin to till, to plow and to sow, well, then he would ask Ferenc: "Well, you fool, why don't you brush your teeth now?" And you see, Mother, you can't blame the war for this. After all, the army needs soldiers not to clean their own teeth but to knock out the enemy's. Mátyás had another idea about this queer habit of Ferenc's. The Jewess told him that she saw Ferenc go to the schoolhouse twice lately, and both times it was the teacher who asked him to come in. So most probably that's the matter with him. Well, if he goes in there only to warm up a bit, there's nothing in that, Ferenc is young, and when a man is young he does things like that, especially nowadays, when folks are so mixed up with each other. But Mátyás thought he ought to warn him not to take her to the altar. She hasn't got anything in the whole wide world to her name, nothing but her two big, frightened eyes; she is so thin she doesn't even throw a shadow.

Mátyás pondered over these problems a great deal and then one day it occurred to him that he had found a way to open Ferenc's eyes. He had a little money in the chest, a little in the chiffonier, a little in the garret, wrapped up in oilcloth. Then he had a few pennies in the bank, not in one but in several of them, everywhere a little, so that if something happened to one bank, his money would not all be lost. So Mátyás collected his bankbooks and took them over to Ferenc.

"Will you look them over for me, Ferenc? See if they are in order. I never know when they cheat me."

Ferenc had a little notebook, and a pencil in it, and it took him but a minute to figure out how much money Mátyás had.

"Eleven million two hundred and eighty-two thousand."

Mátyás pulled down his vest, a gesture which meant, in every language in the world, in the city or on the farm, "The devil of it, so we are somebody, aren't we."

But it was not easy to move Ferenc. He did not show the slightest excitement over the fact that so great a leader of the financial world as Mátyás had trusted him with his confidence. He shook his head.

"Everything is all right, the interest is added too, but you have been cheated just the same."

Mátyás grew hot; he opened a button on his jacket.

"What did you say? I am cheated, eh?"

"Yes. But you are cheated by yourself. How can you leave so much money in the bank? It's getting worse all the time and soon it won't be worth anything."

Mátyás did not understand just what Ferenc told him about inflation and devaluation, and so he did not care to mention the garret and his other banking institutions. He turned his talk into another channel and began to speak about what he had come over for.

"You learn a lot of wise things in those newspapers, and yet you can't give advice to yourself."

"Can't I?" asked Ferenc, rolling a cigerette.

"You never think that you ought to marry, eh?"

"No, I don't," and he looked at Mátyás with honest surprise in his eyes. "What made you think of that?"

Mátyás embarrassedly mumbled something. He had just thought of it. He used to talk about it with Mother, she said that so handsome and decent a man as Ferenc could easily find a good wife for himself.

"I had enough of them," Ferenc shook his head. "I don't feel the need of them, and you know, Uncle Mátyás, it's good to have a wife, but it's even better not to."

"And the child? Do you want him to grow up without a mother?"

"He doesn't need to be suckled any longer, and as for other things, I can attend to them myself. Look here, Uncle!"

And he opened the pantry door. The smell of freshly baked bread streamed out of it. Six loaves of bread were on the shelves.

"I baked them today," boasted Ferenc.

"Six at the same time? Do you want to feed the poor too?"

"You know, Uncle Mátyás, I don't mind baking them, but I do hate to knead them. So I mixed enough dough to fill the trough. I won't have to trouble about bread until Easter."

"But they will be so dry you'll have to split them with an axe!"

"I have brains, Uncle Mátyás. I sprinkle them every week."

Otherwise the pantry was in order, and the house too, the room swept, the bed made, there were even a few stalks of Christmas wheat growing in a pot in the window. Mátyás was forced to conclude that there was but one fault with it all.

"Cold is the quilt that isn't warmed by a woman."

Ferenc said he did not like heat, and if it hadn't been for the child, he would have kept the window open night and day.

Mátyás thought that this was another gentlemanly notion and rose to go home, a little out of humor. He had settled nothing, six oxen wouldn't move this stubborn fool an inch.

"I am going too, Uncle Mátyás, I'll walk you home,"
Ferenc said, brushing his hat with his elbow.

"Coming to us?"

"No, I'm going over to the teacher."

He even dared to tell about it, the shameless scoundrel!

"What have you got to do with her?" growled Mátyás.

"I want to buy some saplings from her in the Spring.
That is to say, not from her, but from her fiancé. He exchanged rings with her a couple of weeks ago. He is a
clerk at the general post-office in the city, but he also has
a tree nursery. We used to be together in the same company in Wolhynia."

Mátyás realized that he was on the wrong track when he
suspected Ferenc with the teacher, and his pipe began to
draw better immediately. He asked him what trees he
planned to plant, and where. For it seemed to him that
there were plenty of them in the vineyard already.

"No, I don't want to put them there," Ferenc explained.
"I was even thinking of throwing out those that are in
there. They are old, those trees, and not the best of them
either, and trees aren't good in a vineyard."

Mátyás shook his head doubtfully.

"And I always heard that a vineyard is never nice without trees, just as a wedding is no wedding without music.
All the old people used to say so. Just look at my big apri-
cot-tree, it paid me forty hundred-weights of fruit the last
year."

"I believe you," said Ferenc. "But it threw shadow on
forty vines, and you didn't harvest much off those, I am
sure."

That was true, Mátyás could do nothing but acknowledge it. But poor men can't be very finicky about things
like that. The land is small, one has to get the most out
of it. That's just the trouble, they don't get the most of it,
answered Ferenc. He saw it in foreign countries, how they

do it, and those people aren't fools either. In Japan, for instance, there is a whole garden on the lot covered here only by one apricot tree. They like dwarf trees there. Mátyás was greatly surprised at this, he had never heard of dwarf trees, only of dwarf dogs, although only big dogs are worth anything. But he liked to see that Ferenc was so experienced. Of course, those who had a chance to look around in the war were lucky; too bad poor Rokus wasn't so lucky, then Etel wouldn't have to work so hard.

"It's a nice slice, though, just look at it," said Mátyás, pointing at Etel's land with a wide sweep of his arm. "And good land, too. It's worth almost as much as yours. It's smaller by an acre or two but there is no soda in it."

Ferenc suggested that the land bordering on the lake should be planted with paprika, that was to be more profitable than wheat.

"But the poor woman can't do all the work herself," Mátyás pursued, trying to herd him back to the right path. "Of course, if only the right man would put a kerchief on her head! And she deserves it too, she is a modest and decent woman, not one of those loose hussies you can see about nowadays."

Ferenc nodded; yes, he knew it.

"She has a little money by her own right, and our money won't be put to the grave with us either, she'll get that too, after our granddaughter. She has lots of suitors, you know, one for every one of her fingers, but she is too finicky. One is too young for her, the next one too old. She says she has plenty of time to wait for the man God is keeping for her."

"Every sack finds its patch," suggested Ferenc wisely and shook hands with Mátyás.

Mátyás reported to Mother that there was nothing the matter with Ferenc, he was flinching from the yoke only because he was too bashful, but that could be helped too, he would find a way.

On the last Sunday before Lent, Mátyás buttonholed Ferenc in the Club and invited him to supper on Shrove Tuesday, to bury Carnival.

"Thank you ever so much, Uncle Mátyás, but I don't think that I feel like merrymaking."

Mátyás assured him that the time of big merrymaking had passed, the world wasn't the same now that it used to be. Ferenc was to be their only guest, but if somebody happened to drop in, of course, he wouldn't be thrown out. They were counting on him to come with the child; let him eat his belly full once in a while, too, then he could go on living on cabbage until Easter.

Very well, Ferenc accepted the invitation, and sent his best regards to Aunt Roza. He would show up on time, together with the child.

But on Shrove Tuesday, Marika called for Peter early in the afternoon. Mother sent her over with a little popcorn and bade her return with Peter while it was still light. That of course didn't mean that Ferenc should wait until after dusk.

He walked over after sunset. Rain was in the air, and steam rose from the meadows. Somewhere somebody was playing a bagpipe; it squeaked hoarsely. That was a sign of rain too.

Ferenc found the women in the kitchen, busy around the fire. Mother received him exuberantly, but Etel was pale and had rings under her eyes, scarcely recognizable as she stood there, with drooping shoulders.

"Are you sick?" asked Ferenc.

"Heavens knows! I don't feel any particular pain, but the cold nearly eats me up."

"Love's cold, my child," Mother threw in very innocently, stirring something on the fire.

"That's easier to cure than poverty," Ferenc picked up

the joke. "You ought to marry!"

"Carnival is over," answered Etel, and stopped to blow a little at the moist twigs. As the fire flamed up, Etel reached to her eyes. Smoke went into them.

"It isn't yet! Why else should I be here?" Ferenc went on with the jest. "Where is Uncle Mátyás?"

"He's educating the children inside," explained Mother, opening the door for the guest.

Mátyás was a practical educator. He held to the opinion that a man had to begin to harden himself early, and nothing hardened one better than wine.

The two children were wobbling in the middle of the room, holding hands. Marika, her face flaming red, tried to sing, but her tongue hardly moved. Peter was as green as a lizard, and waggled more and more with every step. Mátyás enjoyed them from the corner of the sofa, and clapped the beat to their dance.

"You say it too, Peter!"

Peter said it, by heart:

"The devil take you, the devil take you," but just what he wanted the devil to take was not disclosed. When he noticed his father he made a rush for him, and stretched out on the floor in all his two foot length, as it behoved a serious man bidding good-bye to Carnival.

"Poor little beetle," his father said as he lifted him up and put him on the bed in the corner. Marika needed no help, she climbed up to Peter right away, embraced him, and fell asleep in a second.

Mother noticed that Ferenc had become serious and that his eyes looked angry-like. She shook her head disapprovingly.

"Oh, you old guzzler, how could you do a thing like that to those innocent little souls!"

Mátyás, as befitted an old guzzler, laughed loudly. The cap on his head slid to one side and threatened to fall down.

"Let them remember Carnival! I wasn't any bigger than Peter when I first got drunk and yet I can remember it. Put down your *suba,* Ferenc!"

Ferenc controlled himself, he even clinked glasses with Mátyás, but he only touched his own with his lips.

Etel brought in the chicken soup, and Mother placed a small loaf of bread next to Ferenc's plate. It was baked especially for him, Mother was sure he had not eaten the like of it in Russia.

"No, I didn't," Ferenc answered, staring at it with strange concentration.

"What kind of bread do the Russky's eat?" Mother pursued the point in question. "Did they have war flour there too? Did they mix it with corn flour?"

"Sometimes," answered Ferenc curtly and bent over his plate. He ate his soup very fast now but still without bread.

Whereupon Mother remarked that it seemed to her Ferenc was not very fond of bread.

"No, not much," Ferenc said, swallowing hard.

"My poor Rokus was very fond of it," sighed Mother, "he could have died for bread."

At this point Ferenc coughed so much that he turned blue in the face. A splinter of bone must have stuck in his throat.

"Swallow a bite of bread," advised Mother, "that will push it down. Don't you turn me down, I've baked it for you."

Ferenc thanked her for it but it was already down. Nevertheless, he took a piece of the loaf and even carried it to his mouth, but then he put it down again and drank a glass of wine, this time without any water.

Etel noticed that Ferenc only crumbled the bread but ate everything without it. It was good that Mother did not notice this, because she would have been sad to see the

failure of her charm. For she had baked into that loaf a
thread or two from Etel's skirt. Mátyás had also eaten a
loaf like that once upon a time and it had contained two
threads from Roza's skirt, but of course neither Mátyás
nor Roza had known anything about it, for if they had the
charm would not have worked.

All Mother saw was that Ferenc broke a bite off the
charm and she was so happy over this that she did not
mind that Ferenc took but one helping from the stuffed
cabbage and made very little damage in the roast.

"You eat very little, Ferenc," Mátyás gave vent to his
disapprobation.

"Enough is as good as a feast," Ferenc defended himself. It was not always like that, he had a pretty good
appetite once upon a time, but he starved so much in
Siberia that his stomach shrunk, and now whenever he ate
too much he thought it'd burst.

"Well, we've got to eat up what's on the table because
we can't do anything with it during Lent," Mátyás remarked.

Just as he said this, the dog began to bark. Mátyás reached
for his glass greatly relieved.

"I'll give you a capful of devils if Boisi isn't barking at
a friend."

The dog's barking indicated that the visitor was a decent
man. He did not snarl, as was his business when a gentleman showed up; he didn't snort as he did when a beggar
was at the gate. He bayed, and that meant friend.

The decent man began to bless Jesus already in the
yard, and he did that in a rumbling bass voice. The two
old folks looked at each other satisfied. Etel smiled irritatedly:

"How does he get here at this time of the night? It's
Gyurka Messzi," she added, for the benefit of Ferenc.

Etel was not very fond of the old wine-sack. When he

was drunk he clung like a burr, and when he was sober he was such a thief that even the nails trembled in the walls at his coming. Ferenc and the old watchman had been great friends once upon a time, Gyurka Messzi had always looked in the other direction when Ferenc, then a little shepherd's boy, stole corn. But they had not once met since Ferenc's return.

The watchman staggered in. Water was just streaming from his hat and his *suba*. One could hear through the open door the Spring rain coming down in torrents. Gyurka Messzi was a tall, lean man, and considering the fact that he was a watchman that was a wonder, for men in office never starved, and had plenty of time to sleep. Furthermore, he was "in the neck," but that was no wonder.

A person who is "in the neck" is not drunk; just illuminated. This is not to say that he has already drunk himself silly; he merely has not poured the wine into his boots. His head does not tremble, only his feet stumble. In short, he is in that state when he thinks that even God was happy when He created him, and that it is his own personal duty to be happy about it also.

The watchman was so happy to see Mátyás that he asked him whether he had knocked over the bottle or the bottle had knocked over him; he was so happy to see Ferenc that he addressed him with a "servus," an address he did not bestow upon many; and he was so happy to see Etel that she was obliged to slap him on the hand with the handle of the fork.

The watchman shook his head as a horse does in his oat-bag.

"You see, darling, if an old bee can't eat of the ripe honey, at least he buzzes around it. Am I right, Roza?"

Mother agreed that that was true and after letting the watchman buzz round her for a second, she pushed the dish before him.

"Have a little of what's left, Uncle Gyurka."

The watchman protested that he could not eat another bite. Ever since noon he was going out from one friend's house and into another and, to be frank about it, his stomach was filled to its brim.

Mátyás came to his rescue, suggesting that Uncle Gyurka had never been known to be a man with a great appetite.

"He doesn't need more for supper than a little bird and a little calf."

But since Uncle Gyurka did not want to leave Mátyás in shame, he pulled the dish in front of him and gobbled up everything that was in it. He did not think he could eat of the poppyseed-*rétes*, either; he hated poppyseeds ever since Sadowa, when they had to put gunpowder on their rolls instead of poppyseeds. But purely out of politeness, he sent down some nine pieces of it. And when Mother screamed out: "Oh, I forgot all about it, you should have had a little *kocsonya* before the *rétes,*" Uncle Gyurka modestly advised her to bring that in too, because that was a typically Lenten dish.

After he had laid waste to everything, he turned to Mátyás:

"Well, brother, how did the devil ruin his son?"

Mátyás considered himself a better man than the devil, nor did he want to ruin Uncle Gyurka by keeping him from wine. The watchman did not drink little, but often. True, he did not forget either Mátyás or Roza, he filled their glasses every time he drank. But he did not fill up the young folks' glasses.

"You ought to have brains enough for yourself to know what to do."

The two young people were lost in a quiet conversation. Etel had troubles with her war doles, they obliged her to bring in a certificate of poverty, though they said nothing about that to the other widows, although some of them had four times as much land as she had. She did not know when she could go to the office, although she had to admit that they were rather kind to her, they told her she did not have to go in during office hours, she might come late in the afternoon, or rather, she should come only then, when the clerk would be in the office all by himself, and they could talk the matter over more quietly. What did Ferenc think, she was so stupid about these things? Ferenc said that he would go with her, he had something to attend to in the city anyway, he was buying a threshing machine on part-payments.

The watchman was telling news to the old folks. The son of the distiller, that bricklayer fellow, you remember him, he was always a rascal, well, he is now a sort of Lord Lieutenant in the city, called a government commissioner or something, and he wants to give him, Gyurka Messzi, a job too, he wants to make him Chief Watchman in the City Park. But he did not know whether he should accept that big office.

Mother was greatly surprised at this, but Mátyás, who was already beginning to lose his head, winked at him, desperately as if to steer him on to some goal.

"Did you—wish—to say something—brother?"

But the watchman did not heed Mátyás's winks. He didn't know what to do. Big office, big office, board, quarters, clothes, pension, everything, the only trouble was that he wouldn't be allowed to keep dogs, and what is a watchman without a dog?

Ferenc, to his misfortune, interrupted him in his self-torture.

"Well, if the watchman has no dog, he will have to bark himself."

The watchman at once rose to the height of the situation.

Ferenc's hand was hot, Etel's cold as a corpse.

The rain stopped. Ferenc, sunk in thought, walked cautiously with Peter round the small puddles. So the Mátyáses wanted him to marry their daughter-in-law. He had been suspecting for quite some time that something like that was in the back of Mátyás's head. Well, Etel might marry him if he asked her. She was a handsome, modest woman, anybody who married her would fare well. But Ferenc did not feel like marrying. He did not want a woman, neither Etel nor anybody else. He was tired, he wanted nothing but peace and quiet; he wanted to enjoy the fields, he wanted to sow, to work. Later perhaps, after he had completely forgotten these four years and a half, when he got rested, back on his legs. Maybe then. And if Etel was married by then, there'd be somebody else. Ferenc was convinced that as far as men were concerned women were all much the same.

# VIII

THERE was a banquet in the Club on the evening of the Fifteenth of March. In former days, they used to celebrate High Mass in the morning and listen to speeches delivered by an attorney from the city and several other friendly gentlemen at the *Honvéd* Monument. The attorney told them who the *honvéds* had been, and what the Hungarian nation wanted, and they placed a wreath with a ribbon in the national colors upon the monument. This year, however, there was no celebration. True, several old women and old men did gather around the monument, but they waited in vain; there was neither mass, nor wreath, nor speeches. The Reverend sent word that he was ill in bed; the attorney sent no message at all, just did not come. It was possible that he could not come, because the lake had inundated; fortunately not toward the fields, as was its custom, but in the direction of the highway. It flooded the road so completely that several wagons bound for the city had to turn back.

The leaders of the community agreed however that they could not possibly let the Fifteenth of March pass by without any celebration whatsoever and so they decided that they would not cancel the usual festive supper at the Club. After all, the poor Jewess had made preparations already, and it would be rather mean to let her throw out all the delicious *bürge paprikás*. And a few toasts had to be drunk in honor of Father Kossuth, too, even though the city gentlemen had left him in the lurch.

Ferenc went down to the Club following the path that

led along the shore of the lake. He watched uneasily the dirty yellow waves which had already reached the wheat-fields. There had been a cloudburst in the afternoon, and although the rain had ceased, the field-gray clouds still hovered menacingly around. From afar came the sound of the bell; the Reverend had not forgotten, despite his illness, to give orders to ring it. And the bell rang out, reminding and warning the people to fall to their knees, to pray to their angry God who alone could command the winds to sweep the skies and the sun to dry up the rain-soaked fields.

But who is he who, around St. Gregory's Day, un-fastens the chains of the waters and lets the lake loose upon the houses, the sowings, the farms? Who is it bids it sneak stealthily, destroy thunderingly, break open the cemeteries, uncover the dead and destroy the living, crumble down houses, heed not whether the people pray or curse, whether they be good or bad? What is this lake, who has put it here in the center of desert sand, who has appointed it a scourge of God, a terror of men?

The scientists claim that it is a basin of little wild streams which, running in the womb of the earth, gather here, in the hollow of the land, from higher planes. The people living on its shores say that there are secret springs at its bottom which occasionally spout forth. But they know nothing of sunken cities, or sunken bells ringing in the depths. There have never been any monasteries in this vicinity; no bishops, no princes, nor any other spiritual or worldly potentates have ever lived there—this spot of earth has no history, nor any folklore. At times, after an inundation, the lake leaves behind on the shore queerly shaped, peculiarly bored stones which the tide has washed up from the bottom. The peasants say they are chips of stones which fell from the skies; the archeologists argue that they are stone axes with which early man beat the roes to death. Poor men have lived in this neighborhood for ten thousand years, nameless slaves of the soil have loved, been born, lived, and died here for ten thousand years, races have blended into one another, all trying to tame the desert with their work, to fertilize the sand with the sweat of their brow, in Summer, picking flowers for their children at the shores of the reed-oasis, in the Spring, asking the water in horror, "Who are you?"

Old maps bear witness to the fact that the lake has always been what it is today: a playful monster—one day an innocent puddle, the next an awesome sea. Some maps show no trace of it, it was so small a pond in those days that the map-designer did not even notice it. Another draws it an inland sea as big as a county.

Sometimes it is blond like ripe wheat, like the hair of a woman, at other times it is angry-green, like young shoots on the fields in early Spring; and when it is most frightening, it is as gray as a coffin. Sometimes, for years on end, only the marsh marigold yellows on its shore, and only the white lace of wild carrot covers the little islets in the marsh. Then, all of a sudden, strange red and blue flowers appear in the swamp, flowers never before seen thereabouts, and vines thick as trees. Where have they come from, who has ordered them up from the mud? Sometimes, for long months, only the wailing cries of the pewit are heard from the swamp, then, from one day to another, the marsh begins to echo all sorts of strange noises, the night is filled with creaks, screeches, quacks, whistles; with hissing, buzzing, cackling, chirping, howling, chuckling, grunting, hooting sounds, and, in the pink of the dawn, or in the copper-colored mist of the full-moon, strange birds soar, flutter, dive, circle, spin, hover, and glide above the water. Who has sent them? Whence have they come? Whither will they go? Has God sent them to frighten mankind, or has He sent them to warn us that if we do not follow His commands we shall be punished? Or are they merely messengers from far-away, huge seas, bringing tidings to this impoverished relative, late descendant of ancient oceans, now wedged in between wheatfields and vineyards?

Ferenc was not occupied with such vain thoughts as he stood, leaning against a gnarled, old marsh oak, which was hard, stubborn, and strong to his back and gazing at the visibly swelling lake. All Ferenc thought of with his veteran brains, sharpened in foreign countries, was that it was rather queer that this lake, which, after all, despite all its mysteries, was nothing but a lowland marsh, had never yet found its master. Ferenc knew nothing of past ages, and to save his life, he would have been unable to conceive how many the thousand years had been that had elapsed since our conquering ancestors had held their first national assembly somewhere in this neighborhood. But one thing was sure, and that was that ever since Ferenc could remember, there had always been none but peaceful, work-loving people living here, people who gave unto God and unto men what was their due, people who honored the king and respected the law, people who even kept the rules and regulations concerning pastures, especially when they were forced to do it. They paid taxes to the city, they paid soldiers to the state, they fed their superiors out of the palms of their hands. Nevertheless, neither the city nor the state, neither the county nor the deputy had ever said to them: Well, men, why shouldn't you have a good time too, once in a blue moon? We'll drain, dry, and fill up this ugly hole down in the hollow, we don't want you to fear it every Spring; it will no longer swoop down upon you to eat up your houses, lands, cats, dogs, sparing only your tax-books. (For that is so light and winsome a little book that it always remains on the top, like foam.) Ferenc could not understand why it was like that, but he somehow felt that it was not good as it was, at least, it was not so abroad. In foreign countries, they cared for the poor people too, and not only for the barons. Not like here—for, lo, yonder across the lake, northward from where he stood, a dam protected the Baron's estate. The wind brought to Ferenc the merry voice of a piano, submerging now and then the feeble screams of the village bell.

Well, this certainly was a more complicated problem than all the theosophy and geology in the world combined, and the best that Ferenc could do under the circumstances was to cut a dried branch off the oak tree and to continue his way to the Club in the rain-smelling, rain-soaked twilight.

The branch was cut as a weapon against the dogs, but dogs are so created that sometimes they are wiser than their masters. They not only feel death three days before he steps up to the foot of the bed, they even receive accurate advance information concerning such curses of the elements as floods and earthquakes. They cannot very well explain to us why, but it is a fact that at such times they always look well in advance of the oncoming catastrophe for places where they may feel themselves secure, for shelters such as the bottom of a wagon, or the roof of a sty. Ferenc heard nothing but the hoots of an owl and all he could rouse from the fields was an occasional early-rising bat. The houses squatted silently in the darkness, scattered beneath the night, like chickens who feel a hawk above them in the air.

The Club, on the other hand, was not dark. The Jewess had lighted up both windows to serve as lighthouses for the thirsty souls—thirsty for knowledge, of course—slowly emerging from the dusk. But the cautious Jewess hung out the flag only after it had become completely dark. At night, all flags look black; the red flag of the

enlightened umbrella-maker as well as the red, white, and
green of the true patriot. She, poor creature, would have
best liked to hang out both, but neither in heaven nor
on earth, not even in the garret was there anything but a
fifty-year-old campaign banner, still proudly displaying the
name of a long-forgotten deputy, proving conclusively that
there is nothiing more beautiful than immortality.

Ferenc stopped in the doorway for a second, for the
dense cloud of smoke rising from the pipes bit his eyes.
The Club was full of people and the Jewess, whirling
hither and thither, carrying wine to the old folks and
beer to the youngsters, felt extremely happy.

"This way, neighbor," she winked to the newcomer.
"Here is a place for you, next to Uncle Mátyás. I'll bring
the *paprikás* in a second."

Mátyás had taken care that Ferenc should sit next to
him, among the old folks. It was not the custom to mix
with the young men, but Ferenc looked a good forty with
his graying, not-yet-thirty head.

St. Anthony's fire had already turned red the faces of
those who had arrived first, but there was not much
noise yet, they all talked quietly. And not much of the war.
At the most, they mentioned whose son, or son-in-law, or
godson, had fallen in the war, who had left his arm out
there, or his leg, who had brought home a bullet or two
in his chest, who had any medals, and how many. Also
there were one or two lucky ones who had brought home
other things than mere shots or medals, things even worth
money. A fattish little man proudly boasted that his son
had brought home from Montenegro an iron stove as a
souvenir. It was not a big one, it could easily be put up
in a knapsack, but it weighed about sixty-five or seventy
pounds. The boy had found it in a deserted house, and
had been carrying it on his back all the way home; he
would not have left it anywhere, not for the world, not

even when he had been wounded, because he had thought that his mother would like it. She did, because it was giving heat beautifully.

"But only when you build a fire in it," a miller sarcastically remarked. Whereupon quiet laughter tumbled along the tables. For it is a great pleasure to make fun of a boasting man in the proper way.

There was no talk of heroic deeds of arms, of brave exploits. Someone mentioned the son of the distiller, the bricklayer, and said that he was the master now in the City Hall. That couldn't be true, remarked another, there were many such inventions nowadays. But, no, it is true, I saw him with my own eyes, said the first one, I heard him with my own ears, he delivered a speech on the market place and told the people that hereafter they will be the masters.

"Who, the bricklayers?"

"No, but generally all the workers who were below until now."

"Well, if that's true, the bricklayers and chimney-sweeps will be shut out, because they were always up."

It was Mátyás who remarked this, for although he was not quite friendly toward the government, he simply could not stomach the thought that pasture rent and taxes should be collected by bricklayers. The older men shared his views, but there were some among the youngsters who leaned toward the new order. The conversation grew louder, they were already shouting from one table to another. A young man in a blue shirt and with a military cap on his head was banging the table with his fist, and yelling that now was the time to teach the gentlemen how to behave, he had seen in Russia how to do it. A fellow on his left, a street-cleaner, fully agreed with him, he even declared that though he was an official he would be there with his spade when they beat the Road Commissioner to death, he was the worst of them all, the other day he made him pay a fine because his pig was digging in the roadside ditch. An old farmer shrieked that they should string up the requisitioners rather than the Road Commissioner, he would assist in that business himself. Whereupon Mátyás burst out:

"All this is just empty talk, men! Don't you know what day this is?"

No, the men did not know, they did not want to know, they did not even listen to Mátyás. In fact, they could hardly understand one another, there was such a hubbub in the Club. Mátyás rose and attempted to sing the Kossuth Song, as always on the Fifteenth of March, but in former years it was the cantor who had led the choir, and the others merely followed him. Mátyás had never yet tried to give the tune himself, so he did not succeed this time either.

"Damn this song!" he turned to Ferenc, complainingly. "I just can't strike the right tune. Help me, will you!"

"I don't know how to sing," Ferenc answered and, taking the old man by the arm, made him sit down. "Let it go, Uncle Mátyás, that's done with anyway."

Mátyás sat down dubiously.

"What's done with?"

"The Kossuth Song, and Father Kossuth. We live in a different world now."

Mátyás turned red in the face. He even forgot, in his wrath, what plans he had for Ferenc. He even called his neighbor to his aid, a sleepily blinking rich farmer who owned six oxen. "Listen to this, listen to what Ferenc says." Whereupon the rich farmer opened up his eyes; sleep had left him at once.

"Never, sonny, never. Father Kossuth will never be done with."

"Tell me, neighbor, who did you vote for in the last

elections?" Ferenc asked him quietly. "For the government or for Forty-eight."

"That's different," said the rich farmer superciliously, and stopped for a second. It was already on the tip of his tongue to tell Ferenc, "You're too green, sonny, to know anything about that," but then he remembered that Ferenc had bought a machine and that sooner or later he, too, would become a rich man. So he just looked haughtily at Ferenc. "That's different. The Baron came to visit me personally, I had to vote for him."

The others around him nodded assent. At least those who knew what the argument was about.

Yes, that was different, they too had voted for the Baron. One because he had gotten a permit to distil brandy at home, another because he had been given a lease of land, a third one out of necessity, a fourth one out of friendship. But all of them believed in Forty-eight only, for the Spirit of Forty-eight could never die. A pockmarked man, a hired hand, a great adherent of Forty-eight, burst into laughter:

"Guess if Father Kossuth would visit you, you would vote for him too."

They told him to shut up, because he was a nobody, perhaps not even the shirt on his back was his own. Then Ferenc spoke up again. Silently, quietly, because when everybody is yelling, soft words are heard farthest.

"I doubt it. Suppose Father Kossuth would call on you, like it is in his song, would you go?"

"I sure would!" Mátyás bellowed enthusiastically, banging the table. The great emotional upheaval even brought the tune out of him. He began to screech the song:

*"Father Kossuth sent a message . . ."*

The men rose, pushed their chairs back, and began to sing. But not all of them. The fellow with the military cap, and two or three other youngsters, remained seated and listened to the song with a contemptuous smile on their lips. But when the others reached the line, *"If he sends another message——"* they could not stand it any longer. They did not rise, but they began to hum the tune together with the others.

Ferenc sang too, but he did not participate in the toasting and drinking that followed the song. The devil had risen within him. He yelled out:

"But Father Kossuth never said to you to divide up the land!"

He did not say this directly to anybody, he just said it. But the fellow with the military cap shouted to him from the other end of the room:

"You're just another one of the Baron's hogs!"

Ferenc leaped to his feet; he was as pale as a sheet. He picked up the branch from behind his chair.

"Who said that?"

"I did!" the fellow with the military cap replied and leaped to his feet too. "You're also living off the Baron's hogwash. But we'll tan you together with your master!"

The oak branch came down on the table with such force that it split into two. Ferenc's voice was not like the organ's sound now, it was hoarse like a leaky bagpipe.

"God damn you! Did you say it?"

With this, he jumped across the table, into the center of the room, overturning glasses and bottles.

The fellow was there too by that time, with both of his hands in his trousers' pockets.

"I said it. And I'll say it again if you want me too."

The Jewess entered the room with a trayful of black coffee.

"Jesus Christ!" she screamed, because she slipped on something, and served the black coffee on the floor.

The men tried to hush her up. They thought she screamed because she was frightened and wanted to throw herself between the two opponents. And that could not be done. One could only look at a fight, but not butt in under any circumstances.

"You'd better get out of the room, missus," they advised her. After all, she was not a Club-member.

"You won't say it for long, you bastard!" Ferenc yelled and flung the branch into the corner. He would not attack a bare-fisted man with a stick.

Thereupon the lad also let go of the knife he had already opened in his pocket.

"Don't curse my mother, you dirty pig!"

The door creaked loudly, as if someone had hurled something against it. That Jewess just can't stay quiet!

"Lock it!" somebody yelled. All looked at the door, even the two angry adversaries.

The door flung open and a man, wet, soaked to the skin, muddy, tumbled in. It was the man with the burr-like moustache. The man nearest the door turned to him:

"You seem to have drunk a hell of a toast in honor of the holiday."

"Yes," the man tottered, "but not with wine. With water! The lake chased me out of the house. Come on in, you, it's warm in here, get dry!"

A barefooted old woman, with a child, clad only in a shirt, on her left arm and with a duck under her right, shambled in. Then came a young woman in high boots, carrying an infant in her arms. A cross-eyed little girl hung on to her skirt.

The men mumbled, cursed, and leaped for their hats and coats, jostling and pushing each other. No one cared a fig any more for Father Kossuth or for the battle of principles.

Ferenc jumped upon a table.

"Don't run away, men! Listen to me!"

All turned toward him.

"There's no hope for us unless we cut the Baron's dam!"

"Yes, sir!" the burr yelled, then, realizing that the room was as silent as a graveyard, he shut up.

"The Baron's dam?" The rich farmer came to with a shudder. "Hm. Eternal jail."

"I'll risk it," Ferenc shouted. "I'll risk everything. All I need is a few men with pickaxes and spades!"

But the men all crowded toward the door, there was no use in listening to Ferenc. Mátyás excitedly plucked Ferenc's trousers; he thought the wine had gone to his head, for no one in his right senses would so heedlessly challenge trouble.

"Ferenc, Ferenc, listen to me!"

But Ferenc misunderstood the old man and waved him aside:

"You are too old, Uncle Mátyás, there are stronger hands than yours here. Well, are you coming?"

He addressed the fellow with the military cap who was cooling his ardor with a bottle of deserted wine. But when Ferenc turned to him he suddenly became so great a respecter of law and order that he put down even the wine. Yes, he'd tan the Baron, and all his henchmen, too, but he wouldn't do so foolish a thing as to cut the dam, for that was against the law.

"I thought so," Ferenc laughed and climbed off the table. He patted the burr on the shoulder.

"Well, brother, will you come? You've plenty of time, and it's all the same to you now anyway."

For once the burr answered not with a "Yes, sir." He said it wasn't so. He didn't care a rap what happened to the others; as a matter of fact, it would be only just if the others would suffer too, now that he had been damaged.

The pock-marked man was the only one who knew

what to do. He asked Ferenc what would be his wages?

"What wages?"

"Why, that's how I make my living! Anybody who pays me regular wages can tell me what to do, but he's responsible for it."

"You'll get five thousand *korona* in the morning. Get a pickaxe and a hoe and run to the dam. Wait for me at the three birches. I'll bring a spade. I guess the Jewess has one."

But the Jewess had already withdrawn to her room and locked the door. She did not want either to hear or to see anything. She would give neither spade nor hoe, both were in the stall, she couldn't help it if somebody took them.

Mátyás ran moaning after Ferenc as fast as his old legs carried him. But when Ferenc was lost to sight, he decided to go home. He was frightened and angry, and as soon as he got home he woke up the women and told them, ornamenting his speech with long curses, that Ferenc must have suddenly gone crazy. Mother screamed, but Etel kept as silent as the church bell on Good Friday; she even wept a little in the dark. And as soon as the first cock crowed, she stole out of the house and went down to the lake. But she couldn't see anything. Tired, she sat down on a knoll and gazed at the lake at her feet until she fell asleep. She woke with a start only when the sun shone directly in her face. She rubbed her eyes: the water was a foot lower.

So Ferenc did cut the Baron's dam; She ran home like mad across the sodden fields and wet furrows.

They knew more at home than she did. The Baron's friend, the rich farmer, roused the gendarmes. But by the time they reached the dam, it was already cut. The pock-marked man ran away, but the gendarmes arrested Ferenc and took him straight to town. Mother did not

wish anybody any trouble, but she was quite surprised
when Mátyás told her that Ferenc would not get more
than two or three years, perhaps not even that much, because he would testify, together with several neighbors,
that Ferenc was drunk, he didn't know what he was
doing.

But when they did not hear anything about Ferenc the
next day either, Mother thought it advisable to try to remember the prayer for doomed men. It was a beautiful
prayer, she had heard it quite often in her childhood.

But, praised be God, it was unnecessary for Mother to
put up any prayers. A week later, the red flag was raised
on the Court House and on the City Hall and Ferenc
was set free. The Baron personally intervened on his be-
half, he said he had always been a great friend of the
poor. He begged Ferenc's pardon for all the trouble, it
was a regrettable misunderstanding, he couldn't be held
responsible for it, it was his intention, too, to cut the dam,
he had already sent out instructions to the steward to
do so; after all, he was richer than the farmers, he could
easier suffer damages than the poor farmers. He offered
Ferenc a cigar, but Ferenc did not feel like smoking a
cigar. Then the Baron asked him whether he would care
to shoot deer in his game preserve, but Ferenc told him
that he did not fancy venison. Would he like to have a
nice slice of land for lease then? Ferenc said that he was
happy to be able to tend to everything on his own little
farm. Finally the Baron asked him to do him the pleasure
of accompanying him down the street to the beer-garden,
but Ferenc had no time, he had to go to the barracks,
because the other day he had received a notification to
call for his medals.

Ferenc went straight to the Mátyáses because he felt
that they had taken Peter to them. Peter was sitting in
Etel's lap, but the moment he noticed his father he rushed

to him, rolling like a ball. But Marika was quicker.

"What did you bring from the fair, daddy?" she greeted him.

All last week, Marika had listened to Etel consoling Peter with the promise that daddy would bring him something from the fair. And now Marika thought that she had to ask Ferenc the same way.

"This here, children, look," Ferenc answered, pulling the two medals for bravery in action out of his pocket and giving the bigger one to Marika and the smaller one to Peter, according to their ages. Peter immediately bit it, thinking that it was chocolate in tinfoil, and he expressed his indignation over the medal which could not even be eaten in no uncertain terms. But Marika discovered at once that it could be hung around the neck, and thanked Ferenc properly for it.

"Thank you very much, daddy."

Ferenc was so happy to be free again that he paid no attention to the last word of this remark, but Etel did notice it, and when she bent down to pick up her needle she grew as red as the coral in her earrings. And Mátyás heard it too, and the wheatfields of his hopes turned into green again. He even began to figure.

"Before the new wine," he said to himself.

But it did not take that much time. By the time new bread arrived, Marika had already all the right in the world to call Ferenc "daddy."

# IX

THE best way to learn how Ferenc and Etel finally got together is to let Mátyás tell his own story. Originally, this story must have been shorter, most probably it was nothing but a bare recital of actual facts, but Mátyás told it often, and every time he told it he added to it, so that, as it stands today, it contains not only the historical events but reflects also Mátyás's criticism of these events. His criticism, undoubtedly, is no more objective than the criticisms of other historians usually are; on the other hand, the events are perhaps less distorted in his story than in the work of the so-called idealistic historians. At least, Mátyás claims that his story is truthful, and he never forgets to add that God may strike him dead on the spot if he isn't telling the truth.

\* \* \*

You can't very well say that the Reds made much damage hereabouts, let the hellfire of the Almighty eat them up wherever they are, although, if you come to think of it, it has already eaten them up; I myself know where at least three of them are buried, mighty big mulleins grow over their graves in the hollow, the cows don't even eat them, I guess they can feel the taste of blood.

There weren't many of them here, because the peasants who joined them didn't count, they were just poor trash who owned no house or land, they thought that their day had come to eat their bellies full. Because, you know, there were some among them who had had no meat to eat ever since the war broke out. But they just didn't figure right, because the Reds didn't much appreciate the peasants, especially the ones who joined up, they used them for sort of messengers only, run here, run there, take this letter to the city, show us some hidden wine, and all that kind of business. They themselves, I mean the soldiers, there were about thirty of them, and all quartered in the schoolhouse, well, their business was supposed to be to watch the Serbs on the demarkation line, but all day long they didn't do anything, they just lay beneath the mulberry tree and played cards and sang, especially that cobbler, he sang so beautifully that you couldn't hear the like of him even in the city. Especially when he sang "Christians, weep," why, your heart just trembled when he sang that. He could even whistle the high mass from beginning to end, have you ever heard anything like that? I told him myself that if he couldn't make a living as a cobbler why didn't he become a cantor, or a musician, or something, because he knew how to play the flute too, why in hell did he give himself to such an ugly business?

"Uncle Mátyás," he used to tell me, "believe me, I'd like to do something else, but I got a rupture on the Italian front, on the Doberdo, and now I am no good for anything, so I thought I might as well become a Red soldier, they at least leave me in peace."

I don't know what's become of him, it's possible that he also went to his grave on a ladder, like the rest of them, because he couldn't even run well, but I liked him because he could patch up any kind of a shoe or boot or slipper you took to him and all for a pipeful or two of tobacco. But, as I said, they didn't do much damage during the day, they went out at night only, and then they stole chickens, and visited women, of course, only those who let them come in, but there were many of them like that, because many a woman became unfortunate during the war, and I always say when a dog grows accustomed to licking fat he'll stay lickerish for the rest of his life, unless you shoot him.

Well, as I said, we got along somehow with our Reds, because they didn't ask us for taxes, and they didn't touch the cattle, not like in the next county where they collected all the milk and eggs and fruit, and paid just a trifle for them, and then took them to the city, and sold them at a great profit. So people from that county came up to us and said why don't we join hands, if we joined we could just pitchfork the whole bunch of them hellhounds out of here. But we told them that they'd better tend to their own troubles themselves, the best they can, after all, why should we take the thorn out of their sole and stick it into ours, am I right?

But, all the same, I knew that everything was not as good as it seemed, some day our turn might come, and then I didn't like their money either, because the smaller and whiter it got the less they gave for it, so that some people didn't even want to take it. And everybody paid with it, they saying they had no other. I myself stuck the old banknotes into reed stalks and thatched them up in the back of the barn in the wall. Well, I slept very little on account of all these things, and I couldn't fall asleep on that night either, which was the night before Peter and Paul's.

It must have been round about eleven o'clock, and all of a sudden I heard somebody knocking on the door, I mean, on the kitchen door, that gave to the yard. We never used to lock up anything, but ever since this topsy-turvy world had come upon us we got used to bolting the doors. The dog wasn't barking, so I knew it wasn't a stranger. I thought it was Etel, because in the summer she used to sleep in her own little house out in the garden. She could more easily watch the poultry from out there, and I don't mind saying it, even if I have to say it myself, she wasn't getting on very well with Roza either. You know what kind of folks women are!

"What's the matter with you—did you forget something?" I asked her from the bed. She must have heard it because the door from the kitchen to the room was open for the night, yet she didn't answer anything, she just kept on knocking on the door. And I thought that Marika was also with her, because I heard some scratching, you know. So I thought I'd better get up and see what was what.

I opened the door, and there was no Etel there, and no Marika, only the dog was lying on the ground. Hey, Boisi, I said to him, but sort of quiet, because I didn't know what had happened to him. As I said his name he began to whine. I bent down to him and then my hand got wet from his hair, but it couldn't be water because my fingers got sticky. I smelled it and then I saw it was blood. Tch! Tch! where have you been? I patted his neck, and blessed if he didn't lick my hand, but, of course, he couldn't say anything, just kept on moaning, and I couldn't understand him. I thought I'd bring him some water and I felt my way back to the kitchen. I didn't want to bump into anything, it was very dark, and then I heard the knocking on the door again. Yes, sir, they were knocking on the door, but not on our door, they were knocking on Etel's. And not with fists, either, because it sounded like blows, you know, like thumps. And then I heard a crash also and I knew it was the butt of a rifle. So that's what it was, Communist soldiers. Out again for chickens! I thought. They banged the door again, two or three times, and then I heard them talk and laugh.

"Will you open it, darling? The sergeant can hardly stand on his legs, he would like to lie down!"

Damn it, they weren't out for chickens, they were out for women! Now what shall I do, I thought, and I grabbed this and I grabbed that, I grabbed the broom, then I took the scythe off the hook, just wait, you bastards, I said, and really, I'd have gone out to them, whatever happened, but then I heard shots, three in a row. I got so surprised, you know, I didn't even know what I was doing, and all of a sudden I noticed that something was pricking my waist. I looked there, and I saw that it was a branch of the mulberry tree. Now what do you think of that! Well, I was so surprised I'd climbed up the tree in my surprise! There I listened to them, how they were laughing. One of the gallows-birds began to sing and the rest of them laughed at the song. He sang the song, "I'll knock on your window tonight, dear," and then I heard a crash, and bang went the window pane!

"Shall we go in or will you come out, darling?"

Then I heard Etel's voice too.

"Can't you be patient for a minute? I am not even dressed yet."

"That's just the way we want you—without clothes," the soldiers said and laughed again.

Well, I thought, I'd better speak to Roza about it, and tell her to bring help from somewhere; the door would stand the banging for a while, and there were crossbars on the window. So I sneaked off the tree, went into the room, shook up the old woman, told her to hurry up; run over to Ferenc, I said, he's got a shotgun, and wake up everybody you can. What for, she asked me angrily, why don't you leave me be, I want to sleep. I shook her good and hard, didn't you hear the shots, eh? Run, or the soldiers will break in the door on Etel in no time! Well, what of it, said she, she's strong as stone, you don't have to be afraid for her. But your grandchild is also there, woman, don't you understand? She understood it all right, but she was so afraid that her teeth chattered and she didn't want to go out in the darkness; she told me I should go. I got angry at that, how could I go out, I said, how could I leave the farm at such a time, the horses were here, and there was the cow in the stall, I couldn't leave *her* all alone! So then she got up, and put on her underskirt, and went out. I loitered about the house for a while, but when I heard that the door was already crashing in, I just began to sweat cold. Poor woman, poor woman, what will become of you now? I thought I'd yell at them, tell them to stop their godless business, there were lots of other women all around, why did they pick just our Etel, but then I realized that wouldn't be so wise either, because then they would shoot me too, and instead of one damage there'd be two, and nobody would profit by it. God Almighty, help us, I said, and I looked up at the sky, the dawn began to break already, so I started out in the direction of the light, toward the fields, and suddenly I heard the rye rustle. I shuddered, to be sure, because I was sort of alone, so I looked there, and, lo, there was Marika.

"God in Heaven," I said and made the sign of the cross, "is that you, Marika?"

"It's me, granddaddy."

"How did you get here? Weren't you with your mother in the house?"

"I was, but when the soldiers came mother picked me up and put me out through the window, and told me to go and tell you about it."

"Through the window? Why, there's crossbars on it."

"Not on the pantry window, granddaddy."

You see, that's the kind of a leaky old sieve an old man's head is! I clean forgot all about that pantry window. If I had remembered it sooner I could have told Etel that we were up.

"And what's happened to your mother, my child?"

Well, she didn't know that. So I said, too bad your mother is such a handsome, big woman. If she were as skinny as your grandma she could pass through the window too.

"Granddaddy, I'm cold," said the child, hanging on to my legs, and I noticed only then that the little one had just one single shirt on her back. True, I wasn't wearing very much more myself, and I began to feel the weather too. Yes, it was Peter and Paul's, but dawns are cool near a lake even in summer, and dew began to settle on us already. Good that I noticed the scarecrow in the field, so I took the rags off right away and wrapped up the child in them. Then I told the child, let's go.

But that girl is clever, you know, she has so much brains she could easily pass for a judge in Budapest. She looked at me with her two black eyes and asked me:

"Where are we going, granddaddy?"

Why, I didn't know where to go, I just stumbled about like a blind fly in a bottle. So I asked her:

"Where shall we go?"

"Let's go to daddy," she said, meaning Ferenc, because she was always calling him by that name. This alone shows that she has plenty of brains for herself; my dear mother, blessed be her ashes, was like that, she used to say that if you're not innocent before you're ten, pretty before you're twenty, strong before thirty, clever before forty, rich before fifty, and saintly before sixty, well, you'll just never be any of them.

What was I saying? Oh, yes, the girl said let's go to Ferenc. "All right, let's," I told the child. "I meant to go to him anyway when I started out, I just forgot about it." So the two of us started out, or rather, the three of us, because Boisi had found us in the meantime, although the poor beast could hardly drag himself along. His hinds were just one big wound, but he came to look for us just the same. And that was good, because without him we would never have found Roza. But since he was with us, the minute we got into Ferenc's field, he barked at her. She was kneeling at a stack of sheaves, because Ferenc did not wait for Peter and Paul's, he had to go by the machine, and had already mowed down a few sheaves of rye, so there was Roza in her underskirt. I yelled at her, what are you doing, but she just motioned to me with her folded hands that she was praying, and I could hear for myself, that the bell was ringing for the morning prayer.

So I stopped too, and made the sign of the cross, although I do it every morning, but now I got a little sad, I thought the bell might be the passing bell for Etel, poor creature, she might not even be alive any more, who could tell?

Roza must have thought the same thing because her eyes were full of tears, but we didn't dare to say it aloud, neither she nor I, so I asked her what she had done, and what help she had got? But that was nowhere because in some places she couldn't get in on account of the dogs, and at other places she just couldn't rouse them. There was one man who wanted to come, and had already picked up his axe, but then his wife wouldn't let him go, she said he shouldn't butt in other people's business, and anyway why were we so excited about it, Etel wouldn't die of what other women could stand so well, at least she wouldn't hold her nose so high in the future. Because, you know, that's just like people used to say in the old days, that you shouldn't look for knots on a blade of grass, nor for hair in an egg, nor for sympathy in one woman for another.

"Did you go to Ferenc?" I asked Roza.

Sure, she did, but only lastly, because first she ran heedlessly in the other direction, and when she was refused everywhere, then she thought of Ferenc again, but there she couldn't get any farther than the fence.

"And Ferenc hasn't got any dogs, either," I said.

"No dogs, to be sure, but there's that confounded gate!"

"That's right; that damn Russky fixed it up so you can't open it."

"Not only that, but there is something pulled up against it, a winepress or something, so that you can't push it in."

Wine press, wine press, I thought, why, the harvest was far away yet, what in hell did Ferenc want with that wine press?

Then I asked Mother whether she had knocked on the window. Not the one giving to the yard, but the one that was facing our house. No, she forgot all about that one, she was so scared it just didn't occur to her. Well, I said, don't be afraid, woman, not as long as you see me, because, you know, the minute the sun shines in your eyes you sort of get back your courage, and the sun shone nicely by that time. It'd be best to ask Ferenc to bring out his shotgun, why, the bandits wouldn't dare to lift a finger at him then!

We got to the fence, and sure enough, there was the wine press. We went up to the window and the curtain was drawn, we couldn't look in. Damn it, right there and then I began to suspect what it was all about, sort of smelled it, like greyhounds smell hares. I tapped on the window pane, just with the knuckle of my finger, but nobody answered. So I tapped it with two fingers. Nobody. Then I knocked on the jamb with my fist three times. Then somebody lifted the corner of the curtain and Ferenc looked out, blinking.

"It's us," I told him loudly.

Ferenc lifted his finger to warn us not to shout, then he winked to us with his head to come around to the door. He was coming too, we could hear the kitchen door creak. But the corner of the curtain remained drawn up, and I pressed my nose to the window pane. Then I burst into laughter.

"What's that?" Roza asked surprised. "Do you see

angels?"

"You'll laugh also in a second, woman! But come on now, I see Ferenc is at the gate already."

"Well," I said to Ferenc, "you know what's what, don't you?"

"I do."

"Is Etel here?"

"Yes, she is."

"A long time?"

"Quite long."

"How did she get away?"

"She picked up the big pot, filled it with lye, then opened the door when the soldiers didn't expect it, and threw the lye in their faces. And while they were looking for their eyesight, she ran over here."

"Well done," I said, "praised be God! Isn't she coming home? Nothing will happen to her now."

"Let her be," said Ferenc. "She's just fallen asleep, let the poor soul have a little rest after the excitement."

"To be sure," I said.

Then we went home. Of course, everything was wide open, but there was no damage done at all, except that the door was cracked a little, and the big pot was lying smashed to bits on the ground.

"Take away that dog," I said to Roza, "he'll lick it if you don't watch out."

Because considering how much brains a senseless beast like that has he might even have lapped up the lye in his joy. To be sure, I wouldn't have needed much encouragement either, I was happy myself that God had at last helped us.

So that was how it all happened, men, and if you don't believe me, just ask Roza.

\*    \*    \*

Well, as far as she is concerned, Roza at such times just takes her lower lip between her thumb and forefinger, and, with just a touch of tartness in her voice, declares: "That's true, that's how everybody got a good bite of the apple." This may seem a little cryptic to the ignorant, but Mátyás is a sensible man, so he adds that "If there were no milk, we couldn't have cheesecake." Whereupon Etel usually bursts into laughter and hides her head behind Ferenc's back. Ferenc merely smiles, and if he says anything at all, all he says is: "Men are men as long as they live."

# X

UNTIL the next spring, the two young people lived together without the benefit of clergy; both the Reverend and the Registrar told them that without the proper procedure of declaring Rokus dead there could be no wedding. And this procedure took so much time that if anyone lived long enough to await its end, he could call himself most fortunate. For a while, indeed, there were no authorities at all, the Communists foolishly knocked the wheels out of the country's clock, and the wise men who followed them, brought so many kinds of new wheels, all revolving in different directions, that no one could ever tell what time it was.

"The only thing in which they all resembled each other whatever their name was that they all wanted money from us," Mátyás declared, embittered, for he considered the various expenses a little too high. After all, it was obvious to everybody that Rokus was dead, for if he were still alive he would either have come home, or sent a message, or at least written a letter. And then there was Ferenc also, a living witness to the fact that God had called Rokus to His throne. Then why in hell did they need an official record of it? Mátyás was convinced that the whole business was conducted for no other earthly reason than for the sake of the expenses, and because of the various stamps he had to put on the documents and records. Ferenc tried to explain to him what the procedure meant, but his efforts were in vain; Mátyás would not retreat one little bit from his position. Yes, if that procedure could call his son back to life, then it would be worth while, although the expenses would be too much even then. Quite a lot of people had died since the Revolution, what was the use of spending money on people who had died in the war, far away from home, perhaps even a thousand miles away, one couldn't tell.

Otherwise, the farmers had little reason to complain. The harvest was very good, and all the farm products commanded high prices. True, Mother whined even now, she used to say that it was foolish to waste the pumpkin on the hogs in by-gone years. Now she baked four or five of them, took them to town for the weekly fair, and sold them for so much that, in the old days, she could have bought a cow on the profit. The city people paid anything they were asked, they had not had much to eat while the Communists had been the masters. And milk and eggs brought in such profits that Mother began to worry that the prices would be limited again, as they had been during the war, when Mátyás had preferred to turn his apricots into the roadside ditch than sell them for less than what he wanted for them. One couldn't very well do this with the eggs, because the hens, unlike the apricot tree, had to be fed during the winter. Of course, Mother belittled the apricot tree only at home; in the city, on the market-place, whenever a lady asked her how she had the nerve to demand so much for a basketful of sour cherries when one had neither to water nor to feed the trees, she invariably answered:

"But it's mighty hard to pick the cherries off the trees!"

Mother told Mátyás about this, adding that she was sorry for the lady; for what's the use of a nice hat when she could not eat her bellyful every time she liked to. But Mátyás only shrugged his shoulders.

"That's the way of the world," he said. "The wheels are turning around, now the bottom is up and the top down.

We've been down long enough, let them try now how it feels to be down."

But they didn't know what to do with all the money. Mátyás at last realized that Ferenc was right; the money had eaten itself up in the savings bank. He would have liked to buy land, but nobody sold any. So he invested his money in cows and pigs, and bought himself a meerschaum pipe, but he thought so much of it that he did not use it, he just kept it on the cross-beam.

Ferenc fared far better than Mátyás did; he won more because he played for higher stakes. The machine brought in its cost in the first summer, but Ferenc kept on paying the instalments and bought a wagon and horses and a cutting machine, also on instalments, on the rest of his profits. He made changes on his land, threw out the old vines in his vineyard, planted dessert grapes instead of wine grapes, and an orchard, too, and told Mátyás that he would try cultured wheat both on his and on Etel's land next year.

Mátyás could not be persuaded to try these things, but he did not object to Ferenc's doing them. He was young, he said, let him experiment. When he grew old he would discover for himself that it isn't wise to leave a trodden path for an unknown one. There was, however, one thing Mátyás did not like.

"It's too bad you can't stretch the land like you do rubber."

"But you can," Ferenc answered, smiling.

"Unless you go into the lake——"

Mátyás said this jokingly, but Ferenc answered quite seriously that that was just what he was planning to do. But first he wanted to fix up his house.

"It's fixed up all right," Mátyás suggested. "Why, Etel has even run morning-glory up its walls, although I think that Roza is right when she says that if she wants to be a lady let her run up beans, because one can at least make some use of them."

But Ferenc was not speaking of morning-glories when he was talking of fixing up the house. He wanted to build a new house, with two rooms, planked floors, a cellar, and a tiled roof. Whereupon Mátyás sarcastically asked him whether he did not want to buy a piano too? Because the *other* Baron had a piano. Sure enough, there were quite a number of crazy peasants who bought pianos and kept flour in them. But Ferenc was neither a baron, nor was he crazy, and he did not feel like wasting his money on things that were not made for him. On the other hand, he claimed he had a right to a decent home, like all men.

"Say, who lived in your house until now, march wolves? And men and human beings can manage to live in my house. And in all the other houses, all around the lake."

Ferenc attempted to enlighten Mátyás. He told him that the Tartars also lived in houses and that they were also men. But even their priest's house was worse than a stable in America.

"We must progress, Uncle Mátyás. Etel told me the other day that you want to buy a watch for yourself. Well, your father measured the time by looking at his shadow."

This went straight to Mátyás's heart. He could answer nothing better than that it was not he who wanted the watch but Mother, because she said that everybody in the neighborhood had a watch, only her husband had none. But since he suspected that Ferenc would reply, "See, everybody wants to progress," he decided that it would be wiser to keep silent.

Ever since Ferenc had gotten together with Etel, the three farms counted as one. Ferenc took care of Etel's fields, and this was to Mátyás's advantage, because the two of them paid the hired hand together. Nevertheless, Ferenc never mixed Etel's money with his. He sold and bought for her, but he always accounted to her with every single penny. And this saddened Etel. They lived on the same bread, even though Ferenc made little damage to it; she had given herself to him body and soul, why did he then act like a stranger when it came to money? The rule was that what belonged to the man was his property, and what belonged to the woman, was also his. Etel was so ashamed of this that she feared the world would find out about it some day; after all, Ferenc was not her servant, he was her husband.

"I am not your husband yet," Ferenc said whenever she brought up this matter. "As soon as I am, everything God will give us will be common property. But you know very well that we first need that death certificate to do that."

Ferenc's stubbornness hurt Etel more than the fact that she was not his lawfully wedded wife, although that hurt her too. Not on account of the folks, because they are more lenient on the farms than in the city, if the woman is not otherwise immoral. Etel hoped that after the wedding Ferenc would change, although she could not very well explain why, nor could she tell why she wanted Ferenc to be different. He was good to her, nobody could be any better, she never heard him curse, he would have covered her with stars if he could only have done it, he never came back from town empty-handed; one day he brought her a silk shawl, the next day a pair of earrings, or roast chestnuts, or gingerbread. And he loved Marika perhaps even more than he did Peter; he liked to fondle her, to stroke her cheeks, to call her by all kinds of pet names—indeed, he played more with her than with her mother, and, well, it was this that hurt Etel. She often pondered over this, after dinner, out in the vineyard, when she lay down in the sand in the shade of the vines for a few minutes, or at night, when she stretched out alone in her bed, for they were not living together yet. Ferenc did not play with her like other men did with young women! She could remember how Rokus used to open her apron-strings from behind while she was standing before the trough, or how, when she happened to be in the garret, he took the ladder away, and when she was forced to jump he caught her in his lap. Rokus could never rest; he was so playful sometimes that she had to slap him on the hand. There were times when she slapped him so hard that Rokus broke into curses and turned to another girl. Etel did not mind that, she was glad when Rokus left her alone—and now she discovered why. She had found out, now that she was in love with Ferenc, that she had never loved Rokus, though he had been mad about her. Ferenc was not like that, he never even pinched her. Rokus sometimes embraced her so hard that she nearly cried; true, he did that only when he had too much to drink. Sometimes he took her by the neck and drew her toward himself and said, "How pretty you are, will you give me a kiss?" But Ferenc drank wine only with water, and he drank but little, and he never told her that she was pretty. One evening, when she went over to him to show him how her new earrings looked on her, she asked him, tossing her head coquettishly, "Am I pretty?" But even then all Ferenc answered was: "That red stone is very becoming to you; it's good that I didn't buy the one with the blue stone. The jeweler wanted me to buy that." Why was this so? Was it in his nature to be like that? Would he change after the altar? Oh, God, when were they going to get that death certificate!

But Etel yearned for it only when she was all alone, and even then, only silently. Mother, on the other hand, would not let her be.

"How long will you go on like this?"

"Do you want to live like gypsies all the rest of your

life?"

"Well, I wouldn't like to live on bought mush until you'll be blessed by the priest."

"You'd better go after him to get that paper for you. Not that I wish it, but if you happen to die, you'll go to Hell, surely, living the way you do!"

Fortunately, this was the one thing Etel was not afraid of. As long as the flowers were in bloom, she placed a nosegay on the altar of the Virgin Mary every Sunday, and she knew that the Blessed Mother knew their hearts were as pure as the altar cloth. There was no necessity to urge Ferenc to go after the certificate more diligently, he would have gladly worn his legs to the knees if that had only helped.

On the evening of All Souls' Day, Ferenc went over to Etel. He saw already from afar that there was a candle burning in the window.

"Who's that for?" he asked Etel, who was bidding beads in the corner of the sofa.

"For Rokus."

Ferenc had forgotten all about him. Of course, if one can not go to the grave personally, one has to light a candle for the departed at home. He made the sign of the cross, but did not sit down. He said he just dropped in to see her for a second and was going right home, because he had caught a cold in the cemetery in the afternoon; he had taken Peter to his mother's grave.

Hardly had Ferenc left, someone knocked on the window pane. From the gendarmerie headquarters. Etel asked him what he wanted. Wasn't Ferenc here? No, he had gone home just this minute. The messenger said he would go over to him at once, he had been looking for him all afternoon, a very urgent summons had come in, so urgent that he was commanded to wake him up even at midnight.

Etel suddenly forgot all about the dead, the candle, the rosary. She grabbed her shawl and ran to Ferenc. What was it? Ferenc didn't know it himself, he would be told about it only in the morning. Perhaps it's the death certifiicate! My God, if it were only that! Ferenc did not think that was it, if that arrived it would come either to Etel or to Mátyás. Then what else could it be? Ferenc did not know. There were so many barbed wire fences all around one these days one never knew where one might bump into one—all he knew was that he had been summoned to headquarters. Etel was in despair, and she swore that if anybody dared to touch him, she would strangle him to death with her bare hands. Ferenc said nothing, he only smiled, calmly.

Nor was he perturbed when he was told the next day what the barbed wire fence was. It was a strong and high fence; the Baron's dam. They wanted to lock him up for cutting the dam last Spring. There was no need to be afraid, however, the attorney who used to come out on the Fifteenth of March had taken the matter in hand, he assured Etel nothing would happen to him.

And nothing did happen. Mátyás and Etel roused the neighborhood, "You wouldn't let the man who saved you from the flood go to jail, would you?" No, they vowed, we wouldn't, he is one of us! Ferenc was commanding respect already; he owned a machine, had built a new house, knew what he was talking about. So they decided that, if it came to it, they would all swear that he had been drunk when he had cut the dam. Even the rich farmer, the one who owned six oxen, came out squarely for him. Ferenc was not guilty at all, he said, it was that barefooted ragamuffin, that hired hand, who had done it.

Not that this meant anything to Ferenc. He calmly confessed that it was he who had cut the dam; he would neither deny what he had done nor pass the buck to someone else. And so it was again up to the Baron to save him. He had already announced that he would be a candidate at the next elections, for no other reason than because he had the farmers' interests at heart and wanted somebody to represent them in Parliament. He wanted to go arm in arm with the peasants and if Ferenc promised him that he would persuade his fellow farmers to vote for him, he would see to it that the gendarmerie should drop the matter of the dam for good and all. Whereupon Ferenc replied that if the Baron would stand by him and help him found a company to drain the lake, he would in turn help the Baron.

The Baron agreed, and the aristocracy and the third estate sealed their friendship in the beer-garden at a banquet. This was a double holiday for Mátyás; first, because he sat on the Baron's right, and secondly, because he had received Rokus's death certificate that very afternoon. He had it in his pocket all during the banquet. Later Ferenc found it advisable to take it out of there, so that nothing should happen to it. For Mátyás had never tasted any but light beer in his life, and even then only when somebody else had paid for it, for he himself would never have spent a single copper on that bitter stuff, he could never understand why anybody had ever invented it anyway. But the Baron ordered dark beer for him and that flowed smoothly down Mátyás's throat; it was as sweet as if sugar had been soaked into it. He drank one stein after another, and it was no wonder that the beer knocked him out.

The Baron took them home in his car but Mátyás had little pleasure out of his first auto trip; his stomach had suddenly become revolted against the black beer. By the time they got out of that devil's wagon, at the foot of the little hill where his land crossed the highway, Mátyás could not differentiate between his right leg and his left.

Ferenc wanted to help him, but the beer had made Mátyás stubborn.

"Go away! I—I can—stand—on my own legs—like Mount Sinai——" he said, and fell flat among the weeds.

So Ferenc went up the hill alone, and when he noticed Etel standing in the kitchen door, he waved the death certificate to her.

"I've got it, Etel!"

The sun went down just then, far, far away, beyond the timidly greening fields, and was lost in the cloud of mist hanging over the bald poplars. As Ferenc reached the top of the hill he hid its glowing disc from Etel. Only a few sparks showed above his shoulders.

"As if he had stepped out of the sun," thought Etel.

They were married two weeks later. There was no wedding, however, because Lent had already arrived; the Reverend had to ask for a special permission from the bishop to do it at all. Mátyás therefore slaughtered only three lambs for the kins and relatives and the women belonging to them. No one invited Gyurka Messzi, but he showed up just the same, and at last he had a chance to deliver the speech he could not tell the winter before on account of tongue trouble.

"When the Lord Almighty invented Holy Matrimony——"

It was a beautiful speech, several of the women present began to cry, and Mother, sitting next to the bridegroom, sighed:

"My God! If Rokus had only lived to see this!"

"If only he had——" Ferenc said, staring at the plate in front of him.

Etel looked at him, but by that time Ferenc was already clinking his glass against the watchman's.

# XI

IT was Sunday. The church bell proclaimed it so, but even if they had taken out its tongue, or had had it recast, as they had done in the war, to herald the glory of God in the form of a gun, even then it would have been Sunday, and every beast would have felt it, and not only the beasts but the sand on the highway also. The golden particles of dust glistened in the sun as merrily as if they had remembered the times when they had still been lofty mountains, with snow caps on their heads and Christmas trees on their sides. On weekdays, the dust cannot possibly have such playful thoughts, for then its job is to creak the wheels of the wagons. But there are no wagons on the highway of a Sunday morning, and the yellow bells of the cowslip and the blue blooms of the chicory swing their dew-laden heads far more courageously than they do on any other day, for they need not be afraid of the whistling wagon drivers' whips. The acacias and the poplars have already washed their leaves of the dust of Saturday, and gently invite the jays and the shrikes to settle on their branches. Now tell me, upon your soul, they seem to ask, isn't it better to rock on our branches than on the twigs of those spoiled, finicky city trees which are watched even during the day by paid guards? Naturally, the shrikes and the jays are also dressed in their Sunday best and festive feelings fill even the soft, crustbacked insects ordered by the Creator to serve as food for the shrikes and the jays. Everybody celebrates the holiday as best he can; the flies, for instance, celebrate it by sharpening their bayonets even more carefully than on other days, and by sinking their stings deeper into the skins of those lazy Christians who still lie in bed when the bell has already rung once for the eight o'clock mass.

Though Etel had hung her skirt on the curtained window, enough sunrays pierced the glass, the linen, and the gayly printed gingham to show the flies how to find their way to Ferenc's head. They could have alighted on his hair, or—those who preferred the smooth skin—on his chin shaved only last night, but they picked out the spot where his two bushy brows met and they thrust their stings into the drawn wrinkles, as if trying to find out what was behind them.

This was something Etel would also have liked to know. She had been up already for quite a long time, had already swept the room clean, the kitchen, and the yard, and had given water to the cattle and the fowl. She had even dressed the two children and sent them off to church. Now she was sitting on the bed, in shirtwaist, chasing away the impertinent flies, and gently wiping Ferenc's forehead with a piece of soft cloth.

Ferenc was not a bit annoyed by the flies, but the minute the cloth touched his brow, he opened his eyes with a start and looked around frightened in the half light.

"What did you dream of, dear?" Etel asked, bending over him.

"I?"

This was a rather queer question, since only the two of them were in the room; but not so very queer if you consider that this is the reply generally given when one has to think over what to answer.

"Yes you. You. Who else then?" Etel slapped Ferenc on the shoulder, as he deserved it, but then left her hand there, transforming the slap into a caress, to soften it.

"Why, who else would I call dear?"

Ferenc assured her that he had not dreamed of anything bad at all.

"But you moaned so loudly," Etel said, and took the skirt from the window to let the sunshine pour in. Then she went to the chiffonier and stooped to take out clean linen for Ferenc. Ferenc gazed darkly at her; his eyes seemed riveted upon the woman—but he could not have seen her, for one strains one's eyes that way only when one wants to see far-away things, things a hundred, or even a thousand, miles away. But before she could have noticed his intent gaze, Ferenc's good humor had already returned.

"Guess it'll be pretty hot today."

"Yes, I didn't take out a necktie for you either. You are handsome even without that, dear," Etel said and put down the clean white linen on the bed. "Do you want to get up now? Shall I go out?"

"Makes no difference," Ferenc answered, sitting up in bed. "I'll go out myself."

But Etel was already out of the room. She leaned against the door jamb and began to play with the red blossoms of the bean-vine which faced the sun only after the morning glory had already closed its little bells. The wedding had not changed Ferenc much, he was still as bashful as a virgin girl, but Etel did not mind it any more. It was in his nature and Etel liked him the way he was. She was the red bean-flower and Ferenc was the morning glory which is closed more often than open. One could not always look into him: he was like the cattle well in the pasture; sometimes the water stood high in it, at other times there was hardly any in it at all, and that only on the bottom.

A gray hen rose into the air and landed on the brim of the well; she was watching out of the corner of her eye whether the white cockerel would follow her. Etel smiled and decided to ask Ferenc whether he would go after her into the well? Although she knew in advance that Ferenc would only smile and answer nothing.

The white cockerel indeed followed the hen and Etel ran to the well to chase them off the brim. Get off, you fools, or else you'll fall into the water. She was worried because a a turkey chick fell into the well the other day and was drowned. Ferenc then remarked that a year hence they would no longer fall into the water, for he would drill an artesian well, if God only helped him. Mátyás, who had just dropped in to borrow the fig sieve from Etel, overheard it and was beside himself with excitement. An artesian well here? Just like the one the miller had in his yard? Yes, one just like that, and a mill too, but the mill will not be like that, it will be a better one. Ferenc then explained to Mátyás how he wanted it, he figured that it would pay its cost in about ten years, the savings bank would extend a loan for it, if he mortgaged his and Etel's lands. Whereupon Mátyás remarked that if Ferenc really wanted to become a miller, why didn't he buy the windmill, which was for sale just then, and to which people were already accustomed to go. The miller wanted to sell it, he had made enough money on it already and was going to live in the city; the flour had gone to his lungs and he wanted to get them back in shape again. But Ferenc argued that people would go where they'd get better service; he said his mill would bring in more money in one year than the windmill did in ten. Mátyás was dubious, and cautiously replied that Ferenc had a very restless nature, and that it was never known to be good to hurry anything, but Ferenc declared that when somebody wanted to catch up with things he had to hurry, and they were all way behind in everything. Thereupon Mátyás asked him what they were behind of? There was

plenty to eat, plenty to drink, never before had so much
bacon got rancid on one's neck as nowadays. That's just
it, came back Ferenc, why should one eat rancid bacon
when one didn't have to? Mátyás flew into a rage; who
did Ferenc think he was anyway, he had been brought
up on rancid bacon and not on fancy pastry; Mátyás failed
to understand where Ferenc had picked up all these gentlemanly ideas. Others had been away in the war,
and got knocked on the head, and got tarred with
the same brush, but none of them was so greedy about
novelties as Ferenc was. These youngsters nowadays all
thought they knew everything better, they thought they
could wax everybody's moustache, but everybody knew it
was not wise to let a calf lead the oxen.

But no matter how often and how much Mátyás scolded
Ferenc when they were alone together, he was hotly in
favour of electing Ferenc president of the Club. They did
elect him, too, and Mátyás was mighty glad of it, although he did not consider it sensible of Ferenc to lead
a delegation to the burgomaster the minute he was elected,
and ask him to rebuild the schoolhouse. Nor did he approve
of Ferenc's pressing the deputy, the Baron, to throw in his
influence too, to appoint a new teacher because the old
one had married. Mátyás had never been a great friend
of schools, he argued that they wanted the children just
when they were big enough to use them around the house.
One could hardly get a gooseherd's or a cowherd's boy
anywhere nowadays. It was quite different when he was
young, although they had learned to read and to write
even in those days. Mátyás himself was an educated man;
when he was a child, the teacher was a choir leader at
fairs, and since there were no fairs in the winter, he had
plenty of time to teach. For a basket of apples or a small
bag of nuts he would teach any child to write all the letters
of the alphabet, except the "y" which, he claimed, was

not a Hungarian letter. Consequently Mátyás, whenever he was forced to pick up a pen, wrote his name thus: Mátás. Mátyás was never afraid to tell anybody what was on his mind, and he told Ferenc that it would have been much wiser if he had asked for a cut in the taxes, which were incredibly high for a poor man like himself. Several club-members agreed with Mátyás on this point, but Ferenc swiftly made an end to the argument, declaring that taxes were necessary and never before had the poor man paid his taxes as easily as he did now.

Etel often overheard these arguments although she did not understand them, nor did she ever ask what they were all about, because it was not becoming to a woman to get mixed up with things that only concerned men. But she liked to listen to them; Mátyás often grew angry, and sometimes started to yell; but Ferenc always remained quiet and smiling. Etel knew nothing except that nobody in the whole wide world had a husband like hers; he was handsome, and good, and clever, perfect in every respect, and she could not find enough words to thank God for having given him to her.

"Etel!" cried Ferenc, and although there was neither impatience nor anger in his voice, Etel leaped like a spark and rushed in.

Ferenc, washed, in his Sunday boots and in a nice white shirt, sat astride on a chair in the middle of the room.

"Go ahead, dear," he said, bowing his head like an obedient child.

Etel brought forth the comb and the bottle of olive oil. This was her greatest Sunday joy: to comb her husband. While she was at home, with the Mátyáses, she used to clip Mátyás's eyebrows every three months. Once upon a time, it was Mother's office to clip those huge brows, but ever since Roza had been forced to use spectacles, and since sometimes there were glasses in them and sometimes there were not, she had to relinquish her job; for she either left Mátyás's brush-like brows in a most disorderly state or she clipped off a little of the skin too. Mother took it quite to heart when she had to resign, and though Etel obeyed she was not very overjoyed. Indeed, she did it only with disgust. Ferenc's hair was not much blacker than Mátyás's white eye-brows, nor could any one contend that it felt like velvet, for it was coarse like the hair of all outdoor people; nevertheless, Etel could not have resigned that Sunday morning combing to save her soul. She rubbed the iron-gray hair with oil and carefully parted it on the left side, smoothing down with the palm of her hands those hairs which would not dutifully let themselves be brushed down. Ferenc protested at first, he said he was not Peter, and if he could comb his hair for six days in a week, he needed no guardian on the seventh either, but then he surrendered himself to Etel's whim—let her enjoy it if she liked it.

"Tell me, dear, when were you last combed like this?" she asked, diligently wielding the comb.

"When? Well, when the barber was combing me for our wedding."

"I didn't mean it that way. When was a woman's hand last brushing your hair?"

"Well, it must have been more than twenty-odd years ago! Poor mother combed me last, if she did it at all. I can't remember it anymore."

Etel took a step back and contemplated her work. It was funny; somehow it didn't want to come off the way she would have liked to have it. But it was also possible that she was thinking of something else, while she stood there staring at him. At any rate, she began to comb him all over again.

"Did anybody ever comb him like this? Some Russian woman? I mean Rokus, the poor man."

Ferenc tossed his head uneasily and reflected for a while. "Why, yes."

Etel put down the comb and placed her hand on Ferenc's shoulder. She spoke in an earnest tone, but not at all resentfully.

"You've never said anything about that. I've never asked it, to be sure, and I really don't know why I asked you now. But, tell me, how was it out there in Siberia? Was he really living with a woman?"

"Who?"

"Rokus."

"The devil only knows," said Ferenc. So much had happened since, there wasn't much to talk about, he couldn't remember very much of it, didn't much care for it, he never liked to intrude on other people's affairs—in one word, Ferenc did not feel like talking about the Tartar innkeeper. But Etel wouldn't let him be. Was it true that everything over there was just like it was here? Couldn't the men stand it without women there either? And did the grass-widows live just like they did here? He could tell her all about it, she had already heard the whole story.

"What story?"

"About Rokus."

"Well, if you've heard it, you know it."

"Did he really have a woman?"

"Yes, he did."

"An innkeeper?"

"Yes. She was very rich."

"Was she pretty?"

"God knows. Like most of them. Sort of Tartar. She came from far-away, from Asia. Fergana, that's how they call her country. She said her father was a khan or what-not and that he had a hundred camels."

"And you?" Etel asked, and her hand, although against her will, grabbed Ferenc's hair fast, "did you go a-visiting to her too?"

"Rokus asked me once to go with him. For supper."

"Did you also like her?"

Ferenc laughed. One could hear that it was a hearty laugh.

"The hell! She was a skinny little woman. And she had a moustache."

"You must have looked her over carefully!"

"I had to notice it. It was as if she had eaten a cat and the tail of it had stuck to her nose."

Etel laughed too. The comb now sailed smoothly over the hair.

"And poor Rokus, well, how did he get stuck to her?"

"It wasn't he, it was the woman who went after him. She kept him well, gave him money. And as Mother likes to say, not every pestilence is the same. Perhaps Rokus liked her."

"Did he kiss her?" asked Etel, blushing.

Ferenc didn't know about that because he wasn't asked to be present when he did. But Etel wanted to know more. Did he live with her?

No, he just stole out to her from the camp. Often? As often as he wanted to. Anybody who had money to bribe the guards could sneak out easily. And the others too? Did they also sneak out to sin? Yes, to teahouses, to inns, to the streets, just to look around, to see men, people— depending on one's tastes. If, for no other reason, just for the sake of going out, the prisoner would give everything to get out. Dogs can lie around their houses all day long, but the minute they chain them they want to run away.

"Well, it's done," Etel finished the five-times-ruined parting on the sixth try. "Now I'll just put the pot on the fire and then we can go."

And while she put the pot on the fire and chopped the kindling wood, she reflected that this was how she would have liked to chop to pieces and put on the fire all the bad women in the world. She was angry with herself, because she had been so cowardly, and had just been beating around the bush. What did she care what poor Rokus had done with the Tartar woman; what she longed to find out was what had Ferenc been doing with women? But she knew that she would never, never in her life, dare to ask him that—because she was afraid that Ferenc might tell her the truth. For Ferenc, as in so many other things, was different in this regard too; he had never yet told a lie, and she knew that if Ferenc confessed to her that he was just like all the other men—oh, but it was silly even to think of it, oh dear, her axe again missed the log, good that it just touched her finger, now let's put some salt on the wound, quickly.

Ferenc was already waiting for her on the threshold, with Etel's embroidered silk shawl and blue kerchief on his arm and with her prayer book and rosary in his hands.

"The bell has rung twice already."

"Just a second, dear, just a second," Etel said breathlessly, and laughed at the shawls, "I have to get dressed first. I noticed only now that I was still in my shirt-waist."

Ferenc started slowly to go ahead. And when Etel overtook him, she walked behind him silently for a while, admiring the narrow footmarks his boot made, and putting her white satin slippers into them, and staring with shining eyes at the sturdy legs, the broad shoulders, the bowed head lost in thought, till she could hardly restrain herself from shouting at him: "I love you!"

"Dear——"

Ferenc turned around—one could see that he enjoyed looking at her—and he took her left hand with his right, and they went on side by side walking silently on the road in the glistening, glittering sunshine. Etel was happy that

Ferenc was holding her hand and she would have rather let her left hand be cut off than tell him he shouldn't play with her wounded little finger. Although Ferenc noticed neither that the little finger was wounded nor that he was playing with it.

# XII

THE one-legged mail carrier was a frequent guest at Ferenc's. She used to be a well-to-do woman once upon a time, but then her husband went off to war and did not come back, and she, in her sorrow, gave herself to drink, and began to live fast, wasting away her money and her land, one of her legs, and losing even half of her wits. What else could she do then, the poor soul, but to become a mail carrier, for what else is a one-legged woman good for? People hereabouts have no time to read letters before the evening anyway, even those who do waste their time on reading, and by that time, the old crone has either finished delivering the letters, or she hasn't. And if she hasn't, well, then she delivers them the next day.

For Ferenc, she usually had nothing but seed-catalogues, and catalogues of agricultural machines, things highly adaptable to make Peter and Marika acquainted with the triumphs of modern engineering as well as with the secrets of the cultivation of roses. This time, however, the crone was carrying something she judged important enough to tell about to Roza, as she was passing by Mátyás's farm.

"Look what I'm carrying to the youngsters!" she said waving an enormously big letter. "There must be gold in it, because it's heavy, and hard."

Mother, of course, immediately hurried to the fence.

"Let me see it!"

"I can't. It's got to be delivered personally. It's written on it in Turkish."

"Then get the hell out of here," said Mother, highly

insulted. "They are out on the fields mowing hay anyway. Mátyás is out there too, and if you hurry you may get
there by nightfall."

"God, that's too far. Are they going to eat out there?"

"What else could they do? They took cheese with them
and bread."

"And drinks?"

"Yes, that too. Pickles' juice."

The mail carrier began to think.

"I don't know what to do now. Shall I go? I'm so thirsty!
I'll die of thirst in a minute!"

"Why don't you drink? There's the well."

"Why, after all, I could leave this Turkish letter here
with you, if you don't mind. I can't drink water in the
morning. It just gnaws at my stomach."

Mother immediately understood the connection between
the leaving of the letter and the gnawing effects of morning water on the mail carrier's stomach. So she brought
her a glass of drink—one couldn't very well call it wine,
because half of the nectar was pickles' juice, and not the
sourer half, either—and the mail carrier handed her the
letter. Indeed, it was heavy and hard.

"Where did it come from?"

"From the post office."

"Donkey! From what country?"

"Turkey or China, that's what the miss said at the office.
And she said that I should take care of it like it were my
eyes, because there's something valuable in it."

Mother tried to judge the letter's contents by weighing
it in her palms. The mail carrier came to her rescue.

"If I am present you may open it right now. God, but
it's hot."

Mother became so excited that she forgot all about the
pickles' juice and the mail carrier got a glass of clean wine.
It made her shudder more than the first drink had.

"This must have been sleeping with vinegar when it was young! Just look at it!"

Mother wanted to look at it but the envelope wouldn't open.

"There's a sack in it, or something. Help me, will you?"

With the old crone's help she broke open the envelope. A yellow tinplate, wrapped in linen, came out of it. It glistened like gold, and almost blinded the old eyes. Mother was the first to recognize what it was.

"Why, that has the Blessed Mother's picture on it! The Black Mary! And there are red stones in Her crown!"

Mother kissed the picture twice, first the Holy Virgin, then the Little Jesus, and then declared that she had never yet seen such a beautiful thing in all her life.

Yet there was nothing extraordinary on the picture. It was a factory made Black Mary of Kazan, stamped on a thin copper plate. But even the blind could see that it was of gold! And the red stones, how they sparkled! Diamonds, at least!

"Who could have sent it?" Mother pondered, holding it at arm's length so that she could examine it more carefully.

The mail carrier picked up a sheet of paper from the ground.

"Here's the letter to it."

"Read it."

"Just a second, I must just lean myself against this ladder. I don't know what's the cause of it, the heat or something, but I see rings of fire before my eyes. God, it's hot. My tongue just sticks to my mouth."

Mother hurriedly served a third glass, and the rings of fire immediately ceased to bother the mail carrier.

"It's Jewish writing, upon my soul! Genuine Jewish writing, from Jerusalem!"

Mother bent her gray head nearer to the mail carrier's

gray skull.

"Gracious God, thank you for permitting me to live long enough to see this!" she said, deeply moved. "You know, until now I've heard only of Jerusalem rosaries, and Jerusalem water, that's a good medicine, I still have a little of it left, I use it to rub my back with when it hurts."

The mail carrier sat down on the lowest rung of the ladder and, putting the palm of her hand like a shade over her eyes, looked up at the sun.

"It must be going on toward noon, I guess. I shouldn't mind eating a little of a beautiful woman's cooking. Even if she isn't as beautiful as your daughter-in-law. The other day even the gendarmes talked about her at the post-office and they said that you can't find the like of her even in the city, the king himself might be happy if he could look for fleas in her bed!"

The mail carrier made herself very comfortable on the ladder. She was beginning to feel sure of a dinner. But Mother shattered her dreams in no time.

"Get out of here, you fool! To say a thing like that in the presence of the Blessed Mother!"

The mail carrier corrected her moral testimonial.

"I didn't mean it that way, Aunt Roza! I know that Etel isn't like that! You are an old woman, but you must admit yourself that you've never yet seen such a clean living, pure woman as she is."

Mother was a patient soul, she could stand a lot of things, but this was too much. She left the mail carrier, went into the house, and slammed the door behind her so loudly that the mail carrier immediately forgot all about her thirst and hunger and rolled down the hill as quickly as her one leg allowed her, although she didn't know, the fool, what she had done. This alone proves that she was crack-brained. For if she had not been half-witted, she would have known that it is easier to make a horse's tail grow heavenward than the ear of a mother-in-law to listen to praises about her daughter-in-law.

Though Heaven will testify that Mother was very kind to Etel, and if anybody had said anything bad about her in her presence she would have scratched their eyes out on the spot. If, for instance, some knave had said that Etel was thievish, or that she had put fire to somebody's crop, or had cut somebody's throat. Etel had never done anything like that, Mother could put her hand in the fire for her. But as far as a clean life was concerned, that was a different matter, Mother would discuss that until the crack of doom, if she felt like it, never forgetting that Etel was a member of her family, and not even a bird, if it's a decent bird, ever dirtied its own nest.

No, Mother wouldn't speak badly about Etel to any stranger in the world, but she just couldn't help it, she had to lay bare her soul to Mátyás. Not that she wanted to talk about them, but it was positively indecent, the way they carried on, they were always together, always kissing, always embracing each other, and no matter when one went over to them, they had always just jumped apart. She had never seen the like of it, she was ashamed even to look at them.

"Then don't look at them," Mátyás answered from behind his pipe. "And anyway, that's a kind of disease everybody gets cured of sooner or later. Just look at ourselves."

Mother then stopped talking and vowed that she would never open her mouth again; she would rather bite her tongue in two than say anything to this old man who made fun of everything. But when she saw that she was waiting in vain, she began it anew. Did Mátyás ever notice how Etel was always following Ferenc around? Ferenc was a very well-built man, God must have created him when He was in a particularly good humor, but he was not thinking of naughty things all the time, it was the woman who could never rest, the woman who was like a bubble on water. They say that women are of fire until they are twenty-four, but Etel was past that age already! She wanted to tell Etel that so much hot blood was not becoming to her any more, but she knew that if she mentioned it Etel would fly into a rage. Mátyás, on the other hand, could easily speak to Ferenc about it, like man to man, and tell him that a new woman, like a new mill, should be regulated before it's too late.

Thereupon Mátyás turned his back on her—because Mother usually laid bare her soul at night—and sighed:

"I must have made a very great mistake forty-odd years ago when I forgot to regulate your tongue."

Then Mother discovered that Ferenc was not such genuine velvet as he had seemed at first either, and that if Etel had not been in such a hurry she might have had a better husband than this broken man who looked so old that he could have passed for her father. The funny part of it was that Etel nearly wore herself to death for him. What shall I cook, dear? Shall I broil or roast the chicken, dear? Do you want fresh feathers in your pillows, dear? No, I won't wear this kerchief because that isn't the color my darling likes! Oh, no, I can't sit down, dear must be home by now! No, I won't go, don't even ask me, Mother, I don't like to go anywhere without him! I'll split your heads in a minute, children, if you won't keep quiet when your father is asleep! Now have you ever heard anything so foolish, Mátyás?

For once, Mother's talk was very much to his taste.

"Now you can see for yourself, Roza," he said shaking his head, "how little you like me. When did you last ask me which I liked more, roast chicken or baked potatoes? Old as you are, you might learn a little from your daughter-in-law."

Thus Mother, unable to find an understanding heart in

Mátyás, could do nothing but keep everything to herself, and even then in such a manner that the young people should not notice it, because the truth was that Ferenc always gave Mother all the respect due her and whenever Etel cooked *rétes* she always sent a generous slice to Mother to taste it. And when a new kerchief was not in Ferenc's color, only Mother profited by it, for then the kerchief was deposited in Mother's chiffonier. Not that Mother was very particular about what Mátyás's color was, but it is a great pleasure to know that after one's death there will be plenty of things in the drawers, even kerchiefs, for the sexton and the palbearers.

Even now, as Mother went over to Ferenc's with the picture of the Blessed Mother, Ferenc immediately brought out for her the chair she liked best to sit in, and put it down in the little garden next to the lavender bush, because he knew that Mother liked to crumble its leaves.

"What's that under your arm?" Mátyás asked her.

"This!" she said as proudly as if she had made the picture herself. "And this Jewish writing came with it, too, straight from Jerusalem."

"That's in Russian," Ferenc ascertained, but he couldn't read it either. "I wonder who sent it?"

Mátyás was the only one who could guess.

"Why, Spirituto, of course. He owns a hundred acres, it's easy for him to send anything like this!"

"That's right, it's from Spirituto," Etel smiled. "He always dreamed about this Blessed Mother with the red stones."

"It's very valuable," Mother added, in an instructive tone of voice. "They sent a message from the post-office that you should take great care of it."

"We will," Ferenc said merrily, looking at the tin picture glistening timidly in the moonlight. "Perhaps it'll bring us luck."

"Perhaps it will," Etel echoed quietly and pressed the Holy Virgin to her heart. Let the fruit of Mary's womb smile at the fruit now budding under her heart.

But Ferenc was thinking of a different luck. He had been harrassing the Baron for so long now and had talked it over so often with the more well-to-do farmers that he had all the hope in the world that the corporation to drain the lake would soon be realized and that they could start working on it by the end of the summer. And the lake, as if sensing the approaching danger, withdrew. It left behind only a few little, round pools covered with sea-weeds and algae, hardly perceptible among the green weeds of the fields; the rear guards of a retreating enemy.

## XIII

THE Field Inspector is a very big person, the worm a very small one. This may lead a rash person to the conclusion that the Field Inspector is the more powerful of the two. But that is not the case!

There is only one Field Inspector, but worms are numerous, and no matter how strong a Field Inspector is he cannot possibly deal single-handed with all the worms eating up the plum trees. The Field Inspector, therefore, runs to the City Council and alarms them with the news that if the worms ruin the trees what's going to happen to the revenue from the plum brandy? Then the City Council hurriedly gets together and deliberates until a brilliant member cries out:

"We'll have to worm the trees!"

And just as the Lord gives orders to the dog which the dog forwards to its tail, so the City Council issues commands to the Field Inspector, which the Field Inspector, in turn, transmits to old Mátyás: Worm the trees, or pay. The Inspector places a big law book on his desk—to be sure, he puts it out there merely because he needs something on which to knock the ashes out of his pipe, for he knows the law by heart—and besides he does nothing from morning to noon but collect fines:

"You've again neglected to worm your trees! You'll pay so and so much or you'll be locked up for so and so many days."

Mátyás, and the others, grumble, pay the fine, and worm the trees. But, in a year, the worms are back again, although no one has invited them. Then follow fines again, and what with going to the city and harnessing the horses and unharnessing the horses, the day is wasted and no work is done—a five years' crop of plums isn't worth that much trouble.

Mátyás had realized this already some time ago, just as the gypsies usually realize their mistakes after they are hanged, but what with this topsy-turvy world, and no masters, no authorities, he did not think it important enough to worry about worming. But everything comes to an end one day, and when Mátyás was summoned to appear before the Field Inspector, he knew that order had been restored—the devil take it. The Field Inspector knocked the ashes out of his pipe onto the big book and turned to him.

"Well, my friend," he pronounced the sentence in a friendly voice and not at all angrily, "you've again neglected to worm. Will you pay or will——"

To be locked up now when one could make a neat profit even on grass blades? No, it wasn't worth while. Mátyás did not even wait for the end of the question, he put the fine on the desk.

"Here's your money!"

His little eyes squinted so shrewdly, laughed so merrily, that the Inspector could not possibly suppress his surprise.

"You seem to be happy to pay a fine!"

"Why not? This is the last fine I'll ever pay."

"Are you so sure of it?"

"As sure as there is but one God."

So, early the next morning Mátyás began to worm. By the time Ferenc's new wagon stopped before the farm, he had done quite a lot of work already.

"What are you doing?" Ferenc asked.

"Worming!"

"Now, when there are no worms?"

"That's just it, I don't ever want to have any. That's why I worm now."

"With an axe?"

"Of course. I've cut out three trees already, and I'm going to cut down the rest of them too."

Ferenc burst into laughter. Well, we'll plant better ones the next year, fine dessert plums that will sell for a higher price.

Mátyás noticed that Etel and the children were also on the wagon.

"And you? Going to town?"

"Yes, but only with Etel." The first meeting about the lake was going to be held at the City Hall. Several gentlemen from the Ministry of Agriculture had come down from Budapest, although it would have been better if the government had sent some money instead of the gentlemen, but there was a possibility that money was forthcoming too. Etel was taking two baskets of early grapes to the market; quite a novelty at this time of the year, it would be sold in no time. They expected to be back by noon.

"Keep an eye on the children meanwhile, will you? You won't have much trouble with them, they'll be playing by themselves."

The two children were already climbing off the wagon. Peter nearly fell under the horses because he tried to catch a dragon fly while getting off.

"Oh, you little tramp," Etel said, smoothing the boy's disheveled hair out of his eyes, "all your hair is in your aching eyes."

And indeed, the child's left eye was quite swollen.

"What's happened to him?" Mother asked anxiously. "Did a spider walk on it at night?"

"I don't know," answered Etel. "We'll bring him eye lotion from the pharmacy."

"Who needs that?" grumbled Mother. "By the time you find it, it'll be cured already. Am I right, little boy?"

Because Mother, although she loved Ferenc's son as much as she did her own granddaughter, never called him by his name, as she did Marika, but always as "little boy."

Etel pulled a good-sized loaf from under the driver's seat and asked Ferenc for the knife.

"Fresh baking, of new wheat. I'll leave half of it with you, Mother, give it to the children when they get hungry. It's still warm."

"What do you want to leave it here for? We have bread ourselves," Mother fretted, but she took the half-loaf just the same and smelled it. "Just like cake. Did you bake them by the pair?"

"Just the way you do it."

"That's why it's so nice."

Then Ferenc and Etel climbed back into the wagon, but before they started Etel turned back and promised Peter—Marika was taking the loaf into the house with Mother—that if Mother should complain about him when they got back, she'd chop him to pieces.

"I'll be good," the boy answered irresponsibly, but his serviceable right eye was already greedily taking in all the wonderful things that promised sin and enjoyment. There was a jay's nest on the birch tree, for instance, and little chicks chirped among the horseradish plants, the cat was lying-in on the straw in the byre—Peter had already noticed yesterday that, with a little help, the eye of one of her kittens could easily be opened—and there was a strong possibility that grand-daddy would go into the house for something and leave the axe unguarded. All in all, Peter could look forward to a forenoon offering a huge variety of manly pleasures, not to mention the joys to be invented by Marika. But nothing is ever given free of charge on this earth: Mother was already approaching him with a little pot in her hand, and although Peter would have liked to mistake it for a pot containing jam, it seemed perilously like something else.

"Come here, little boy!" Mother said. Her voice was always authoritative when she spoke to the children, because one could not possibly start early enough to teach the youngsters respect for their elders, but this time she mixed it with a dose of purposeful sternness. Because sternness makes the doctor and Mother was now present in the capacity of a doctor: the pot in her hand contained Jerusalem water. There wasn't much in it, in truth, because she had had a splitting backache last night, her spine must have felt a coming change in the weather, but there was still enough in it to cure Peter's eyes before Etel could get at him with her eye lotion. "Don't be afraid, you donkey, I won't eat you up."

With Marika's help, she succeeded in bringing back the little donkey who, being sensible enough to entertain a natural dislike toward the pot in which there was no jam, had sought safety behind the fence. Forced to yield to superior strength and power, Peter even folded his hands, much against his better judgment, because he had already prayed once today, and he was not a friend of soliloquies. But Marika folded her hands too and while Mother's trembling fingers washed the swollen eye with the medicine, the three of them recited the prayer composed for such special occasions.

"Now you can go and play," declared Mother after the "Amen," and the two children ran off to pick flowers. But in a short while, barely enough to recite a quick "Paternoster," Marika was back, dragging Peter behind her, who creaked like an old wheelbarrow and smudged the tears coming from his Jerusalem-watered eye all over his face with his dirty fists.

"Peter says his eye hurts him, he says it itches!"

"We'll fix that itch in a minute."

Peter resisted the contemplated new attack heroically but finally succumbed to the majority. Mother soaked a piece of cloth in cold water, put it on the aching eye and then bandaged it up with an old apron. Peter was rather unsympathetic toward the wet cloth but he found the apron very much to his liking. For the first time in his life, he viewed the world through only one eye, and he found it decidedly interesting. Marika watched him enviously for a while, then casually remarked that she could bandage her eyes too, if she only wanted it, and then she could also watch the turkeys through one eye, but Peter shattered her hopes with the declaration that that bandage would not be made of Mother's apron.

"Yes, it will be, because after dinner, when Mother takes a nap, I'll steal her black apron out of the lowest drawer, and that'll show even nicer things than yours."

"Yes, but that apron will not smell like sausages. This one smells just like sausages."

There was therefore nothing else for Marika to do than to humiliate herself before Peter and to beg him to let her tie up her eye with that sweet-smelling apron. She promised him apricot-stones in exchange for the apron. Then she offered him a red apple, one that had no worms in it, but Peter resisted even the apple, with an obstinacy to be observed in men only when they are less than six years old.

They wrangled over this question delightedly for quite some time and stopped it only when they heard Mother's call:

"Come in, children, here's bread for you!"

But before the children could reach her, Mother remembered that there was still a piece of their own bread left in the bread-basket, and somebody ought to eat that too. True, that was brown bread and somewhat dry, but the little boy had good teeth, he could conquer it. So Mother cut for Marika a slice off the fresh white loaf and gave the dry bread to Peter.

"Here you are, children. But don't go down to the lake, you'll get muddy!"

Now, if Mother had only told them to go down to the lake, because it was nice and cool down there and the sun would not scorch them so much as it did up here, then, quite certainly, they would have climbed the barn and sat down on the roof. Thus, however, taking each other by the hand, they immediately walked round the farm and sauntered down to the lake. They sat down on a little knoll of dried bog and began to munch their respective slices of bread, each one his own.

It would never have occurred to the little boy to make comparisons between the two slices of bread dealt out to them by Mother had Marika not remembered that she was now eating bread baked of new wheat; she had overheard her mother speaking about it the morning. Consequently, according to the ancient ceremony, she slapped her belly and cried out:

"New fruit, go in my tummy; fever, go to hell!"

Peter was so amazed when he noticed what Marika was saying that he simply dropped his jaw. Then he also bit a big chunk off his slice and slapped himself on the tummy.

"New fruit, go in my tummy; fever, go to hell!" he chanted.

Marika burst into laughter.

"Oh, Peter, but you're a fool! Why, you're eating old bread, and then the wish don't count."

"Then give me a piece of your new bread."

"I won't!"

"Just one bite, Marika!"

"Not one bite. Just for spite."

The little boy stared with aching heart at the white bread in his sister's hand.

"Gimme just one teeny-weeny little bite and I'll give you all mine."

"I got this from Mother. Go and ask her, she will give you some too."

It occurred to Peter that it would be wisest to send not only the fever to hell, but the new fruit too; the house was far away and he was not so certain of Mother's generosity. So he thought of a better idea.

"Marika!"

"I told you already I won't give you anything. Not even the priest preaches twice."

"But if you give me a little of your white bread, I'll take the apron off my eyes and tie up your eye with it."

Marika's mouth was full of bread. She couldn't answer before she swallowed it; she had time to reconsider the offer.

"All right. But just one bite. And you'll tie up my eye first."

Peter decided not to bargain. He accepted her terms without hesitation; he wanted to play fever very badly. The sooner the better. He leaped to his feet, pulled the apron off his head, stepped behind Marika, and began to untie the knot. All this time Marika was imperturbably stuffing the white bread into herself as fast as she could. When Peter noticed her treachery, she had only a little piece left. Now, more mature men than Peter had been known to break their agreements under similar circumstances, so it was no wonder that he tore the last bite out of the girl's fist and ran away to place the prey in security.

"I've got your bread, I've got your bread!"

He even boasted of his deed, the little bandit. Although, as wiser men say, it all depends from what vantage point we look at the thing. From Peter's point of view, it was heroic temerity and eternal glory. From Marika's point of view, it was nothing but a dastardly outrage and eternal shame.

"Thief, thief! Gimme back my bread!"

And she sprang after him. He was quicker, and more alert, but Marika was bigger and could run faster. Peter did not want to lay his prey open to the risk of a counter-offensive. So he stopped for a second, took a deep breath, and leaped forward again. His little white shirt sailed behind him, as if a little angel were flying above the fields. He lifted the bread high with one hand and, with the other, slapped his tummy:

"New fruit, go in my——"

He got no further; he fell into a pool covered with weeds and creepers and disappeared in it in a second. It was a small pool, a grown-up man could have easily jumped over it. But Peter sank, and the green scum crinkled, as a tablecloth would if a beetle got stuck beneath it; then not even the scum moved any more, it was once again the pretty, smooth, green, velvet-cover it had been a minute before.

"Peter! Peter!" the little girl cried out. She waited for a second, then ran madly up the hill, to her grandfather.

"Hurry up, granddaddy, Peter has fallen into the lake."

Mátyás ran, with the axe in his hand, but: seaweed here, scum there, which pool was it? The little girl did not know. Mátyás waded into four of them before he finally found Peter in the fifth one. He pulled him out and laid him down on the dried bog.

Peter was no longer a white-haired little angel; he lay there, covered with seaweed and moss, like a crushed green worm.

Mátyás made a trumpet out of the palms of his hands and cried out horror-stricken at the top of his voice:

"Roza! Roza!"

Mátyás's voice was hoarse, but even if it had sounded like a bell, Mother would not have heard him; she was washing in the house and loudly slapping the wet linen against the washboard.

But Ferenc must have heard the drawn-out shout as he brought his wagon to a stop before the farm, for as Etel ran into the house to give Mother the salted pretzels she had brought her from the city, he looked around. Boisi rushed up to him, then turned on his back in his joy and kicked his legs wildly in the air.

"Where's your master, pup?" Ferenc asked, scratching the dog's belly with the handle of the whip.

The pup understood him. He leaped to his feet, jumped forward, and scuttled downhill in the direction of the voice, yelping merrily. Once in a while he looked back to see whether Ferenc was following him. Ferenc walked spryly behind him, he could hardly wait to tell the good news to Mátyás: the draining corporation had at last been realized, he had been elected a member of the board of directors, and now it was certain that the lake was doomed.

As they reached the cornfield, Ferenc noticed that Mátyás was bending over something; his axe and his cap were lying on the ground next to him, and the bald top of his skull glistened in the sunshine. Ferenc knew nothing yet, but he no longer ran: he flew down the hillside, almost overturning the old man.

"Peter!" he bellowed, then added in a quieter voice: "Little Peter—you——"

He wanted to bend down to him, but Boisi sprang at him and embraced his knee with his forelegs.

"Get away," Ferenc shouted and kicked him so hard that the pup turned over three times. He croaked for a while, then he got up again and sneaked back to Ferenc.

"There must be some misunderstanding here," the dog thought, and he put his forepaws on the kneeling man's shoulder. Panting, his red tongue hanging out of his mouth, he lifted his two shiny eyes up to him, as if he wanted to reproach him: "But, man, isn't there enough decency in you to pat me on the head for bringing you here?"

Ferenc looked vaguely around, he did not know exactly what he was looking for but he knew it was something he had seen just a minute before. But what was it? Yes, there it was: the axe! He picked it up and split the pup's head in two. Then he lifted the dead child's head into his lap and began to clean the knotted, ruffled, blond hair of the green lichen that clung to it.

"Go, call your mother and your grandma," said Mátyás poking the trembling Marika.

Before the girl could reach the cornfield, Mother and Etel were already breathlessly running down the hillside, crying.

"Dear," was all Etel could say, and she embraced her husband. Ferenc said nothing. Mother patted him on the shoulder: "Calm yourself, my son, it was God's wish."

Marika feared only Mother, and now that she heard her say that God's wish was responsible for it, she felt reassured. With stubbornness and obstinacy in her voice, she spoke up:

"I couldn't help it, he took my bread."

"Shut up, you fool!" Etel screeched and picked up the axe.

The glistening blade woke Ferenc and he grabbed the woman's arm just in time:

"Etel! What do you want to do?"

Etel did not know what she wanted; she just crumpled up and dropped her head into her husband's lap, face downward, next to the dead boy's head. A few locks of her hair escaped from under her kerchief and mingled with the child's hair. She lay there as if dead, only an occa-

sional jerk of her shoulders, only her fingers scratching
the sand showed that she was still alive.

Mátyás wiped his eyes and broke the silence, because,
after all, somebody had to speak.

"Poor little beetle! He would have grown up into a
fine man. He showed already that he was the stronger."

"What do you mean, stronger?" asked Mother.

"He got what he wanted! He was the frailer of the
two and yet he got the bread. Look, it's still in his fist!"

Ferenc lifted his head with a start, and gazed, with
glassy eyes, at the piece of bread which had not yet had
time to dissolve, but had merely turned brown and spongy
in the mud, and which was still held fast by the little fingers. His eyes started from their sockets, the veins of his
forehead swelled out, and a moan broke from his lungs,
a moan as bitter as if it were his last, and he covered his
face with his hands.

He did not notice that Mother had gone, nor that Mother
had returned, nor even that she had crumbled the bread
out of the child's hand and put a small beaded cross in
its place.

"We'd better take the poor little thing away from here,
children."

Ferenc rose, helped Etel to her feet, and lifted Peter
in his arms. As he carried the little body into the house,
his face was paler and more ghastly than that of the
corpse.

The green water of the lake grinned mockingly and
coldly after them.

# XIV

THERE is no piece of smoked bacon that will last forever and no pain that will not vanish some day, thank God—Mother used to say, especially after the tragedy. But such is human nature that nobody wants old potatoes and nobody minds what old women say.

"Why do you cry all the time, my child?" she asked Etel, in a gently scolding voice. "After all, you were only his stepmother; he was Ferenc's son; and yet it is Ferenc who has gotten over it first."

"Yes, but he's a man," Etel answered, wiping away a tear.

"And you are a woman, and you ought to know that one shouldn't mourn a child. It's quite different when God takes him away when he is a full-grown man, like our Rokus. Though He might as well have taken Mátyás or me, we are only a burden on the earth, anyway."

At such times Mother also sniveled a little into the corner of her kerchief, but that was different: she cried for a man and not for a child. It was Mother's firm conviction that Etel should have mourned for Rokus to the end of her days, and another woman in her place would have done so—but then, of course, not even our own fingers are all alike.

"We women say," Mother went on, and she was already smiling, "that a little child is like glass. It breaks easily, but the easiest thing in the world is to buy another in its stead. And then they say that a mother buries the little child only in the foot of her bed, and whenever she feels

177

like it, she just picks him up alive again."

Etel knew she would never feel like that again, at least that was what she used to say in those days. She spent most of her spare time in church, and when she was alone at home, she knelt before the picture of the Black Virgin for hours. It was standing on the chiffonier, between the photos of Rokus and Ferenc, leaning against a china crucifix. Mother scolded her quite often for her negligence; how could anybody leave such a valuable piece lying around like that. Then Etel began to grow white. She had always been pale as buttermilk, but now she whitened even more and, after a while, she looked like a loaf of unbaked bread. Then she began to spread out, like overleavened bread on the breadshovel. And the first blades of grass were not even out on Peter's grave when the new child was here already; the one buried in the foot of the bed, the new glass taking the place of the old one.

Mother was thinking of such things while bathing and swaddling the little red titmouse. What a titmouse was Mother didn't know, although she had always heard that it was some kind of a bird, and most probably a beautiful bird too, as birds go, but anybody who looked like a red titmouse in the water couldn't very well be called beautiful. Of course, Mother would not have told this conviction of hers to anybody, except to Mátyás, and even he disagreed with her.

"Now don't say that Roza, because he's a very pretty little mite, even the midwife says it looks just like me. I guess she refers to my white skin, because otherwise I don't look much like a baby."

Of course, that was just what a midwife would say. She told Etel that the child must have sprung straight from her heart because his hair, eyes, nose, and mouth were just like hers; she told Ferenc that the baby looked as if he himself had spat him out, one only had to look at him to see that he'd grow up into the biggest farmer in the neighborhood; and the cry told her that the infant's voice was just like Mother's.

But as regards that she was not quite right. The child was not a cry-baby at all, most of the time he kept silent— and though that is considered a sign of stupidity by imperfect grown-ups, in reality it is nothing but dreaming of the deserted Heaven he had left behind—and he cried only when he demanded what was due to him, and he did that energetically, as it behooved a man-child.

"Go on, give suck to the child," Mother said handing the child to his mother, "he cries like a hawk chick."

"Like a swallow chick, mother dear," Etel corrected her, but, just the same, she kissed Mother's wrinkled right hand twice over, because Etel loved everybody very much those days. She had nice words even for Marika, although she could not have looked at her without growing glum for a long time, though that didn't bother the little girl at all. She was no longer a baby in arms and she had never been much fondled, because Etel had brought her up severely, as a poor man's child should be. But the love the mother took from the girl the father gave back a thousandfold. It was really amazing how Ferenc had become completely mad over the girl, ever since Peter had gone to meet God. One might almost say that he fondled and petted her as if she hadn't been a child at all, but a puppy, or a filly. He brought her candy and St. John's bread, picked eggs for her from the shrikes' nest, drove her around in the haywagon, took her wherever he went, showed her how the engineers from the city were working with all kinds of looking glasses down at the lake, and, on Sunday afternoons, he told her tales of little Chinese boys with twisted pigtails, whose names were not Pista and Joska, but Cheng and Ching, as if they had no real names at all, but just tinkled them with little bells.

Etel was very glad that Ferenc so completely forgave the girl and she blessed him to his face; there was not another man in the world who would have done a thing like that. Ferenc answered that one could not grow angry with a child, and anyway, the girl was not to be blamed. Sometimes he added that it was God's will, but, on the whole, he did not like to talk about it at all.

"Why talk about something that's passed and gone?" he used to say wearily.

He would not baptize the newcomer Peter, either, although he rarely opposed Etel's wishes. No, that would be like challenging God, He might even resent it—and Etel was surprised to hear this. Because Ferenc, although he kept the Commandments, as much as any weak mortal creature could possibly keep them, was not much of a pious person, which would have been a rarity anyway among men on the farms, that being strictly a woman's prerogative.

"Then let's name him Ferenc, after you, dear," Etel said, and took his hand into hers.

Ferenc objected to this too.

"We'll have time for that, when God gives us another child. We'll name him Mátyás. Let's give the honor to the old man."

Even Mother liked this suggestion, and Mátyás was deeply honored. True, it was a very fine name, even the almanacs said so, and his father had been called Mátyás too.

The question of who should be the god-parents was harder to solve; it was complicated by the fact that the Ferencs were on good terms with everybody around. Most of the folks in the neighborhood were kin in one way or another, but the Ferencs did not go a-visiting often; Ferenc had no time ever since he had started to do so many things at once, and Etel did not feel like going alone. People used to say that she held her nose high and generally behaved as if she were God Almighty, but, of course, they said this only behind her back, and the more prosperous Ferenc became the more they flattered her to her face. It was difficult to select a god-father; there were too many candidates. Every neighbor, cousin, friend, relative who brought a bite to eat to the expectant mother, asked her:

"Who will take the baby to church, Etel?"

"I really don't know it, Ferenc hasn't made up his mind yet."

"Because, if you don't mind my saying so, there's always us, you know. Funny that you didn't pick someone a long time ago."

Etel did not know herself why they had not, although in every decent household the godfather is assured long before the child is. So she said to the inquirers that they had forgotten all about it on account of the tragedy. But then they found out that all Etel's explanations were just so many lies, for Ferenc had already asked the Baron to be the child's godfather.

As a matter of fact, Ferenc had not asked the Baron; the Baron had offered himself to Ferenc. Of course, they did not come to church, they were merely put down in the register as witnesses. The Baron sent a bouquet to Etel, forgetting that bouquets were sent to brides only, but these gentlemen liked to send bouquets all the time. The Baroness-godmother sent a golden medallion because the Baron could not tell her whether she had a godson or a goddaughter. This made little difference to Mother who emphatically declared that, in spite of all that, the medallion could have been larger and the chain thicker. But Mátyás was very happy that things had turned out the way they did, for thus it was he who held his namesake under the baptismal water, and in a truly baronial fashion, too, wearing a silver-buttoned waistcoat, a necktie, and his new silver watch. Thus he denounced, in the name of the little namesake, the devil and all his works, which he did far easier than the Baron could have done because the devil had long ceased work on Mátyás.

Although one could never know. Old Mátyás, with little Mátyás in his arms, walked down the aisle so proudly, gave him such smacking kisses with his toothless old mouth, and winked so wickedly at Mother in front of the church after the ceremony that not even the Reverend himself could withhold a smile. But the Reverend did not hear when he whispered to her, after he had finally grumblingly let go of the namesake and had put him in Mother's arms:

"Ah, Roza, Roza, what a pity that every cloth gets threadbare when it grows old."

When they reached the farm, Mother handed the child over to his father:

"Before you cross the threshold with him, lift him three times to the sun and say three times: Sun-king, shine on him, Holy Virgin, bless him!"

It was high noon and the Spring sun shone brightly. Ferenc did not want to let the sun shine into the half-open, feeble little eyes and looked around for a shady place. His eyes alighted on the young pear-tree he had bought from the post-office clerk two years before. It was in full bloom for the first time now. It had peculiar blossoms, curious looking white stars; quite different from other pear blossoms—the clerk had said its name was war-pear, a new stock. A Belgian gardener had bred it, it bore extraordinary fruit.

Ferenc stepped beneath the war-pear tree, lifted his son three times toward the sun, high up among the star-shaped blossoms and the buzzing bees, and recited three times, according to Mother's wish:

"Sun-king, shine on him, Holy Virgin, bless him!"

When he lifted him for the third time, the little man

sneezed, feebly, queerly, like a blind kitten.

"He'll be a lucky man," Mother prophesied, and taking the baby from Ferenc, went into the house with Mátyás.

Ferenc walked down to the stable to feed the horses. When he came out, the one-legged mail carrier yelled at him from the gate.

"I've got another letter from Jerusalem!"

She did not stop, just threw the letter across the fence. Ferenc picked it up and looked at it—it was addressed to Mátyás. The address was in Hungarian, written by a heavyhanded, rarely writing person; its letters were even more scrawly than his own. But there were Russian letters on the quaint blue stamp.

"Who could that be?" Ferenc wondered and broke open the letter. He began to decipher it on his way to the house so that he could read it more fluently to Mátyás.

"My dear parents," the letter began. Ferenc faltered as if stunned by a blow and did not read any further but looked at the signature. "Furthermore I send kisses and regards to Etel and I remain faithful to her and furthermore I send kisses to my child and remain respectfully your son Rokus."

Ferenc wiped his brow, turned back from the threshold, went into the garden, way back as far as the apiary, dusted the bench with his handkerchief, sat down, and started to read the letter from the beginning.

"My dear parents, I pray to God that these few lines will reach you in good health furthermore I let you know that I am here in sad prison," and then he went on telling how sad his prison was, and how much it rained, and that everything was full of mud, and that bread was very dear, and that if they sent him five million the Polski consul would let him go home. Then followed the regards to Etel and to the child, but there was not one word in the letter about where the sad prison was. The sad prisoner had forgotten to put that in, the sad prisoner who could be freed for five millions and who claimed to be Rokus.

A deep sigh broke forth from Ferenc's lungs:

"If it was only true!" he said to the bees, because nobody else was around him. But it could not be true! He himself had closed the eyes of the starved man, he himself had covered him with moss before he continued his journey toward freedom with his last slice of bred. No, it could not be true, an impostor, a swindler had written the letter, men like that were not rare in those days, he often read about them in the papers.

Ferenc folded the letter and hid it in the inner pocket of his coat. Why trouble the Mátyáses with it? And Etel?

And by the time he entered the room, his eyes were shining radiantly again, as befitted a father bending over a cradle.

# XV

IT WAS raining. And it was a genuine Autumn rain too, the kind that comes stealthily, like a thief, and usually at night, drowsily, sleepily; neither pouring nor gushing, but creeping and drizzling; not knocking but soaking the leaves off the branches, with drops that have neither point nor weight, but which manage to sneak under the skin, into the hair, into the feathers; into men and into beasts. The drenched sparrows retreat to a shelter under the roof and squat silently shivering. For a while, the crows go on digging among the furrows but when they see that not even the field-mice are so crazy as to come out of their burrows, they soar up into the air and journey off to distant woods with mournful croaks. From that moment on, there is no sound to be heard, and all a man can say is that the rain has come early this year, the devil take it, and since, from one day to another, it grows colder in the house than it is outside, all he can do is to saunter from garret to dunghill and from byre to pigsty, trying to make himself believe he is working. Finally he gets tired of even that, and then he begins to whittle, to carve, to fix up things, stealing an occasional glance at the sky to see whether there is any hope of clearing.

Mátyás had been doing this for a week, and he had already fixed up everything he could; the broken leg of the wash-stand and the handle of the hoe, he had whittled some new prongs for the rake, and was now carving a cradle for his grandson. But if one is not the master of an art one is its murderer, and Mátyás either bored the holes

185

in the rockers too large—the rockers had been barrel staves once upon a time—or he cut the sticks to fit into the holes too thin. But all the time he pondered over things, and found that his grandson was not really his grandson at all, for Ferenc was not his son-in-law, merely the husband of his son's widow, and so the child was nothing to him, only his godson and namesake. Mátyás had had other godsons too and yet he had never before thought of carving cradles for them, indeed, he had not done it even for his own son, or his own granddaughter by blood either. But it was impossible not to love that little mite; hardly a foot and a half long and already trying to get hold of pipes, and whenever he could grab his grandfather's moustache he screamed so happily that it was a pleasure to listen to him. He could have hung on to Ferenc's moustache just as well, because that was also quite bushy, and bleached too, but he liked Mátyás's better, probably because that was completely white. Why is it, wondered Mátyás, that babes in arms like white moustaches better than any other kind? And why is it that though one doesn't mind a woman playing with one's moustache as long as it has its own God-created color, it feels so much better to have it in the hands of a little child?

So Mátyás put down his work and decided to wade over to Ferenc in spite of the slush; he had not seen his namesake since Sunday, and he wanted to see him very badly. True, he wanted to speak to Ferenc too, for it occurred to him last night, in bed, that it was foolish of them to take the wine-dregs to the distiller in Keresztdülö when they could use them themselves. Ferenc could easily get a permit to operate a small still and Mátyás, when he grew old, would still be good enough to sit around in a distillery and watch the still. After all, nobody had ever yet died watching a still! And then there was one more thing that urged Mátyás to put on his *suba* and to shut the door behind him. He heard Mother coming back from the pantry mumbling something about a mousetrap and Mátyás did not feel like listening to her. He knew that whatever was the trouble with the trap, Etel and Ferenc would be dragged in, and Mátyás was tired of all her twaddle and bibble-babble. He would have plenty of it in the winter when womenfolk have no other amusement than gossip, why listen to it now too?

When Mother found that Mátyás was gone, she shook her head disapprovingly. He must have gone over to *them* again. Ever since that titmouse had arrived Mátyás had been spending all his time over there, although he should have known by now, Mother had told him quite often, that the two of them over there were not quite right in the head. Why, one of these days they'd be going into their fifth year—after all, one had to count the time before the wedding too, even though they'd lived together like gypsies then—and yet they acted like young honeymooners.

Nevertheless, one shouldn't misunderstand Mother. She did not exactly want them to say good-night every evening by tearing each other's hair out, God forbid, there was nothing more beautiful than peace, but the law of life said that it was good to rattle knives and spoons once in a while; it kept them from getting rusty. These two never so much as quarrelled; a poppyseed dropped on the floor would make more noise than they did, and that was something Mother could not comprehend. She figured that as the years passed by the milk would get sour a little, and then even Mátyás would have to acknowledge that she was a clever woman, for she had prophesied it in advance. But Mother waited in vain; Etel adored Ferenc more and more day after day, and Ferenc accepted her mad adoration like a stone crucifix the prayer. Mother had absolutely no hope for a break between them; true, her envy never went that far, but it would have been good for her liver if Ferenc had once in a while just grabbed Etel's knot of hair and pulled it good and hard.

Nothing had ever brought Ferenc out of his accustomed mood; Mother had never seen the like of it in all her born days. For instance, when the Black Virgin got lost from the chiffonier, Mother thought that the devil would at last show up. In the morning, the picture was still in its place, in the evening, it was nowhere. The earth had just swallowed it up.

"I told Etel often enough that was to be the end of it; why did she keep it in a place where anybody could get at it?" Mother attempted to lead Ferenc's attention into the right channel. "Hired hands, cowherd's boys, beggarmen, charity ladies from the city come and go, who knows to whose hands it got stuck? Perhaps it isn't the thief to be blamed, but the person who didn't take care of it!"

Etel suspected Marika; she told her that if she had hidden it out of fun nothing would happen to her. The child cried, she said she hadn't seen it yesterday either, whereupon Etel promised her a good whaling. Then Ferenc went to Marika's aid and said that there was no sense in ringing the bell as if the house were afire, it'd turn up sooner or later, even if one wasn't looking for it, and that ended it all.

The outcome of the affair had a disappointing effect upon Mother. Not the fact that the picture had not turned up but that Ferenc cared so little for the loss of so valuable a thing. She told Mátyás that that was just another of those gentlemanly notions of his, like smoking cigarettes, and not drinking, and not cursing, and having a headache! Yes, there again this headache! Was it right, she would like to know, that Ferenc ate so little, drank so little, spoke so little, and when one asked him what was the matter with him, all he said was "I've got a headache." Was that right for a man who was neither a priest nor a gentleman? This was the one point on which Mátyás was in complete agreement with Mother; headaches were for women only, they had been created to have headaches, or else for gentlemen, who were not a whit better than women. Pretty nearly forty years had passed since Mátyás had been stabbed in the head at a ball, and so thoroughly that he had been dizzy next afternoon when he had gone out to mow—and he hadn't had so much as a headache since. What for, anyway? Only people with deep sorrow have headaches, and deep sorrow hasn't been invented for poor men. A sad peasant is like a lonely stalk of wheat that grows by the roadside, he gets trampled on before he can ripen.

Mother had done everything in her power to break up the peace between the youngsters, but what was the use of all her efforts when God's blessing was lacking! She had been envious of that headache of Ferenc's for so long that all at once her head began to ache too, despite the raw potatoes she put on it. And if Mátyás had not gone over to Ferenc without saying a word to her, she had not only showed him what a foolish mousetrap that clever Etel had bought for her at the Fall Fair, but had also asked him to bring her a quince from Ferenc, because the smell of quince was good against headaches.

The next day, however, the headache became so splitting that she felt as if the whole room had been whirling about her like a merry-go-round, as if people had been beating drums, blowing whistles, ringing bells in her ears. She didn't mind the bells so much, because their sound was pleasant and they even put her to sleep, but whenever they began to whistle she came to with a start and woke up Mátyás too.

"You're very hot," Mátyás said, and got up. He became genuinely alarmed when, after he had lighted the lamp, he discovered that the old woman grew cold again and that her eyes remained open. Indeed she recovered only when Mátyás rubbed her forehead with a piece of cloth soaked in brandy and massaged her backbone thoroughly.

That was how Mother's illness began. But she got up just the same, and walked around the house, even her headache left her occasionally, but whenever she took a deep breath she gobbled like a turkey. Then she lost her appetite, and in vain did Etel prepare for her the finest wine-soups and creamed chickens, she could not eat, and in a couple of weeks she was worn to a shadow.

"Well, Roza, the long Friday has reached you too," Mátyás said, sadly, and since he knew that it would be rather difficult to take Mother to a doctor, he just hitched up the horses and, without saying a word to her, brought out the new doctor from the village, a very agile young man. He looked at Mother's tongue and throat, tapped her on the back, put his ear to her heart—poor Mother was so frightened that she was more dead than alive. She had experienced many a horror in her life, but, so far, the Blessed Virgin had always protected her from a doctor.

"Well, there are lots of things wrong with her," the doctor said, twitching his ear-lobe, "I don't even know which one I shall cure."

"Well, the cheapest one," Mátyás said, but only out of habit, because he really did not care for the expenses. He pulled the money out of the chest uncounted and paid cheerily for all the lotions and powders the doctor prescribed. Mother took the sweet ones as well as the bitter ones until she got tired of them, although she had known in advance that no good would come of them, because the doctor was very young; he might be all right to cure a child, but he couldn't have had enough knowledge for old folks.

"Shall I take you to town?" Mátyás asked her. "Or shall

I bring out a better doctor for you?"

Mother said she would rather go, because from the visitors at her bedside she had heard that there were now doctors in the city who had lamps with which they could see one's insides. They called them axe-rays, or something like that, and not everybody could afford it because they charged a lot for them.

"That's all right," Mátyás said and took Mother to the most expensive chief-doctor, who had a big beard like a shovel. If he hadn't worn it one could have used it for shovelling snow.

Mother had one great pleasure out of her visit: the old doctor called the young doctor an ass and prescribed new powders. But they did not help much either. The axe-rays helped her; Mother felt her heart rejuvenated. But that lasted for a few days only. Then her face became wax-like again, and although she did not complain much, the matter seemed very grave to Mátyás.

"It seems we're going to lose Mother," he told Etel and Ferenc, "because she don't even grumble any more. You know that she could never stand the cat and now she don't mind even if she lies on her pillow."

On the morning of the Immaculate Conception she asked for the Reverend; she wanted to confess and to receive extreme unction. Mátyás went off to fetch the Reverend and Etel lighted the consecrated candles.

"Etel, my child!" the patient quietly spoke up.

"Yes, Mother dear!"

"Bring my little godson to me, I'd like to see him for the last time."

"Oh, no, not for the last time! You'll be dancing at his wedding yet," Etel said, lifting her son to Mother's eyes.

Mother panted heavily.

"They say that an old woman could be clubbed to death with a quill. I don't even need a glass blade, my child."

She dropped her hand on the little blond boy's head but the child did not even feel it. His big blue eyes stared calmly at the queer little birdlike face.

"Blessed be thou by Jesus Christ, the Blessed Virgin, and St. Joseph, and the Trinity in Unity, Our Lord."

Etel pushed Marika forward and she kissed Mother's hand. Marika wept, but not because her heart ached very much; she wept because she knew already what death meant.

"Be good, my child. Obey your father and your mother, love your little brother, and be good when you grow up. God doesn't permit me to see you go to your holy communion."

A drop of tear appeared in the corner of her eye; Etel gently wiped it off. The old woman lifted her eyes at her.

"Let Ferenc come near me too. So, in the name of God's eternal mercy, I beg you, my children, forgive me."

"But, Mother dear, there's nothing to forgive," Etel said, stroking the perspiring brow. Her voice choked. Ferenc took the old woman's hand in his own. He assured her that she had never harmed them in her life.

The wax-face became lively for a second.

"I know better, children. I always wanted to cause trouble between you. For no other reason but because we all are mean. Only, only——"

"Don't tire yourself, Mother," Etel said, and she could no longer suppress her tears. "You were mother to me instead of my own, God will pay back to you what I couldn't in your life."

Mother raised her hand, but she couldn't hold it up, it fell to the quilt.

"Aren't you lying well, Mother? Shall I fix up your bed?"

"No, not that. Reach under the sheet, my child. There. No. A little to the left. There. That's it."

"Oh!" Etel was surprised. She showed Ferenc what was under the sheet. It was the Russian holy picture, the Black Virgin.

"I took it. Not because I wanted to steal it. But because I wanted Ferenc to scold you. But he didn't say anything. Not even on account of this. Such a valuable picture. He didn't mind the gold, the stones. He's a rare man. A rare man."

Ferenc's lips curved to a smile.

"But, Mother, this is not gold. It's copper, and glass beads."

Mother became serious. For a second it seemed to her that she had been cheated. But she also knew that nothing mattered any more. Nothing. Only the mercy of Our Lord. She tried to lift her hand toward the picture. Etel touched it to her lips.

"Have pity on us, God."

Mátyás returned with the Reverend, placed a chair for him at the bedside, and then they all went out of the room. Only the infant remained in the corner. A visible angel among the invisible ones waiting to bathe the sinful souls in the eternal waters of Jerusalem, then to take them, purified, before the face of God.

After a while, the priest opened the door.

"You may come in."

Mother was lying in the bed serenely, calmly. Her two hands lay clasped on the quilt, her face was pacified, her eyes closed.

"God's mercy be with the saved soul," the Reverend said and on his way out touched Mother's hand once more.

Mother opened her eyes and, almost with a smile on her lips, asked the Reverend not to go yet, she wanted to make a last will and testament.

In such hours, not only the tear is infectious, but the smile too.

"You don't need a priest for that, my dear, but a notary," the Reverend smiled.

Mátyás smiled too, but only with his moustache, because the tears in his eyes had not dried yet.

"Don't mind that, Mother! You see, our Lord Jesus Christ made two testaments and yet the peoples don't follow either one."

Mother thought she shook her head, but she did not even move it. She wanted to make a testament which needed a priest, and it needed a priest because it was to be kept even after Mátyás's death.

"Say it, Mother," and the Reverend sat down once again.

And Mother said it, clearly, intelligibly. She wanted to have a mass celebrated for the salvation of Rokus's soul every year on the day of St. Rosalia.

"It'll be done."

"But with a choir."

"With a choir."

"The cantor should sing too."

"The cantor will sing too."

Mother's face grew very humble.

"God pay you for it. Although Mátyás will take care of it too. And after that, Ferenc. But don't forget to put in the song 'He rests in his cold grave in Bosnia!'"

"Who?"

"Why, Rokus. My Rokus. My son."

They explained to her that Rokus's cold grave was not in Bosnia, that the Bosnian war had taken place a long time ago, but that didn't mean much to Mother. Once upon a time, when she had been a little girl, they had celebrated Mass for a lad she had known. It had been a heartbreaking thing and she had not forgotten it ever since. The cantor had sung "he rests in his cold grave in Bosnia," and that was why she wanted to have that sung for Rokus too. Why didn't they want to do it for her sake?

They promised it to her, and Mother fell asleep, content and happy, in the Grace of the Lord and in His love.

They buried her the next afternoon. She had a fine funeral. Mátyás bought a metal coffin in the city and many people accompanied Mother to her last home. Then they returned to the house of mourning, ate their funeral supper, and drank a few glasses of wine, reverentially and respectfully remembering the dead. To others, the wine was only sour, but to Mátyás it was bitter too, because his tears rolled into the glass. He was left like a picked tree, and he had nobody to make his bed.

"We are still here, father dear," Etel caressed the old man's head and Ferenc said that hereafter they would be like one body, one soul.

By that time, Ferenc already had in his pocket the second letter from the sad prison. The mud was still enormous and the good intentions of the Polski consul were still to be had for five millions, but this letter was not addressed to Mátyás, it was addressed to Etel, because "my parents don't answer perhaps because they are not alive; it's such a long time that I am here. I kiss you my dear little wife and my little child too and I remain faithful to you Rokus prisoner of war."

Ferenc put the impostor's second letter into his purse, next to the first one. At first he thought he would show it to Etel, but then he changed his mind. He knew that would only lead to talk about the real Rokus, the dead one, and Ferenc did not like to talk about him.

# XVI

IN A corner of Etel's legacy, way down toward the lake, the soil was of lean, poor, white sand, not at all good for wheat. Ferenc thought that if he turned it over for grapes he could get more out of it. So he hired three day-laborers—young lads who worked well as long as one stood behind their backs and watched them. But Ferenc had no time to watch them; the corn was suddenly attacked by smut and he had to gather the crop before it could ripen thoroughly. Thus he could only go down to look at their work on the afternoon of their third day.

But he could not find them. He paid them wages as if they had been grown-ups, gave them good food—and, where were they? Had they made off? No, nothing had happened to them, they were just bowling in the hollow.

"What are you doing down there? Wasting the day?" Ferenc yelled at them. But not angrily because, after all, they had done good work, had turned over quite a lot of land already, four spades deep, just as ordered.

"We're bowling," giggled the boys.

"I thought so. But what are those white things you use for pins?"

"Dog's bones, or something."

From where he stood they seemed to Ferenc to be too big for a dog's bones, and when he got nearer he saw that they were human bones. Arm bones, shinbones; stuck into the earth like regular bowling pins. And the bowl was a skull. Or rather, not one but three, not like in a cheap

196

bowling alley; here every one of the three players had a bowl for himself.

"Let me see it," Ferenc said and picked up one of the skulls.

It was a regular skull, and it must have been quite old, for it was not as frightful as are the skulls of a recently buried corpse, he had seen those often enough in the war; in deserted trenches, by the roadside, some even with flesh only partially rotted off. He had already seen some like this too, in museums, in Siberia, in America, but only under glass. He had never yet held one in his hands. It was yellow and smooth, had regular eye-sockets, a nose bone, a jaw-bone, only its teeth had been bowled out. Or perhaps it had not had any.

"Yes, it had," the lads told him, "all of them had teeth. Some of them sat in the skulls so strong we couldn't knock them out even with the spade. Some of these dogs' heads fell to pieces before we could get them out."

"Asses," Ferenc scolded them. "These are not dogs' heads. Can't you see they are human skulls?"

"Why, yes, the skulls of dogheaded Tartars," one of the lads said, a living proof of the fact that the General Education Bill had not passed in vain.

"How many did you find?"

"Tartars? Oh, five, I guess. But there might have been more, because I took one of the skulls home; it's good as a trough for pigeons."

Ferenc told the boys not to touch them if they found some again, they should be left the way they found them.

They did find another one later that day; he must have been a soldier, for there was a bayonet next to him. Ferenc did not care for that, he picked up only the drinking cup, or what not, that lay near the head, and put it on the shelf in the clean room. As regards the bones, he told the lads to put them all in one heap and later dig a big grave for all of them.

The day laborers spread the news to the farms and Ferenc's reputation was greatly damaged. Others had found dead people too, sometimes even Hussars, together with their horses—it was no rarity in this neighborhood, especially not down toward the lake, one could hear bones and pottery crack under the ploughshare almost everywhere. God knows who they were—Gyurka Messzi claimed that they had been buried at the time of the big pestilence, his grandmother must be among them too, he could recognize her if they showed her to him because she had had a notched eyetooth, although she hadn't been a witch—but it was quite possible that none of them were Christians, because there was no rosary in their hands, and some of them hadn't even had coffins.

Although that didn't matter much, either to them or to those who found them. Children sometimes picked up what the ploughshares turned up, some of them took the skulls home to use them as troughs for pigeons, because people said that the pigeon that drinks out of them wouldn't fly away—but it's better to avoid the dead whenever possible because one never knows when it'll bring a curse upon the house. And so they were quite surprised when they heard that Ferenc not only cared for the bones, but even went so far as to start fussing around with the pottery; he simply stuffed his clean room full of those old pots. Mátyás told him that he had better stop that foolishness because it would end in trouble, but Ferenc paid little attention to him. Instead, he went over to the Reverend for advice, taking with him one of the fancy pots as a present.

But the Reverend merely shrugged his shoulders. He did not think it was an antique. It might be a milk pot, but since it had no glaze on it, it was more probable that it was just a flower pot. At any rate, it was not worth anything, and Ferenc might do worse than throw it out. But Ferenc had already seen things like that in museums, had read that such antiques had been found all over the county, he had even heard that some of them might have been made when Christ was still walking on the earth.

The Reverend patted Ferenc on the shoulder.

"That's all nonsense, my dear friend. Don't believe a word of what you read in the papers. You see, I never take a paper in my hand; I know it'd just contaminate my soul and I don't want to sin."

Ferenc was a little ashamed and tried to excuse himself on the ground that he read the papers only when people brought him some goods from the city wrapped in them. But as far as the fancy pot was concerned, he did not let it go at that, and the next time he went to the city, on the next market day, he took it to the museum where he had never been before. He asked whether he could see the director and as soon as he showed what he had brought they took him to him. The director was an elderly, graying man and looked a little like Ferenc.

"This gentleman looks just like a peasant," was Ferenc's first thought.

"This peasant looks just like a gentleman," thought the director.

And both of them had good eyes, for the director instantly began to beat around the bush like a peasant. He couldn't say exactly that the pot was not valuable, it must have been about fifteen hundred years old, but just the same, it was not much of a rarity, the Museum did not have much money, they could hardly give anything for it, provided he had brought it in with a view to sell it. Ferenc proved to be more of a gentleman than the director; he put the pot on the desk and declared that he did not want anything for it, he had about ten more like it at home anyway.

"That's nice of you! And do you intend to give them to the Museum too?"

No, Ferenc intended to keep them. The director turned a little sour at that, but when Ferenc told him that if he didn't mind coming out he would show him the other pottery, and if he cared to, he might dig for some more in the fields, there ought to be more of them where these came from.

This cheered up the director, and he took Ferenc around, showed him the old arms, armors, pictures, the treasures kept in glass cabinets. Ferenc listened quietly and spoke only when the director pointed out to him a huge piece of bone and told him that that was the shinbone of an animal that lived before the Flood, called the mammoth.

"I know," smiled Ferenc, "I have already seen complete ones." Where? In a museum. In which museum? Oh, in many of them, in the Petrograd museum, and in Tobolsk, and the biggest of them all in Pittsburgh. The director was greatly surprised that Ferenc had observed such things, and he was glad that he had found such an intelligent man.

"Well, when you're in the war, you either get blind, or your eyes open up," Ferenc remarked, and that impressed the director even more.

By the time Ferenc left they were friends. The director promised to go out to him next week, to dig up the field. Was there a place on his farm where he could sleep? Although the nights were still warm, he could sleep in a haystack.

"Oh, we'll give you a better place than that," Ferenc said. "You will stay in Etel's house."

"Who is Etel?"

"My wife. We live in the new house, it has a red tile roof, you can recognize it from afar. Her house is empty, we just keep apples in there, but we can take them out if you don't like their smell."

"That's the one thing I like about them. And have you children too?"

"Two of them. A boy and a girl."

"How big are they?"

"One is going on to three, the boy, and the little girl's just started to go to school."

That surprised the director. He wouldn't have thought that the children were so small. He had thought Ferenc had a daughter about to be married off, and was a little ashamed when he learned that Ferenc could have been his son.

But it was not only friendship that prompted the director to ask about the family; he also had evil intentions, he wanted to buy souls. Indeed, he bought them quite cheaply; the boy cost him a trumpet and Marika, a coral necklace. The third soul was thrown into the bargain free of charge; Etel asked him whether it would be all right for him if she roasted a pigeon for him for supper.

"God forbid," protested the director, and very much from the bottom of his heart, for he was not much of a friend of fowl. But Etel wouldn't hear of his protests and placed a plateful of fruit on the table, while Ferenc went out to fetch wine.

"Make yourself at home with us."

Whereupon the director said that he already did, because the minute he laid eyes on Ferenc he liked him as much as if he had been his own brother.

Etel needed no better encouragement. If you'd only learn to know him better! It isn't nice for a woman to praise her own husband, but my husband is perfection itself. He wouldn't harm a fly, no one has ever heard him curse, and whatever he says is like the Scriptures.

The director enjoyed listening to the beautiful, bright-eyed woman who, leaning against the chiffonier, boasted so enthusiastically of her husband. Then he noticed the two pictures.

"Who are those two youngsters? Your brothers?"

"No!" Etel burst into laughter. "This one was my first husband, but he got lost in the war, the poor soul, and this is Ferenc, but he is more handsome now because he looks more like a man."

And she wiped the picture with her apron. Not the dead man's picture, but the one of the living one, who, with his graying hair, wrinkled brow, slightly drooping shoulders, and tired, weary smile was much more handsome now than when he had challenged the world with glistening eyes, a proud moustache, and a youthful head.

"Oh, women, how good it is that you are all alike," the director smiled to himself, and he was not surprised that Etel roasted chickens for him, not one, but two.

If one had been permitted to choose between two roast evils the director would have taken the pigeon, because it was smaller, but one had to do many things in the interest of science.

So he began to eat the chicken, with not much enthusiasm to be sure, and devoted most of his attention to the soft, crumbling, freshly baked rye bread, when he noticed that the host never as much as touched the bread and ate the chicken with lettuce only.

"Don't you eat any bread?" he asked him.

Ferenc answered nothing; he merely shook his head. It was Etel who explained the matter to the director.

"You know, he ate too much bad bread in the war, especially in Siberia, that's why. Bread baked of all kinds of flour, corn, and oats, some they ground of treeroots, isn't that so, dear? Then he got so sick of them that now he can't eat even our own bread. Especially since that catastrophe, you know, perhaps you heard about it."

No, the director had not, he hadn't been around here for a long time. Ferenc waved it aside:

"Never mind it, Etel, the director isn't interested in that."

But Etel looked at the director and saw that he wouldn't mind hearing it, so she told him how Peter had fallen into the lake.

"And now I'll show you what happened afterwards," she said and beckoned the director to the sofa where the boy slept. And while Ferenc went out for wine—although the pitcher was still half full, for the guest was not drinking much—Etel pulled up the little boy's nightshirt and showed the director his tummy.

"Do you see this birthmark, here, on the left side?"

The director saw it. A brown mole, a rather ordinary mole. He had seen many of them, some looked like cherry pits, others like plum stones, but this one had a jagged edge, it looked like a strawberry.

"You must have picked a lot of strawberries while you were with child," the director remarked jokingly.

"Ferenc says it's because I stared too long at that piece of bread in Peter's hand. He can't look at it at all and when I bathe the boy he always goes out. That's why he went out now, so that he shouldn't have to look at it."

"Then let's cover him up quickly," the director said, because he did not like to cause sorrow to anybody.

By the time Ferenc came back they were already talking of the flowers on the window sill.

The director did not meet Mátyás until the next day. While digging in an ancient grave, they found a curiously shaped vessel lying next to the skull of a skeleton. It was like a radish; big-bellied, small-mouthed, pointed down below. What was it?

"Children's toy," suggested one of the laborers.

"A money box," said another.

One said it was an old fashioned brandy jug, another said it might have been a jar holding paprika. Mátyás,

who was sitting on a knoll of earth, watching the director
work, just couldn't hold his tongue listening to all that
stupid talk. So he began to explain:

"That used to be a substitute for pipes in the old days."

"Do you think so?" asked the director.

"Now just listen to this, sir. There was no tobacco in
those days but one always had to smoke. Am I right?"

The director readily acknowledged that. He was also
an addict to the devil's straw.

"Now then, how did our ancestors do it? Easily. They
poured water into a jug like this, stuck a reed into it, and
blew bubbles. That's how they whiled away the time."

"Well, that's quite possible," the director said. "No one's
ever thought of it yet; how people smoked when there
was neither pipe nor tobacco. I'll mark it down and write
about it in the newspapers. Let's teach something to the
ignorant city folk."

But while he was taking notes, he told them that some
time long ago it might have been just as Mátyás said, but
when they had buried these ancestors here they had used
the pottery for another purpose. They had put food and
drink in them.

"For the dead?" Ferenc asked.

"Of course! So that he shouldn't starve on his way to
Paradise. They were better men than we are, for we
grudge the bread even from the living. I don't say that
all of them do, only the scum of them. I am sure that
you, Ferenc, would give your last bite of bread to somebody who needed it; you don't eat bread anyway."

Ferenc went pale and tottered. If the director had
not caught him in time he would have fallen into the
grave.

"What's the matter, Ferenc? Are you sick? Bring a
little water for him, boy, hurry up. Lie down for a while
on the grass."

"That's all right, it's over," Ferenc said, wiping his brow. He felt like that sometimes, he didn't know why. But he hoped nothing worse would ever happen to him.

With this, he went back to the house. But Mátyás remained with the director. He felt very friendly toward him; he must be a fine man if he considered his opinion good enough to write it down. And by the time they returned to the farm, they were great friends.

"Come and see my house too," Mátyás invited the director.

The director went over to Mátyás's and admired the famous well, despite the fact that it was already doomed because the engineers were scheduled to start work on the artesian well on Ferenc's farm the next week.

"Etel is taking care of it since Roza left me; she even comes over every night to make the bed. Sit down for a while."

But the director excused himself. He bade him good night.

"You get sleepy soon out here, don't you?"

Not exactly that, but the director wanted to work, he had a lot of work to do yet tonight.

"I saw your lamp burning quite late last night. I thought it was because you were afraid of being alone."

In the evening, Mátyás knocked on the director's door. "Well, how are you getting on?"

"I want to work, Mátyás," the director answered. There were paper and pencils on the table and a handful of cigars.

"Just go ahead, never mind me," Mátyás said and lighted the cigar the director offered him. Then he sat down and waited patiently; he wanted to see when he would start to work and what work he would do. For that was why Mátyás had come over, he had never yet seen a gentleman work, especially not at night; and now that one was here, he thought he would come over and look at it, since it didn't cost him anything anyway. But although the director smoked a good many cigars, he didn't do any work; he just wrote, and wrote, sheet after sheet, with incredibly tiny letters. At last Mátyás realized what it was all about. The director must have been some kind of a notary, a chief notary or something, that must have been his regular job. Well, it certainly was an easier job than hoeing, although he wouldn't swear to it. Just listen to that sigh he gave when he put down the pencil and leaned back!

"Finished it?" Mátyás asked him in a friendly tone.

The director smiled, wearily. His work was never finished, he said.

"Why, you couldn't even read that much! What did you write, if you don't mind telling me?"

"A book."

"Book? Well, God help you. I suppose it's a nice job, if one knows how to go about it. And what kind of a book?"

From what the director answered, Mátyás figured he was writing a story-book.

"Well, with one's head at rest, it's easy."

"That's just the trouble, Mátyás, it isn't at rest any more. I'm a tired man, nervous."

Mátyás snapped at the word. That was just it! In bygone days only horses were nervous; he had had a horse that was so nervous that sometimes one couldn't start him off even with a pitchfork, and sometimes an acacia leaf dropped on his head was enough to make him so wild that he almost shook the plow to pieces. Nowadays one often heard that people were nervous, even out here on the farms. Especially the young ones who had been to the war. They had their hands and feet and appetite and everything, they didn't look sick at all, yet they were nervous. Why, what was this nervousness anyway? Some kind of an imperfection inside?

"Well, something like that," the director consented and looked at his watch. It was past midnight.

"The next time I won't keep you up so late when you want to work," Mátyás promised him.

And he came to visit him every night and never left before midnight. The director taught Mátyás things about the world, and Mátyás perfected the director's knowledge in the poor man's sciences. Both of them were very satisfied with each other.

Ferenc went so far in his friendship that one day when he and the director were alone in the apiary, he suddenly asked him:

"You know the law, don't you?"

"As much of it as I have to, Ferenc. I know what they lock you up for if you don't know it. Why do you ask me?"

"I just ask it. Suppose a prisoner of war is declared dead. His wife marries again. Then the prisoner turns up. What's going to happen then?"

"He ought to be happy that he got rid both of the prison and of his wife. But why do you want to know that, Ferenc?"

Ferenc just wanted to know it. One could often hear of such things as that. Once they had asked him about this in the Club but he hadn't known what to answer, so he thought he would ask a man who knew more than he did.

The director fell to thinking. He said that as far as he knew the law, the first marriage would be held valid under the circumstances and the second one would be nullified. But then the woman could divorce her first husband and marry the second one again.

"You don't mean to say you're in that fix?"

"God forbid! That would be a tragedy."

"On account of the children, eh?"

"Well, you could separate them somehow, but the house, the farm, the fields, all the common property, and everything else are so mixed up that it would be hard to tell what's Etel's and what's mine. I heard something that in such cases that husband wins with whom the woman sides, that that is the law."

The director held to the opinion that it was not wise to shake anybody in his faith, so he just nodded. Later in the day, however, he walked up to Etel while she was peeling fresh nuts.

"Tell me, Etel, how did you live with your first husband?"

"Very well," Etel answered surprised. "Why do you ask it?"

"Well, I just wondered what you would say if he just turned up one day and demanded his rights. Which one of the two would you choose?"

"The Lord Jesus Christ protect us from that!"

Etel turned greener than the nuts in her lap. She had never thought of a thing like that, not even in her wildest dreams.

"And don't even think of it again," said the director. "I asked it just out of fun."

It was not a fair joke on the part of the director. Etel broke two glasses on that very day and lost the key to the garret so that it had to be opened with an axe. Ferenc, on the other hand, couldn't remember where he had hidden the cellar-key, and while looking for it, he knocked his picture off the chiffonier. Its glass broke too.

"Don't get nervous," the director warned them and smiled. He remembered Mátyás's theory about nervousness.

This was his farewell supper; the next morning an auto

came to fetch him. They loaded the car with sacks full of bones, with baskets full of pottery. Ferenc even gave the director the pots he had on the shelf in the clean room. He decided not to keep them.

And just when the director was about to start, Ferenc remembered Spirituto's letter. The one he had sent together with the picture of the Black Virgin. Perhaps the director could read it. No, he couldn't either, but he offered to take it with him, he knew somebody who could translate it. He would either bring it out personally, or if he didn't have the time to do that, Ferenc should fetch it from him the next time he came to town. The director then took leave, hoping that they would remain friends. But Etel would have to promise not to roast any more chickens for him because now he could tell her that he didn't fancy fowl at all.

# XVII

FERENC was very much like Mátyás's nervous horse; an acacia leaf had fallen on his soul. He could not say that he was ill, he had even lost the cough he brought home from Siberia, yet he felt seedy somehow. Anybody could see there was something the matter with him, he was lean and yellowish, his moustache had grown even grayer and his hair had begun to fall out. His mood had turned worse too. What work he did outside the house he did impatiently, angrily, paying little or no attention to it, and although he tried to control himself at home, he became even more taciturn than he had used to be. And when the children so much as opened their mouths he was beside himself. Etel often surprised him staring rigidly, stiffly into space, for hours.

"Something pains you, dear?"

Ferenc answered smilingly, but Etel noticed that when she spoke to him he shuddered like one who had to come to himself first, before he could answer.

"No, only my head aches. But it'll pass if it wants to."

"Let's show it to a doctor. Shall I go with you, dear?"

Ferenc did not object. There was no reason to go, but he thought he would do it for Etel's sake. To which one should they go? It would be best perhaps to go to the one with the big beard, the one they had visited with Mother, at least they knew him. All right, let's go to him. It was all the same to Ferenc.

The big-bearded doctor listened to them patiently, then asked Ferenc whether he had been a soldier? In the war?

At the front, in prison? Yes, Ferenc had been everywhere.

"But your wife was not with you, was she?" the doctor joked.

"No, she wasn't," and they all laughed.

"Of course. I thought so. That's just the trouble. Take off your coat and roll up your shirt sleeve."

He tied some kind of a rubber band on his arm, pricked him with a needle, then told him to come back in three days.

Three days later he received them with smiles:

"My friend, you're a lucky man. There's nothing the matter with your blood."

Of course, there wasn't. Ferenc had known that three days before too, he could have told the doctor that himself. Etel shrugged her shoulders. Don't tell us what is not the matter with my husband, tell us what is.

The doctor thought that the peasants had become a little too fresh these days and ill-humoredly instructed Ferenc to stick out his tongue. Then he rapped and tapped him, made him breathe and sigh, listened to his heartbeat, felt his liver, just as he had done to Mother. Then he gave him some kind of a medicine. Mátyás immediately discovered that it was of the same color and smell as Roza's had been, it was a pity to have spent money for it, there was more than half of Roza's still left on the windowsill. Etel was alarmed, if it hadn't helped Mother, it might not help Ferenc either.

"Don't fear that, Etel," Ferenc said and put the medicine on the windowsill. "If it won't help it won't harm either, at least not as long as it remains in the window. I'm not afraid of death, but I'd like to finish the mill first."

But Etel was afraid. She put the price of two geese in St. Anthony's chest and prayed for Ferenc at all of the three altars for an hour. She told the Holy Virgin that if Ferenc died she would not survive him, she would slit her throat in that very hour. She often thought of that at night too, lying in the bed with eyes wide open, listening to her husband's irregular snoring and nervous tossing. She rarely fell asleep before dawn and then it was Ferenc who woke. He listened to the faint sound the borer made in the door. That was exactly how his worries bored him! Ferenc knew what was the matter with him, and he knew that if he could only tell about it he would feel easier at once. But why should he trouble this innocent woman with those things? God knows how she would take them.

Once, in a night of torment, Ferenc remembered the director. He did not know why he had such trust in him, but all at once he began to yearn for him. In the morning he told Etel he was going to town to see him. There was a meeting of the draining company and he thought he would see the director about Spirituto's letter.

"Don't go with empty hands, dear. Take a little fruit to the director."

"Very well, take some apples and pears from the garret while I hitch up the horses. But pick only the best of them."

Etel filled her apron with apples and war-pears. The war-pear bore less this season than it had in the first two years, but the fruit was large, fleshy, juicy, and beautifully red.

While Etel was wiping them, Matyika stole up to her, staring covetously at the fruit. He was a silent, earnest little boy; he never asked for anything, but his mother could see what he wanted.

"Do you want a nice golden apple?"

"I don't want apple," Matyika shook his head.

"A pear, then?"

"Yes."

Etel picked out a nice red pear and gave it to him.

"Eat it, Matyika. One-two-three!"

Matyika was more obedient now than he was at any other time. He opened his mouth as wide as he could and bit the pear. But he immediately began to howl as if a wasp had stung his tongue.

"What's that?" Etel jumped to him. Ferenc came up just then and he too bent down to the boy. "Who's hurt you, my boy?"

"The pear," the child answered, spitting out the piece he had bitten off, breathing quickly, like one who ate hot paprika. "It burns."

"Oh, you silly," Etel laughed, but then she added, "though there might have been a beetle on it."

Ferenc took the pear out of the child's hand and bit it. He also spat it out at once.

"It's like poison, tart and sour. What's happened to it? Isn't it ripe yet? It's juicy enough."

They tasted three of them but all were uneatable. The first year's crop was small sized but plentiful and sweet. The second year's crop was less, but the pears were larger, although they tasted like water. And now here were these, so beautiful that one couldn't even have painted nicer pears, but apparently filled with vitriol.

"No wonder it's called war-pear," Ferenc said, wiping his mouth, "it carries its name in itself. I wonder what its fourth crop will be like? Well, put only apples in the wagon, Etel."

"Shall I wait for you with dinner, dear?"

"I don't think I'll be back before nightfall. Maybe I'll have to wait a while before I can see the director, I don't know."

But he did not have to wait. The minute he arrived the doorkeeper announced to the director that the elderly peasant who had brought the fancy pottery was here again, but now he had genuine, real apples instead of pots.

The director said he had been waiting for him, on account of the Russian letter. There was nothing extraordinary in it, some Russky was sending them his thanks, what was his name——

"Spirituto."

Something like that, yes, Spiridinov. Ferenc had better keep the letter, if only for the sake of the address, one could never tell when one would need it, perhaps they might want to write him. The Russky asked them to write him, to tell him how big Peter was, he also had a son now, also Peter, but he was too small yet.

"And how are things on the farm?" the director asked, while Ferenc was putting away the letter in his purse, next to the two other letters.

"Well, we just get along somehow, slowly," Ferenc answered, fussing with the purse. Then he suddenly put it away. He changed his mind. He would not mention it, perhaps the sad prisoner would stop writing after all, why should he gossip about it? So all he asked was whether the director would like to come out to them for the harvest. No, the director had no time, he had to go to a meeting even now, and he was in a hurry too, although he would have liked to chat a while with Ferenc. Ferenc understood that he had had enough of the guest, and since he too had to go to the company's meeting, he asked the director to come down to them when they butchered the pigs. But no, said the director, that would be too far off, why not meet after our respective meetings? There was a quiet little restaurant down near the river, he was to have his dinner there, Ferenc was to go there too, and they could talk.

But neither of them would have thought that it would be evening before they left the restaurant. For, after dinner, the landlord sat down at their table and complained that he was in trouble. His son had come home from

Russia last year, got married, his wife was just lying-in, and now the Russian woman the boy had picked up there had also arrived the night before. The devil alone knew what was going to happen now, two wives and one husband was perhaps an even more complicated thing than two husbands and one wife, for that was something women could stand easier and liked more.

Ferenc listened to the story with bated breath. The wine was already working in him a little and when the innkeeper went to another table to entertain his guests, he turned to the director:

"I'm in the same fix myself, if not exactly."

"What do you mean?" the director asked, surprised.

"This is what I mean," Ferenc said with a sudden rush, and gave the two letters to the director. Then he told him the whole story from beginning to end.

The director was not surprised that the sad prisoner had not told where his sad prison was. He had seen several such letters already, with the date-line missing. No one had ever taught the sad prisoners how to write letters, because, in the school, the noun and the verb and grammar were considered more important; which was quite right and correct, since how could a hired man possibly strew dung over a field if he didn't know what a possessive pronoun was and what sort of bread would a woman bake if she didn't know on what tree the nominative case grew? And then it often happened during the war that the soldier was not permitted to write home when he was eating the Czar's bread, because the world would have been immediately thrown off its axis if an old peasant had learned that a hundred miles or even more from him there was a Polish or Russian village by the name of Zrsztrmprszt. This prohibition got so much into the blood of some of the more conscientious soldiers that even when they became sad prisoners they stuck to it, and instead of writing down the date they began their letters thus: "I pray to God," because they had learned in their childhood that a letter which did not begin thus was no letter at all.

The director could make Ferenc understand all this, but he could not understand himself why the letter-writer was still a sad prisoner, when there had been no more prisoners for a long time. He discovered, however, that the Polski consul was none other than the Polish consul, and he thought that he could perhaps follow that clue. True, the postmark was washed away and could not be deciphered, but the Ministry of Foreign Affairs might try to do something about it. Although it was easier to find a pin in a haystack than a lost Hungarian prisoner of war in Russia, nevertheless, if Ferenc wanted it, the director could take some steps in the matter, and it was possible it would not cost very much.

Whereupon Ferenc declared that the cost did not count. He did not mind if his whole farm went away, if Rokus could only be brought back to life. But the dead never wake, and so the letter-writer must be an impostor; all he wanted was to swindle money out of Mátyás.

"Possibly, possibly," the director said, staring at the letters in his hands, meditating. For it occurred to him, although he did not say so, that a person who wanted to cheat had the brains to do it too, and he would certainly not have forgotten to mention where to send the millions.

"Are you so sure, Ferenc, that these letters could not have been written by Etel's first husband?"

"As sure as there is but one God!" Ferenc declared earnestly and raised both of his hands. "I buried him under the moss with these two hands of mine! Why, I've told you already. If I wasn't so sure of it I wouldn't dream so much about it. And it wouldn't come before my eyes every time I see bread."

He reached greedily for his wine but the director put

his hand on Ferenc's arm.

"Wait, Ferenc, don't drink! Etel won't let you go to meetings any more if she smells wine on your moustache!"

Ferenc smiled. Not with his customary, slow smile but with that sudden flaring up which is born only in wine.

"Not she, sir! Not Etel! She's a fine woman! She wouldn't do that!"

The director pulled his chair nearer to Ferenc's.

"Look, Ferenc, you shouldn't keep anything a secret from her. One could tell everything to a woman like Etel. And one should, too. Even if you'd killed a man, Ferenc— you should confess her even that. But you committed no crime, you can step up to her calmly. And it'd be better if she learned all this from you and not from somebody else, because that might possibly have a different effect on her. Confess to her frankly everything, tonight, and then both of you will be calmed. God bless you, Ferenc!"

Twilight had already fallen as Ferenc left the macadam road and turned into the sand. It was a silent, beautiful autumn evening; sparrows hopped on the road, a yellow leaf fell once in a while from the poplars, spinning slowly, thoughtfully in the air as one who knew that there was no sense in hurrying, and that the earth would not run away from underneath it. From afar came the sound of cow-bells, clouds of smoke hovered above the fields here and there, swineherds fried bacon on a fire of dry twigs. Ferenc thought he felt the fried bacon's smell in his nostrils. He cracked the whip above the horses' heads, for he was hungry.

Marika was sitting at the end of the house, on a bench, reading loudly, pronouncing the words slowly, and emphasizing every letter separately.

"Trust God and you will not fail."

"Why don't you stop reading, Marika? You'll ruin your

eyes, it's dark," said Ferenc. "Where's Matyika?"

"He's fallen asleep on the chest. He couldn't wait for mother."

"Mother? Wait for? Where is she?"

"She's in the clean room. She got a letter in the afternoon, the mail carrier gave it to me when I came out of school. When I gave it to her she went into the room and hasn't come out since. I went in once and told her I was hungry but she shouted at me to get out and so I didn't dare to go in again."

# XVIII

A DROWNING man clutches at a straw. Etel heard from the storekeeper that there was a soothsayer on one of the farms—true, she had not always been one, she had been a vender of almanacs before, but she had given up that job and was now in touch with the spirit world. She would not accept any money, only lard and flour, but it was worth it, because she could find out everything in the world, even things nobody asked her. Indeed, sometimes she told only such things, because that was all the spirits revealed to her.

Etel had never tried a thing like that in her life, she had never yet had even her fortune read, but now that Ferenc was not at home she thought she would go to see the soothsayer. The soothsayer closed her eyes and said that she heard loud rattling of chains from somewhere very far, probably from hell. Then Etel interrupted her and said she was not interested in the dead, what she wanted to know referred to the future, whereupon the soothsayer said that a big, black man was following Etel around. Etel got very angry, she said the big, black man should follow the devil and not her, she had already a husband, what she wanted to find out and what she wanted the soothsayer to find out for her from the spirits was whether he would get well or not. The soothsayer grumbled and mumbled, apparently she entered into another hurried consultation with the spirits, and not in vain either. For the spirits revealed to her that Ferenc would not only get well, but so great an honor would come to him that even the newspapers would print his name. Then the soothsayer sprinkled Etel with holy water and asked her to mention her in her prayers, which was a queer thing to ask since it was she who was associated with the spirits and not Etel.

But Etel did not notice this, nor the sprinkling either, all she heard was that Ferenc would get well, and so she was in excellent humor until Marika gave her the letter.

She recognized Rokus's handwriting on the envelope at once. She did not lose her head but she seemed to have lost control of her brain. It had already happened to her a thousand times that an ant had crawled along on her hand. Had she ever stopped and gazed at it? Never before in her life. And now she was standing in the center of the room, with the unopened letter in her hand, and stared at the ant on her hand. How small it was, how thin, how red, how ugly! Why was it so red? Was there blood in ants too? Probably, because it had a head, and feet, and a waist, everything. Had it a heart too? Perhaps. It looked exactly like a little man. Look, how it crawled back and forth. What was it looking for? The way home? To its father, mother, mate, children? Now it lifted its head, looked around, and began to rush upward on her arm. It bumped into a hair. It rose angrily and embraced it. Now it looked like a man wanting to tear a birch out of the ground. What would it gain by it? Then it turned around and ran toward her fingers, stopped for a second, looked around, as if trying to find the right way, finally it selected the index finger, ran the length of it, then leaped from it onto the letter and began to scratch it. Now it seemed as if it tried to bore a hole in it, as if it wanted to get into it, to find out what was in it.

Etel suddenly broke open the envelope and read the letter, read it from beginning to end. Then she started to read it over again, five times, ten times, twenty times, until twilight settled on the window. She stepped nearer to the light, nearer, always nearer, until she knocked her head against the window pane, but even if they had knocked her head off she wouldn't have known what there was in the letter. All she knew was that Rokus hadn't died and that she wouldn't give up Ferenc. No, no, she wouldn't! Not to the Lord Almighty Himself! No!

Marika opened the door; Etel angrily sent her out. His daughter! The daughter of the dead man who now wanted to come back! Well, let him come, let him take his daughter, his house, his field, the whole world, only: he should not touch her, he should not take her away from Ferenc. From her husband, her real husband, the only true one, whom God had created for her, whom she had sought out for herself, whom she had found for herself, whose hand had been tied to her hand with a stole by the priest, to whom she had borne a child!

Yes, yes, her hand had been tied to Rokus's hand first, and she had borne a child to Rokus first, but what did that count? What did she care for that? As far as she was concerned, Rokus was dead, he had left her a widow, she had a paper about it, oh, how good it was that she remembered it! Where was it, why wasn't it here now, to cover up and to hide this letter with it! I don't want you, I can't see you, you don't exist! Oh, where was that paper? No, no one could have it, Ferenc was keeping it in his chest. But what if the paper was lost? Etel smiled. Why, there were enough people to testify that the law had been obeyed; even her father-in-law, Rokus's own father, knew it. Oh, how happy he would be to hear of this, the poor man. Etel did not mind that father and son would be happy; as long as Rokus would be satisfied with his father, she didn't mind him, she did not even mind if he married again. On the contrary, she wished him all the luck in the world. But what if Rokus would not let her go? What if he flared up and forced her to stay with him? Because he had a nasty temper, he had always been quick tempered. But she was not afraid for her husband. Indeed, she would like to see anybody try to harm Ferenc! She would finish him, even if he had a hundred lives! She was ready to fight against everything, man, God, law— for him! But that could not be! Neither God nor law could be so bad as to change everything they had ordered, settled, consented to. But what if they did? If they said: Go home, woman, your place is with your first husband, his rights are the stronger, because they are older, you've only dreamed of the second, forget that you've ever dreamed of it—what then? Well, then she would, on their last night together, fix up her own, dear husband's pillow once more, for the last time, and then go out to the lake— for whatever the engineers had done to it, there was always enough water left in it for her. No, not for the two of them, she would not even think of that! No hell would be a severe enough punishment for her if she took Ferenc's soul with her! She did not want to take any innocent soul with her, but she could do whatever she wanted to with herself!

The wagon rattled outside the window; Ferenc had come home. Etel turned to light the lamp, but it was not on the table. Oh, of course, this was the clean room, the lamp was over in the living room. She hurried over, threw the letter on the chiffonier, and was lighting the lamp when Ferenc entered.

"I hear you've got a letter?"

"Yes. Rokus is found."

Ferenc's voice was alarmed, Etel's calm.

"That isn't Rokus. It's an impostor."

"No, it's Rokus, really. Here's the letter."

"Don't even show it to me, dear, I know it by heart. This is already the third one. I've got two myself that this man has written."

Etel's heart sank.

"Rokus?"

"No, not Rokus. That impostor. Look at them——"

Ferenc brought forth the two letters. Etel looked at them.

"They're from Rokus. I know his handwriting."

Ferenc threw himself on the sofa—its legs creaked loudly.

"Do you believe that the dead can come to life again?" he asked hoarsely.

Etel looked at her husband. How pale he was! Or was it merely because of this bad oil?

She screwed up the wick and, kneeling on the chair, put her elbows on the table. Now she could see Ferenc better.

"God knows. If he isn't dead."

Ferenc wiped his brow with the back of his hand. He screwed the wick lower. It hurt his eyes.

"Listen to this, Etel. I've told all about it to the director already. He said it'd be best if I told it to you, too. I haven't done anything I couldn't tell you."

Etel's lips parted. She fastened her glistening eyes upon her husband. Ferenc's talk started slowly, but it grew smoother as he went along.

"It was when we ran away from the Murman Coast. You know, the five of us. Until only the two of us were left. In the woods. It was so dark that sometimes we couldn't see anything even during the day, just felt our way forward. Then silence, such a silence, that we were afraid to move, we were afraid of our own voices. Only one who has experienced it knows that there is such a silence in the world. And the night was bad because then we heard all kinds of voices in the dark. They sounded like ghosts, but it was only a snowy owl swooping down on a squirrel, and that was what screeched. And then we heard rattling, but not from the trees, from the sky, as if they had been shaking nuts in thousands of sacks, and here it was red, and there it was green, and there again there were blue fires in the sky, like poles, and they burned like ribbons. Sometimes the night became light, sometimes for an hour even, and then we saw the big snow-white owl tearing a squirrel to pieces and the squirrel dripped blood."

Ferenc took a deep breath.

"So that was what you were always dreaming about," said Etel. "Why didn't you tell me this before?"

"No, it wasn't this," Ferenc answered, shaking his head, and went on. "The light in the sky came in very handy when we got accustomed to it. For then the owl got blinded and when we hurled snowballs at it, it dropped the squirrel. And we divided it up, Rokus and I. He liked it, because the squirrel's flesh was just dripping with oil on account of the pine cones on which it lived. But I ate only once or twice of it, because my stomach couldn't stand it. I got very weak, I couldn't even walk. Rokus was stronger than I was, he picked me up, sometimes he carried me in his arms, sometimes on his back."

"My poor dear," Etel put her hand on Ferenc's, but perhaps never before in all her life had she thought of her dead husband with so kind a heart as now.

"We found a farm, woodcutters lived there, and were friendly to us. They gave of what they had, tea, sour cabbage, smoked bear-meat. And then oatbread mixed with ground treeroots, but I told of that already."

"Yes, dear, yes," Etel interrupted him, because she noticed that Ferenc was panting heavily. "Maybe I'd better give you supper now, don't torture yourself with an empty stomach."

"It'll be over in a minute, Etel. Listen. I pulled myself together at the woodcutters' farm, but then Rokus be-

came sick. He had a fever, he was talking out of his mind.
The woodcutters then met Red soldiers who were looking
for us. They sent them away, but they didn't know
whether they wouldn't come back again, and so they told
us that we'd better go on, they didn't want to get mixed
up in trouble. I didn't very much want to go on, I didn't
care if they caught me again, let them catch me, but
Rokus wanted to go, he said he wanted to see his little
family again. Yes, that was how he said it. Well, let's go
then, I said, it didn't make much difference where I died,
because by that time I had already heard how Piros was
behaving. The woodcutters gave us an old knapsack and
two loaves of bread, and said that that would be enough
for four days, in which time we would find a village,
if we continued straight toward the east all the time. If
we got to that village nobody could hurt us any more because the Whites were the masters there. I carried the bag
because Rokus was too weak. And on account of him we
couldn't go fast, and the woods didn't end even after we
had walked for six days. And no matter how I cut the
bread it was only just enough to say grace over. I swear
by the wounds of the Lord Jesus Christ that I always gave
him the bigger slice, because he was the feebler. On the
sixth day I saw that he was too far gone, so I gave him
my slice too, it was only crumbs, I didn't even eat of it, I
just chewed some wild berries. And when we lay down
in the evening on some dried leaves, Rokus asked me to
give him bread, because he said he was starving, and I
told him I was going out of my wits too, because I always
cheated myself, I always cut less for myself than I did for
him, and that day I didn't eat any bread at all, and I asked
him to be patient until tomorrow, perhaps God would
make an end to our sufferings by then. He said that tomorrow he'd be dead. I showed him the bread, it was no
bigger than a roll, and I asked him, Now where will you

be if I give it to you? If we don't reach a village by to-morrow both of us will be dead. But he just kept on say-ing that he wouldn't live to see tomorrow anyway, why shouldn't he fill up his stomach for the last time in his life. But, I said, what's going to happen to me then? If I got this far already, I don't want to die here. And then—then—but you know the rest. He became silent. Died. In the morning. That's all. That was what I did."

Etel did not notice at all when it was that she pulled her hand away from her husband's. But she did, although she remained where she was, her elbows on the table. She rose only when, after the last word, Ferenc dropped his head.

"Did you do that? You? Did you do it?" she asked in a very low voice.

"I did," Ferenc answered and raised his head. His face was no longer pale. His voice was calmer too. It happened just as the director had prophesied. He was relieved.

Etel stared at him.

"You!!" she screamed and ran out of the room.

Was it a cry? A scream? Horror? Hatred? Pain? Love? Ferenc could not tell.

He shrugged his shoulder, stared for a while into the flame of the lamp, then went out too, with weary, heavy legs. The letter which had fallen to the floor rattled under his step. He picked it up and read it. It was like the others except that the sad prisoner asked for fifteen millions and threatened to break his beloved wife's bones to pieces if he ever got home because she did not want to redeem him from the hell about which he couldn't write any more. Furthermore I remain faithful to you, Rokus.

Ferenc smiled and went out of the house.

"Etel!" he shouted into the night.

No one answered. Aimlessly, he turned back and tried to go into the clean room. The door was locked. He knocked but no one answered. He went around to the window and looked in. In the light of the rising moon he saw Etel sitting crumpled up at the table, her head resting on her two outstretched arms. Ferenc rapped on the window, "Etel, Etel, dear," but when she did not answer, he went back to the living room, made the bed, and lay down. Then he remembered Marika.

She was still sitting on the bench, but had fallen asleep.

"What are you doing, Marika?"

"Trust God——" the girl mumbled and fell into Ferenc's arms.

He picked her up and took her inside.

"Just like her father," he thought as he put her to bed and patted the quilt.

# XIX

THE moment Etel closed the door of the clean room behind her she ceased to talk. One word is not very much, but she did not say even one. The next morning, when Ferenc got up, Etel had already swept the kitchen, but she bid him no "Good morning" and when Ferenc asked her where his old boots were, he couldn't find them behind the door in the shed, and he had to go to turn over the dung for the farmhands were busy washing the barrels, she just kept silent. He might as well have been talking to a stone wall; she went on sweeping as if she had not even heard him. He stepped up to her to ask whether she was angry with him and embraced her by the waist, but Etel gave him a look Ferenc swore he would never forget in his life ever. And whenever afterwards he tried to speak to her, Etel behaved as if he had not existed at all. She did not speak to the children either; true, she dressed and combed and washed them, but never spoke to them, and when she wanted something of them she just waved with her hands, or winked, or motioned with her head. She attended to everything around the house, cooked the dinner and the supper, but she herself hardly ate anything, and slept in the clean room, all by herself, behind locked doors. As a matter of fact, the door of the clean room was locked even during the day, no one could set foot inside that room after that evening. And when they peeped in through the window they saw her kneeling before the picture of the Black Virgin for hours.

For a day or two Ferenc thought nothing of it, he figured that she would stop acting so strangely after she had fought it out with herself, when she realized that it was not Rokus writing those letters. But Mátyás became suspicious. During the first few days he had been busy on the field like Ferenc, attending to the autumn sowing, and harrowing, and so he did not notice that Etel did not come over to him to tend the house. But when he went over to visit them on Sunday and found that Etel, who was milking the cow, neither returned his greeting, nor answered his questions, he asked Ferenc what was the matter with her. Ferenc did not want to worry the old man too, so all he said was that she had been behaving like that for some days now, he did not himself know why, perhaps she had some female trouble, perhaps it was on account of that.

"She acts as if she were crackbrained," said Mátyás and there seemed to have been some truth in his diagnosis.

For there were times when she acted as if she had gone crazy. One day, for instance, she cut her best blue silk skirt to small pieces, and then spent several days sewing them together; Ferenc and Mátyás could not figure out why she did that. Then they noticed through the window that she was making little skirts for the Black Virgin out of the silk patches. She dressed up the picture in the little skirts and hung a mantle over it, so that only the Virgin's crowned head showed above them. Another time, while combing Matyika, she began to choke the boy with her bare hands. She was alone with him in the room and Ferenc ran in only when he heard the boy scream. But by the time he got there, Etel had already left and had locked herself up in the clean room. They heard her crying all day long. Otherwise she knew about everything, knew where everything was, she even helped them butcher the pigs, and stuffed the sausages herself. If it had not been for her silence nobody would have noticed that she was crazy.

"God's beaten us good and hard. His hand is heavy upon us," said Ferenc, bitterly, dropping his head, as he sat in the director's room, for he had come to ask his advice.

"If I only knew what made her like that," Ferenc pondered, staring vacantly. "I guess, though, it was that jailbird who claims to be her first husband. She even said she recognized his handwriting, though I told her the whole story, just as it happened."

The director asked him whether it was not *that* story that Etel had taken to heart so much. Not the fact that Rokus was alive, but the way Rokus had died? He did not ask it so cruelly, he did it cautiously, beating around the bush. But Ferenc understood it even so; his face turned gray.

"Do you think so? I thought of it too, but I shook it off. It couldn't be! What business of hers is it? That's only our business, Rokus's, and mine, and the Lord's. Or do you also think that I am a murderer?"

Lucky that there was no glass in the director's room because if Ferenc had seen his face in it he would have been frightened by the sight. The director gently put his hand on Ferenc's shoulder.

"What childish talk! Rokus died because he was ill. He may have died in prison, he may have died on the front, just like the rest of them. Why should you be held responsible for him? Let him who took him away from his child's cradle be responsible for him. You answer only for yourself, and you did only what everybody else in your place would have done. Tell me, who would have gained anything if you had died too? Perhaps he was already unconscious when he asked for that last piece of bread. Calm yourself, Ferenc. You have every reason in the world to face God with your head up."

Ferenc took a deep breath; it sounded like a hiccough. He answered that he had often tried to silence his doubts with just the same sort of talk the director had just told him, but the wound wouldn't heal. If God had wanted to take Rokus, why had He saved him until he had reached the Siberian wilderness? It was easy to talk, but anybody who had not been there that night, beneath the big trees, anybody who hadn't heard what he had heard, who hadn't seen what he had seen, couldn't know what it had been like, shouldn't say anything about it. When that rattling of nuts had waked him, and those big red and green fires like rockets in the skies, why, it had been so light that one could have counted every hair in Rokus's moustache, and there he had been, lying with his mouth still open, as if he had been still waiting for the bread— Why did he always think of it, why did this picture always appear before his eyes if he was not guilty? He had seen thousands of dead soldiers in the war, on the burnt meadows, in furrowed fields, thrown into heaps, lying one on top of another in the trenches, some with skulls cracked open, and some with their guts hanging out, he himself had thrust his bayonet into men for he had been a good soldier—why didn't he ever dream of these things? Why only of him, only of the fellow-prisoner, the fellow-wanderer in the wilderness, of his open mouth begging the last bite of bread? Why did he think of that every time he saw bread, why couldn't he look calmly at the birthmark on his innocent little boy's body, at the mole which looked like a strawberry to everybody but like a bite of bread to him! And Peter, his own son, dead with a last bite of bread in his stiffened fist, with a last bite he had taken away from Rokus's daughter by force? Wasn't it queer that his innocent son had had to die because of that? If he had run into a scythe, if a barrel had fallen on him, if a horse had kicked him to death, it would have been nothing but an accident. But he had died because of a piece of bread that had belonged to somebody of Rokus's blood—if this wasn't God's punishment, then what was a punishment?

He stopped for a second, then continued in a lower voice.

"I don't always feel like this. But somtimes it just gets me, like fever, it runs down my spine, grabs my heart, and no matter how I fight it I can't get out of it."

He banged his chest with his fist.

"When it gets me, like now, it doesn't matter how often I say: It isn't true, it isn't true—here, inside me, somebody says to me: Murderer, murderer! But I am not a murderer, I swear before God!"

He tossed his head stubbornly, but out of the corner of his eyes he waited for an encouraging word like a child.

"No, Ferenc, you're not," the director said. "You wouldn't be a murderer even if Rokus had really died because of you. But all I can say is that perhaps Rokus isn't dead at all? How do you know it for sure?"

"He was stiff already when I shook him."

"That may have been because of the cold. Or perhaps you were so frightened you couldn't see straight."

"It must have taken at least an hour before I scratched together the moss and the leaves for his shroud. I crossed his hands on his chest; they were cold as ice. Those hands couldn't have written this letter."

He threw the last letter, the one that had been delivered to Etel, on the table.

"I'll try it just the same," the director said, examining the envelope. "Now look at this, you can clearly see the last two letters: —sk. Pinsk? Omsk? Tomsk? Tobolsk? No that would be too long. Kursk? Let me have this letter, Ferenc. I'll try what I can do through the Foreign Ministry, although it'll be a complicated matter because we have no diplomatic relations with Russia. But I'll try it."

"It'll help us about as much as a new horseshoe would

help a dead horse," Ferenc said, and took out the other two letters too.

When he shook hands with him the director felt that Ferenc's hands were cold as ice.

# XX

**M**ATYAS was sowing dill. This is not a difficult job, even a cripple with only half a body, from the waist up, can do it. In fact even the lack of a chest will do no great harm, because only the back is needed. And all the investment it requires is a handful of sand. When you hear the first thunder of the year, you bend down, fill your hand with sand, and fling it behind your back. And no matter where you accomplish this agricultural operation, dill will grow out of the sand you scatter. Well, not everywhere. For instance, if you do it in the house nothing will come of it, although there may be sand there too, and even on the top of the bed, especially in a widower's house, where he does all the sweeping and dusting himself. But by the time the first thunder reminds the farm people that the heavens are inhabited too, no decent person is found inside a house.

And since one could not hear of a more decent person than Mátyás even in a sermon, it was only natural that when the first thunder struck, Mátyás was on his way to the vineyard, passing by the dunghill with a pipe in his mouth and a hoe on his shoulder, and like the experienced man he was, bent down and flung a handful of sand behind his back.

It so happened, however, that the sand fell not on the ground but into the director's eyes. Served him right, why was he loafing around where people were busy sowing dill? Nevertheless, Mátyás grew alarmed.

"I beg your pardon, sir, but I really didn't want to harm

you."

"That's all right, Mátyás," the director said wiping the sand out of his eyes. "The pity of it is that one can't sow money like that."

"You're right about that," Mátyás said, and assured the director once more that he had had no intention of knocking anybody's eyes out, least of all his, although there were some people who'd be better off if God were to take their eyesight.

The director was already familiar with Mátyás's philosophy and so he suspected that he was again in a state of war with the government. But he did not want to go into that now.

"I've come out to see the Virgin. I've read in the papers that the Blessed Mother likes to appear to your daughter-in-law."

Mátyás knew about that too; the Jewess had told him that even the Budapest papers had written about Etel.

"Well, when did it begin?" the director asked. Mátyás replied that Ferenc could tell more about it, although he did not like to talk much about it either, not to him anyway, but perhaps he would speak about it to the director.

"It's bad enough as it is," Mátyás added, pushing his cap out of his eyes, "because Etel isn't coming over any more. Ever since the Virgin first appeared to her, she doesn't care a damn about anything. All she does is talk to the Virgin."

"Have you seen the Virgin too?" asked the director.

Mátyás was surprised that the director, a clever and wise man, asked him such a foolish question. How could he have seen Her when that was only a woman's affair and no man's business at all, though he knew a few men who saw Her when Etel pointed Her out to them. But they must have been holy men, most probably, not mean mortals like Mátyás. He was not worthy to have visions.

The director could not make out how much of Mátyás's talk was piety and how much mockery. So he asked him point-blank.

"Do you believe in those visions, Mátyás?"

"Well, look here," said Mátyás, "why should I say that I believe in them when I don't and why should I say that I don't when I do? You know, I believe in God, and in the saints too, at least in those I know, and I pray every evening and every morning, but what Last Judgment will look like and how all those millions of people will find room in the valley of Joshaphat, well, I don't know about that. On the other hand, one thing is sure, Etel's never lied to me, and I know her because we've brought her up, and when she says that she sees something she sees it, and when she says that she hears something she hears it. And then, you know, I've never been a boastful sort of man, but, you know, it's a great honor that the Virgin's just picked on our Etel."

Mátyás now picked up his hoe again and this reminded the director that people on the farms had other things to do than discourse on metaphysical problems.

"Where will I find Ferenc, Mátyás?"

"He ought to be down toward the foot of the hill. They're carrying bricks for the mill, you know."

"So there will be a mill after all."

"That's what Ferenc says. Though it's hard to get money on interest these days."

The minute Ferenc noticed the director he left the laborers he was supervising.

"You know the news of course," he said while shaking hands.

"Yes, I do, at least as much as there was in the papers. That's why I've come out. I should like to tell her something."

"Her?" Ferenc asked with a sour smile on his lips.

"She won't speak to anybody, not even if he were bringing a letter from Jesus Christ Himself."

"Perhaps that is what I am bringing? I'd like to try it just the same, Ferenc."

"What do you mean?" Ferenc asked and he fixed his weary eyes on the director.

"Oh, I just said it, meaning that perhaps she'll talk to me. Where is she now?"

"Down in the pasture. They say she sees the Virgin in the cattle well. Guess there's a lot of people around her again, you'll see them from afar, just follow this furrow here."

"Won't you come with me?"

Ferenc hesitated. He wouldn't like to go, he said, because every time he had looked at them, and he had already once or twice, from a distance, of course, his heart nearly split. But finally he consented. On their way down to the well, the director wormed out of Ferenc how Etel had come into such close contact with the Virgin.

One evening in the winter, toward the end of it, because the snow had already begun to melt, Marika told her father great news. She was making the beds, because Etel cared for nothing and the little girl had to tend to everything, and had even to be taken out of school.

"My, what a beautiful song mother sang for me in her room."

"A song?"

"Yes, and what a beautiful song too! I don't know where she first heard it but I never heard anything so beautiful yet."

"What was it about?"

"Oh, about the Blessed Virgin, and how She pastures the little angel-lambs on the heavenly meadows, and how She cooks supper for Her dear husband."

"You didn't hear it right, Marika."

"Yes, I did! Mother laughed too, very softly, like turtle-doves."

A few days later, Ferenc himself heard her sing, but then she sang a different song. This one was about the holy city in heaven where the Blessed Virgin was sitting on an ivory throne. She was feeding two little soul-chickens out of her apron, a white one and a black one, and the black one always picked up the crumbs before the white one, and so the Virgin told it to get away. Ferenc could not remember the melody because he was not much of a singer, but it was a sort of Lenten song, like *"Christians, cry!"* But not quite like it, this one was sadder. Ferenc himself became so sad listening to it that he almost began to cry. Etel did not laugh then, but he heard a conversation of two female voices, one was high-pitched and the other one low, but he could not understand what they were talking about. The surprising thing was that Etel was all alone in the room; Ferenc didn't see anybody go in or come out, although he watched the door until he went to bed. Ferenc later concluded that she must have been talking to herself.

Then, about a week later, on a Tuesday morning, the women asked Ferenc before the church whether there would be any Virgin visions that afternoon. Ferenc was greatly surprised. He didn't know anything about visions, and learned only then that his wife was having conversations with the Virgin. There was a soothsayer living nearby, a woman, and it was in her well that Etel first saw the Holy Virgin face to face, and this soothsayer was the one who spread the news. Ferenc had never before known that Etel had had any connection with the woman; to the best of his knowledge, she had never had anything to do with sorcerers and charlatans, but this creature had such a power over Etel that she was more often with her than at home, and she even slept there sometimes, so that it was quite possible that she talked to her. The soothsayer said that Etel communicated the Virgin's words and orders to her and to her only, because she alone was allowed to interpret it to the world. Otherwise Etel never spoke a word to anybody, she just sang. At least, this was what the soothsayer said when the gendarmes took her to headquarters after the Reverend had reported it. Because as soon as the Reverend heard of Etel's visions he went down to the well himself. There were some ten old women around, and he scolded them for listening to such a shrewd cheat, that is to say, to the soothsayer, and to such a poor, crackbrained fool, that is to say, to Etel. But the women resented the Reverend's interference so much that they almost beat him, so the Reverend went away. Etel did not do anything, she just sat at the well and hummed and looked into the water. But the gendarmes couldn't do anything against the soothsayer, there was not one single soul said anything against her, not one witness accused her, so all the gendarmes did was to fill up the well with horse dung. But the next morning the well was clear again, and the Virgin showed twice as clearly as before. Even those could see Her now who had not seen Her before, and so the authorities sent a gendarme to guard the well, and out of mockery, he shot into it. The Virgin now ceased to appear in the soothsayer's well and showed Herself in the cattle well only. She even showed Her bleeding heart that had been pierced by the gendarme's bullet. This almost ended in a rebellion; the people rose in a body, but fortunately there was no massacre because the gendarmes got orders from the city not to shoot; let the people have their fun until they got tired of it, when the time came to work the miracle would be forgotten anyway.

"But I don't know whether it ever will," Ferenc said as they stopped at the end of the wheatfield. "Just look how many people there still are down there, although it's over now. There aren't so many as that in church for high mass."

Old women in big shawls were going home in little flocks of five and six on the cowslip covered pasture, but there were still some fifty people kneeling around the well. White locks of hair, blue gingham aprons, threadbare colored skirts fluttered in the playful spring breeze, the warm sun beat down on tanned legs, on soles toughened by walking on fallow, and on wrinkled, dusty faces shiny from sweat staring at the plump woman who, gesticulated with both of her hands, and walked barefoot up and down a plank laid across the mouth of the well.

"Your ancestors must have stared just like this at the shaman in the Turanian steppes," the director thought, and formed a shell out of the palms of his hands to catch a few sentences of the new Word.

"God have mercy on you, you wicked money mongers and rotten souls—You jump at them like dogs at groats— Our Blessed Mother had trod already on the head of the horrible serpent—because the flood is coming—The God-fearing Israelites—are already waiting in the pearl-laden door of the castle on Mount Sinai—His wrath makes even the archangels tremble—"

At the end of the plank, with her back to the crowd, there sat a woman in white with a black kerchief on her bent head; judging by the way she drooped her shoulders the director suspected her to be Etel. She was worn to a shadow. Before her stood a long, lean woman, with a yellow knitted shawl on her shoulders, her hair let down. The home-made church banner in her hands, a blue table cloth with a picture of the Virgin pinned to it, indicated that she was a kind of leader.

"Who is she?" the director asked.

"Modol Boca. Oh, she is just a hussy. Etel would not even have spat on her before, and now she is her banner-carrier."

The soothsayer noticed that a gentleman was approaching, perhaps even an envoy of the horrible serpent itself, so she thought it would be wise to stop the trembling of the archangels. Instead she announced that a week from today, on Lady Day, at three in the afternoon, the Virgin Mary would have a long message ready for the pious. Then she leaped from the plank and motioned to the banner-carrier.

"Let's go!"

Modol tied her shawl a little tighter, lifted the tablecloth-banner on high, and began to sing in a strong, hard voice, toughened by her many wild grass-widow nights during the war:

> *Open are the pearl-laden doors*
> *Of the holy city in heaven—*

The crowd picked up the song and went after her; the budding blooms of the cowslip broke and fell to pieces under their heavy steps.

A woman or two remained behind, circled the well, and kissed the hem of the white woman's skirt. They had always kissed the lace of the altar cloth and so they thought that without a kiss the ceremony was not worth anything. After they too had ambled away, the soothsayer went up to the two men.

"You want to speak to the holy woman."

She did not ask this, she announced it—as it befitted a soothsayer who knew everybody's wishes. She was dressed in black, and her eyes were searching and mean. She spoke with a drawl, yet her words rang hard, like horse-shoed boots on the stone floor of a church.

"Yes," the director stepped forward. "This man is the holy woman's husband."

"I know," the soothsayer said, looking intently at Ferenc.

"I saw him last fall when I first blessed his wife. I told her then that he would get well and that a great honor would befall him. But he didn't understand what I meant."

The director took the soothsayer by the arm. Her eyes looked daggers at him but the director was immune to evil eyes. His eyebrows were knit together too.

"You'll leave us alone now, auntie. We've something to say to the holy woman."

"You can talk to her as much as you want!" she said with a sarcastic glance in her eyes. "She obeys only me."

"Didn't you hear me?"

There were some milk parsleys a stone's throw from the well and the soothsayer walked over, and sitting down, watched eagerly what happened.

"Etel!" the director said gently and patted her slim shoulders. But the white woman did not turn, she did not even move.

The director stepped before her and looked into her face. He was so amazed he could not find his voice for a minute. For he saw a very thin face, white as washed wool, a narrow, smooth brow, tiny lips with an infinitely sad curve, and indescribably sweet sorrow in the tenderly gazing blue eyes. No wonder that when this face bent above the water she saw the Virgin in it!

"Etel, my child, can't you recognize me?"

The blue eyes continued to stare sweetly, but their gaze was directed at something far-away. And though the lips were parted, the sad smile remained.

"Don't hurt her, sir," Ferenc said and turned away, "I can't even look at it."

The director did not want to hurt her. On the contrary. With his left hand, he took her by the finger tips, and with his right hand, he lifted her chin toward him.

"Etel! I've brought you good news. Rokus is still alive. Ferenc is not a murderer!"

The holy woman's gaze remained calm and imperturbable. Perhaps she saw already the holy city in heaven where the Virgin pastured the angel-lambs. The director let her hand go and stepped back sadly. The light white hand, the fine little chin dropped.

"Let's go, Ferenc."

Ferenc took Etel's hand in his own. He had not touched her since that night. She let him do it. She did not even feel it.

The soothsayer sneaked back and stopped three paces away. She did not even look at the two men; as far as she was concerned they were not there at all.

"Etel!" Her voice cracked like a whip.

And she started to go after the procession which had already reached the edge of the pasture. She did not even turn back. She knew that the holy woman was obediently following her. She glanced back only when Etel got to her side.

"Didn't I tell you? You don't know anything about her! You—men!"

And the soothsayer took the holy woman by the hand and carried her away, as a hawk carries a chicken. How did she do it? Where did she take her? Where did she get the power over her? Who had made her the master of this diseased mind?

The two men looked after them until they were lost to sight behind the trees. Then the director looked into the well. It was just like all the other cattle wells; not very deep, and its water was yellowish, brackish from the sand. On one of the protruding bricks in the shaft there sat a frog. Its eyes glistened up to them from among the tiny hairs of moss.

"It's good water," Ferenc said. "There are frogs in it. But no Virgin."

They turned to go home, across the wheatfield. The

sprouts were small yet, hardly out of the earth, but the green velvet cloth covered the brown clumps everywhere.

"Well," the director broke the silence, "it didn't work. And I thought it'd make both of you happy. Although I don't know whether it's anything to be happy about."

"What's that?" Ferenc asked and hurled a lump of earth at a flock of crows picking at the young shoots.

"Rokus is alive."

"Why—why—didn't you say that just to cheer her up?" Ferenc asked with his heart in his throat.

"No, I didn't." The director took a sheet of paper out of his pocket. "Here's the letter. He lives in Minsk, on a farm."

The director had already seen many kinds of sudden outbursts of joy, but never one like that Ferenc demonstrated. He ran forward some ten paces, then threw himself onto the ground and began to tear the sprouts out of the earth with both hands.

But by the time the director caught up with him, he was on his feet again, silently crying.

"Look, sir—" and the director had never yet heard a grown man's voice sound so childish as was Ferenc's, cleansed and purified in tears.

"Let's not look at anything now, Ferenc, because the flood will be on us in a second; the soothsayer saw that also in advance."

Ferenc stopped.

"Now what do you know about that—the soothsayer prophesied this too—that I'll be cured."

"But if this weather finds us here, I'll get sick."

Greenish, white-edged clouds rolled over the sky from the direction of the city. One flash of lightning followed another, so that the sky looked as if it had been afire. And just when they reached the house it began to hail.

"We should have told it to father, too," Ferenc said,

looking at Mátyás's farm.

"You mean, to Rokus' father," the director added. "Because if the boy's really found, you have a funny position here. Then you are only the husband of the wife of Mátyás's son."

"I don't care about anything, let him enjoy the news too."

But the director managed to make him understand that hurry in this particular instance was not very advisable. Rokus had yet to be redeemed from his sad prison. And that needed money. Much money.

"I'll get the money if I have to sell the pillow from under my head."

"Wait a minute! First of all you'll have to figure out whether that pillow belongs to you or to Etel. And then, whose wife will the poor woman be now? Will her first husband want her? Will he want to come home at all when he finds out about her, and when will he get home? And then, we'd better find out what that sad prison of his is? I think that you shouldn't talk about it to Mátyás until we've found out everything. Mark my words there is no sense in worrying the old man."

And so they agreed that the director would notify the poor sad prisoner of what had happened, ask him why he was so sad, and whether he wouldn't charge less for getting cheered up. Then the director got into his car and Ferenc remembered that he had not yet given him anything. Should he put in a basket of apples or a bag of nuts? The dried grapes had come through the winter beautifully, they were sweet as honey, raisins couldn't be any sweeter. No, the director did not want to accept anything, the apples Ferenc had brought last fall had rotted away too. Perhaps a little smoked ham then? Or at least a small keg of wine? He would roll it up from the cellar in no time.

"Don't put yourself out, Ferenc," the director smiled. "I see the peach tree is in bloom already, look, cut a branch for me, will you? Here's the knife too, take care, it's sharp, don't cut yourself."

"Gladly," said Ferenc. His face beamed with joy, his whole frame seemed to laugh. He jumped to the tree which the hail had beaten rather severely. He turned the branches, twisted them, compared one to another, cautiously lest he might knock off a blossom, carefully lest he might tear off a flower. At last he found a twig and cut it off. It was the one most damaged by the hail, there were hardly more than two or three blossoms left on it. It was just the right present for the director.

The director thanked him nicely and perhaps never before had he shaken Ferenc's hand as warmly as he did now, in gratitude for this shabby, niggardly, stingily cut twig, which he knew would wither even before he could get out of the sand. There he threw it away and stopped the car to pick some marsh marigolds in the sodden soil, although he knew for sure that his shoes would get wet and that he would have a sore throat before nightfall. But—as Mátyás used to say—if one had no brains, no blacksmith could make one any.

And while he was tying the marigolds into a nosegay he felt his heart grow slowly warmer. He had just learned something infinitely beautiful. This Ferenc, this sorely tried and bitterly beaten peasant, who had come out of the greatest of all human wars with a sharpened brain, a broadening intelligence, a growing appetite for culture and education, a more human heart, and a slowly awakening, and perhaps already ruined, nervous life, would before the war, have knifed, or killed, any other young peasant without thought, without remorse, without pangs of conscience, without as much regret as he would have felt for a stolen cob of corn—and now the thought that he was a murderer, because he had, in order to save his own life, starved another man to death, had grayed his hair before his time and had nearly driven him mad. This man experienced a joy today greater than any which had been felt by a man in his race in a thousand years, and if the person who, in his belief, had given him his joy, had asked him for his right hand today, or for his horse, or for his tiled house, he would have gladly given it to him, without the slightest regret. Yet this man felt sorry for the bloom which might be fruit yet, provided no frost killed it, no draught burned it, no wind knocked it down, no worm ate it. He sought out the shabbiest, the leanest twig, one on which only four peaches at the most would be wasted, and if he could have found one with only two healthy blossoms, he would have cut that instead for a present. He was of a race that had survived thus a thousand years and the director was very happy when it occurred to him that by now Ferenc was most probably trying to push back into the soil those sprouts of wheat he had torn out in the first overwhelming wave of his joy.

# XXI

A T DAWN, on Lady Day, the holy woman suddenly woke up with a start and found the Virgin standing at her bedside.

"Etel, my daughter, wake up! Etel, my daughter, don't you know what day this is?"

Etel cast her eyes down; she felt ashamed because she did not. She folded her hands, knelt down, and begged the Virgin's pardon for having forgotten it. But she did not remember who she was and where she was.

"You are Etel, my daughter, and you are here in your clean room. See, here is your bed and your chiffonier and your glass, and even your wedding bouquet is here, wrapped up in your bridal veil. Do you remember them now?"

"I do," answered Etel, "but don't know who my bridegroom was."

"Never mind that, my daughter. The earthly bridegroom is mortal and passing like the forget-me-not. But look at me now! Can't you yet remember what day this is?"

Sleep had left Etel's eyes completely. She knew that it was still night, yet even without a lamp she saw everything well. The wreath of seven silver stars on the Virgin's head, and Her big, red mantle illuminated the room. She recognized Her now and remembered that it was Her day.

"Mother, I will go with you," she cried.

The Virgin gently scolded her:

"But my daughter, how do you think you can come with me with only one shirt on your back? If you want to be my servant girl you will have to dress up nicely."

Etel was overjoyed. She pulled out the drawers of the chiffonier, threw out the clothes one after another—taffeta skirts, silk shawls—without finding the one she wanted to wear.

"What are you looking for, my daughter?"

"I have, Blessed Mother, a beautiful, sky-blue dress, but I don't know where it is."

"But, my daughter, you gave that to me. I am wearing it even now, it's under my mantle. Don't look for it. Now, put on your skirt with the red rubies and tie your lavender shawl around your waist."

Etel looked around; she had never known that she had had a skirt with red rubies. The Virgin pointed at her white skirt with red polka dots—that was it! She smoothed it over with her hands, and she saw that what she had always thought to be red polka dots were red rubies, just like the ones in the Virgin's crown.

She wound her lavender shawl round her waist, but as she tried to tie the ends into a bow in the back, she cried out for pain; her little finger ached. She had cut it with the axe once, but she could not remember when. So the Virgin Herself stepped up to her and tied the bow with Her own holy hands. Etel knew that that was a great honor and she wanted to kiss the Virgin's hand for it, but by the time she turned around She had already hidden Her hands under the mantle.

"Put on your slippers, my daughter, because we'll cross the stone road too, and that's full of pricking, sharp starstones."

Etel hurriedly put on her red leather slippers and then the Virgin asked her:

"Do you know where we are going, my daughter?"

"I don't, Blessed Mother."

"To God's garden, my daughter. Do you know who will

be waiting for you there, at the stack of white lilies?"

"I don't, Blessed Mother."

"Your heavenly bridegroom, my daughter."

Etel blushed for joy and could not restrain herself from throwing a secret glance in her glass. She noticed only now that she had not combed her hair. She pulled out the drawer, to take out her comb.

"What are you looking for, my daughter?" the Virgin asked her.

Etel felt ashamed and so she answered:

"My rosary, Blessed Mother."

"You don't need a rosary where we are going, my daughter. You'd better take along your wedding bouquet though."

She Herself pinned on the bouquet and, for a second, Etel could see Her white, thin, glistening hands.

"Let's go now, before the tempters get up."

The Virgin turned around and went out of the room; Her red mantle fluttered behind Her. Etel followed Her in her red slippers. The door opened all by itself; and the lock did not screech and the hinges did not creak. Only the red slippers tap-tapped on the floor.

The Virgin warned:

"You will wake up the tempters with your slippers and then they won't let you in to the holy city through the pearl-laden door."

The threat frightened Etel; she pulled the red slippers off her feet, stuck one into the other, and took them under her arm. The two of them flitted through the kitchen—no, they didn't even flit, they just flew, like shadows on water; no tempter in the universe could hear their steps. When they reached the porch, Etel looked around. She was surprised to see the disorder of the place. The floor was littered with ears of corn, pieces of broken straw, mud carried in on boots. Evidently no one had swept here for some time. Although there were both the big and small broomsticks in the corner. Etel clasped her hands to her brow; she could not understand why all these things looked so familiar to her. And there was the open barrel too, underneath the end of the eavestrough, where water was kept in case fire broke out. Etel was positive that she had been here once before, but she did not know when.

She would have liked to ask the Blessed Mother about these things, but She was already walking among the trees. Her mantle shone so brightly that the trees, the shrubs, the vines threw shadows on the ground wherever She passed. It grew lighter and lighter, one could see that the branches of the peach tree were tied up, only two little twigs hung broken and withered; hail must have struck the tree because its leaves were ragged too. And there was the winter apple tree, oh, look, it was in full bloom. How familiar all this was! And that big, strong tree over there, with its branches reaching toward the sky—the Virgin was just passing by it—now what was its name—oh yes, that was the war-pear tree!

Etel was very happy that she could remember the name of the tree, but then she struck herself on the forehead. She had forgotten something in the house—but what, what? She remembered it so clearly that she thought she saw it, she reached out her hands for it, but she didn't know what it was. But she would find it, surely! She turned back, she was already in the kitchen—she could not see anything now because the red mantle was far away—but she knew she had to go this way, to the right. She tottered into the room. She heard heavy breathing, people must be sleeping here. She bumped her knee into something: the chest. She felt around with her hands, here was a pillow, here a head, a little head, with soft hair, hair like silk—Matyika, Matyika. Yes, then here, on the sofa, with her head this way, must be Marika—how long her hair was, and how ruffled, it ought to be combed. But where was the comb? Where was it? She herself had put it away somewhere only yesterday. Oh, how dark it was here! She went to the window, lifted the corner of the shawl she had hung over the curtain last night so that the sun shouldn't shine into—into whose eyes? Matyika's? No—but, my, there was the red mantle, the Virgin was waiting for her, why had she come back?

She stopped once more on the threshold, thought of something, she did not know what, then rushed out. She even left the door open. Where was the Virgin? She stopped beneath the war-pear tree, looked around, where did She go? She had been here only a minute ago, where had She gone? Etel looked toward the house, but her frightened eyes could not see that a gray-haired man was standing in the window, rubbing his eyes, like one waking from his sleep with a start.

Then the gray-haired man went back to his bed. He was snoring when Etel finally found the way. Yes, there was the Virgin, far away, past the plum trees even, and Her red mantle grew lighter and lighter, it was sun-colored now. And the farther it got, the brighter it shone. It shone so brightly that Etel could clearly see beneath her feet the tender new leaves of the grapevines, the young shoots of wheat. The dry stubble of reed pricked her soles—she had reached the shore of the lake.

The sun rose and Etel began to cry. Where was She, where was She, where was the Blessed Mother, where could Her servant-girl find Her?

A crow took to flight from the reed and screeched. Etel looked up. Holy God, there was the Virgin. She had taken off Her mantle, She was in Her sky-blue silk dress only, yes, there, there, in the reed! Etel stepped into the water, at first it reached only to her ankles, oh, it was good, it was so cool, for she was hot all over. She took another step after the Virgin; the water now reached to her knees. She lifted her skirt with the red rubies, the slippers fell out from underneath her arm, she did not notice that at all, she only went, went after the sky-blue dress that shone from farther and farther away. She was already past the long, slender reed stalks and the water reached to her armholes; the sharp leaves of the rush tore the lavender shawl off her shoulders. She remembered now what she had forgotten: Her crown with the rubies. What would the Virgin say now? But the Virgin said nothing, She only smiled and beckoned to her, "Come, my daughter, come!" Then She spread out Her sky-blue dress and covered Her servant-girl with it.

In the pasture, at the cattle well, the pious were waiting for the holy woman until nightfall. Then the soothsayer and Modol led the trembling old men and the women in their Sunday best to Ferenc. Where was Etel? The Virgin would not appear in the well without her. Ferenc did not know where she was. Hazily he remembered that he had suddenly waked up at the creaking of the door last night, that he had seen Etel beneath the pear tree in her polka-dotted skirt, but he thought it had been nothing but a dream, although the door to the clean room had been open in the morning and Etel's clothes had all been lying scattered around on the floor.

They waited for Etel for a day or two, then they began to search for her. The gendarmes too. At the end of a week, they found the red slippers; a day or two later, the lavender shawl. But she herself was never found. The lake knew how to keep a secret.

Ferenc, and some other unbelievers, said that she had been drowned in the lake, but there were some who suspected the Reverend. They said that he, together with the gentlemen from the city, had put her out of the way. That was the reason why they let the matter pass so easily, for not one single person was arrested. But the truth was that the Blessed Virgin had taken the holy woman with Her, after She had moved out of the cattle well. At least this was what the spirits told the soothsayer, and in a year, there were witnesses to the miracle too. Gyurka Messzi, for instance, was ready to swear that he had seen with his own eyes how the holy woman had gone to heaven alive; two cherubim had carried her on their wings, and if anybody did not want to believe it, he could go to hell, for all Gyurka Messzi cared.

# XXII

A QUEER but human thing happened to Ferenc; he fell in love. It was queer because Ferenc, who had been only fond of the living Etel, now fell in love with the dead Etel.

God knows how it began, or when it began. It is a difficult thing to say even for one whose business it is to tamper with souls. And Ferenc, although he had organized a draining company, was drilling an artesian well, building a mill, and trading with banks, was a peasant after all, and had not lost one single hair over psychological problems.

A hair—yes, perhaps it was that hair that started it. But then it was also possible that the thing had already begun earlier, and that it was only waiting for that hair to come into the open.

The hair was a long, sturdy, strong, black hair, Marika's hair, and it was found in a loaf of fresh bread that Marika had baked out of the new wheat. It was the first bread of her life. And the first bread means a lot more to the Marikas than the first kiss to the Maries, the Marys, and the Marions. It is almost as important as the first evening gown is to them. It is the test of womanhood.

It was in the evening and they were sitting at the supper table, beneath the eaves. It was not very dark, they had not lighted the candles yet, and Ferenc could see the flush of excitement on Marika's cheeks.

"My first baking, dad. And nobody helped me."

"We'll taste it, Marika," Ferenc said stroking the girl's

hair. Then he made the sign of the cross over the loaf and cut it.

"It smells good," Matyika remarked, looking at it with hungry eyes.

"Yes," said Ferenc. "It's leavened well. A clever hand kneaded it. But what's this?"

He pulled out a long, sturdy, black hair, and held it up against the setting sun.

"It's my hair," Marika said. She was not ashamed of it; one could find hair even in cakes sometimes, if not as long a one as this one. And anyway, the hair did not matter. How did the bread taste?

But Ferenc just stared at the hair in his hand.

"Your mother had just such long hair. Only hers was blonde. The color of wheat. And soft."

Then he let the hair go—the wind caught it and swirled it away—and they began to eat. He found the bread very good, and he told Marika that all she had to do now was to learn how to mend an oven. Then she could go to a ball and get married.

When they had finished supper and Marika was clearing the table, Ferenc, like a child, picked one more bite from the loaf.

"See how it makes me eat it?" he winked to the proud girl but then suddenly the idea occurred to him that Etel would have given it a better taste.

Then he forgot all about it. But, in a few weeks he remembered Etel again. The city decided to build a railroad to the farms; they had talked it over in the Club, come to the conclusion that it would be good if they could have one too—it would raise the land prices—and so they asked Ferenc to lead a delegation to the Council and ask for one. He dressed carefully, as always when he went to the city, and when he began to tie his necktie in the glass he remembered her. As long as Etel had been alive, he had never needed a glass. But no matter how he tried now, the tie never looked well. Etel had always tied it from right to left—this way? No. She had left one end longer—like this. No, he just couldn't do it either way. Finally he went to town without a necktie.

At the vintage, he noticed a strange woman among the vintagers; Mátyás had hired her somewhere. She was a quiet, silent sort of woman, did not giggle much with the rest of them; true, the boys did not play much with her because she had such a no-color face. But it seemed to Ferenc that there was something in her carriage that reminded him of Etel, her feet below the ankles moved the way hers had, and Ferenc felt sure that this woman's legs were as white as Etel's had been. He loafed around her all morning, waiting for her to bend down so that her legs should show. Quite possibly she needed little encouragement to do so, but Ferenc was too bashful to start playing with her, and so he just wasted the morning, nigh unto dinner time, with peeping. After dinner, he went over to their other vineyard to watch the presses, but the squatting woman's picture hovered before his eyes all afternoon, and when twilight fell, knowing that the vintagers were about to go home, he hurried back to them. He arrived just in time; the women were washing their legs, sprinkling water all over each other amidst much screaming and giggling, in the trough beneath the big walnut tree, and the strange woman was also among them. He could see her legs up to the knee. But the moment he laid eyes on them, he turned away his head. Not because her legs were less handsome than any of the other legs around here; they were neither more nor less shapely than the rest of them. At least as much of them as was not always covered by the skirt was tanned dark by the sun, pricked red by wind and fallow, and, above the ankles, it was rice-colored, like most women's legs. But Etel's had been flesh-colored; other women could have had legs of such color only if they had soaked them in pink dye. Ferenc knew that for sure, because he had often observed it. And now, as he walked home among the vines, he saw Etel sitting on the threshold, with a big wooden mortar between her knees, pounding poppyseed. But he saw only her round, pink, shapely legs; the rest of her body was dim and hazy.

A few weeks later, Ferenc discovered that he was continually glancing at the women on the market place, in church, on by-paths, on the streets, in the city. But he saw only those who resembled Etel, and thus he learned—watching other women—what Etel had *not* been like. But just exactly what she had been like, Ferenc could not have told anybody. He never thought of the dead woman intentionally, just as in the days gone by he had never intentionally thought of Rokus either. Sometimes, for two weeks at an end, her memory left him alone, but there were days when he could not get her out of his mind all day long. And when he did think of her, it was just as if some one had been constantly saying to him: Etel, Etel—whether he was in the stables feeding the horses, or sitting on the edge of the bed getting ready for the night. Once, while signing a note in the bank, it seemed to him that he saw the little mole Etel had had in the corner of her upper lip, on the paper.

One morning, well toward the middle of Advent, he noticed Marika searching for something in the chiffonier in the clean room.

"What are you looking for?"

"I'm trying to find Mother's big shawl, daddy. We'd like to go to church and I gave mine to Matyika."

Ferenc helped her to find the big shawl; it was way down at the bottom of the drawer, underneath all the other clothes. They had turned everything in the drawer upside down before they found it, then Ferenc told the girl to go ahead, not to stay too long in the unheated room, he would put the things back in their places himself. He did so, and as he smoothed over the shirts, skirts, blouses, it occurred to him for the first time that it was queer that he could not imagine Etel alive, in her entirety, as she had been. Three years before he had had a spotted calf, a very gentle thing, and he could still remember every one of its spots, he could still see it before him as it rubbed its neck against his leg, he could still feel its wet nose in the palm of his hand. And though Etel had died hardly a year ago, he could see her only hazily.

The thought gnawed at him, he could not get rid of it. He had been feeling fine ever since the director had brought him the news of Rokus's being alive, had eaten well, put on weight—but now once more he began to lose his appetite. He became silent, lost weight. So much so that Mátyás could not stand it.

"Anything the matter with you, Ferenc? You are as thin as a cat when it eats horseflies."

Ferenc answered that he could not sleep lately—and that was true. He hardly slept an hour or two during the long winter nights; just rolled around in his bed. Sometimes he felt as if he had been lying on embers and kicked off the quilt; at other times, the quilt alone was too cold and he wound himself up in the *suba* too. His eyelids were as heavy as lead, yet he could not fall asleep.

Ferenc pondered over these things, and one day he decided to see the soothsayer. Not because he believed in her. He had never believed in any superstition, had never seen any ghosts or men of fire in his youth, and had never carried a talisman on his body in the war. He had regarded Etel's visions for what they had been: the revelations of a diseased mind. Ferenc merely wanted to test the soothsayer. If she was on such excellent terms with the spirits she ought to be able to make Etel appear before him. She could easily do that, easier than anybody else, because both of them had been in the service of the Virgin. But he was quite sure she could not do it; God had not given such powers to any mortal creature. Miracles happened only in the Bible, and of course, in the lives of the saints, at least that was what the books said. But they had called Etel a holy woman too, some of them called her so even now—and she had been holy indeed, Ferenc knew that better than anybody else; no woman had ever been like her and no one would ever be. If the soothsayer could show her only once, only once, so that he could say: yes, this is Etel, truly and really—well, then there was nothing on earth the soothsayer could ask of him he wouldn't give her.

Thoughts such as these crossed his mind as he was walking down the snow-covered roads toward the soothsayer's house in the biting wind. He was dubious, yet he hung on to that "perhaps" which so readily springs up in such cases in the dark places of the soul. And by the time he entered her hut—she had neither a dog nor was her door locked; she felt quite secure under the protection of the cherubim and the seraphim—Ferenc did not at all behave like the president of the Club, like the man who used to lead delegations and deputations to high authorities. He did not carry himself erect but crumpled up like the flame in a lamp when the wick had no more oil to soak up, and instead of threatening the sorceress with severe words, or trying to win her to his side with the promise of a suckling pig, all he said was, and he said that in a cowardly, beggardly manner, could she show him his wife.

The woman of the searching, sharp eyes did not indicate with a gesture, a wink, a word, whether she knew Ferenc or not. Perhaps she had recognized him, perhaps she had not. Perhaps she did not expect much of the drooping, weary, shabby-looking man. And so, after she had scrutinized him for a few seconds, she said only this:

"You are a very sinful man in the eyes of God."

Ferenc mumbled something that all of us were guilty in the eyes of God, but the soothsayer did not heed his words—if she did hear them—and continued:

"You haven't made good for the things you did against your dead wife. And as long as you don't, you have nothing to look for here."

Ferenc staggered out of the house like a beaten dog and did not know how he ever got home. What had he done against Etel for which God was angry with him? If he only knew it! He would give his soul for the secret.

He was told of it that night. Etel appeared in his dream; she ran into his room, barefoot, clad only in a shirtwaist and skirt, just as she had been the night when she had fled to him from the Communist soldiers. Ferenc wanted to jump out of the bed just like he had then, except that he was not alarmed now but jubilant. But Etel stopped in the center of the room, threatened him with her index finger, and mumbled something. But Ferenc must have either gone deaf, or she said it to herself—for he could not hear a sound. She had to say it three times before he could understand it, and he understood it even then only by the movement of her lips.

"Spirituto," she said.

Then Ferenc woke up. He could hardly wait for the morning. The minute the darkness rose he hitched up the horses and went to the director.

Late in the Summer, there had come a letter from Rokus to the director, in reply to his inquiry. The sad prisoner wished the director as the letter writer good health and furthermore understood that Etel had gone crazy and asked Ferenc to send forty millions to the Polski consul for him to get him out of his sad prison, but what kind of a prison it was he could not tell, not until he got home.

Furthermore he informed the director that it was very hot in Russia and that the soil was very good and that the wheat was very expensive, a bushel cost fifty thousand rubles, but that money was no good any more, they called it *chervonetz* now, but he did not know how much that was in rubles.

"One simply can't throw away forty millions on a fool like this," the director said, "and we'll never get a wiser explanation from this nincompoop. Haven't you a friend or acquaintance in Russia yourself?"

"I can't think of anybody," answered Ferenc.

"Then I'll try one more thing. I'll ask a friend of mine to write to the Polish consul in Minsk; maybe he will do it for us. But if you think of somebody who lives there let me know, because that would be best."

So that was why Ferenc now came to see the director.

"Have you any news, sir?"

"Yes, Ferenc, though nothing worth while. The Polish consul scolded the Swedish consul, the Swedish consul the German consul, the German consul the Royal Hungarian Minister of Foreign Affairs, and the Foreign Minister who is my friend, each in turn saying to the other that the what-not and why-not and wherefore of international law do not permit the possibility of unjustified interference in the private affairs of foreign subjects. So that's that, Ferenc."

"Well, I have better news. I have a friend in Russia, a Russky, who used to live on my farm when he was here as a prisoner of war. His name is Spirituto. Although that's not his real name, only father calls him by that name, but here's his letter in which he sent the Black Virgin, there's his real name in it, and his address, too."

"That's fine. I'll write to him yet today. I'll ask him to look after that fool and to find out all about him and to tell in plain language what's the matter with him. I'll have somebody translate the letter into Russian so that he can understand it. Wasn't it Mátyás who thought of him?"

"No, because he doesn't know of anything yet," Ferenc reminded the director of his own advice and told him what he had dreamed of last night.

"Why, man," the director jestingly remarked, "take care! You'll see the Virgin yourself yet."

Ferenc smiled too, and assured the director that that would never happen.

Ferenc did not see the Virgin, but he saw Etel again. That very night. She sat down on the edge of his bed and smiled at him and Ferenc observed her much better now than he had at any time during her life. He noticed that two of her front teeth were a little bit bent and that the hole for the ear-ring in her right ear lobe was a little larger than in the left one. He stared and stared at her, as if he had been just a little afraid of her, and was about to ask her whether she was really dead when Etel—as if she had sensed what he wanted to ask—spoke up:

"It's me, dear."

Ferenc jumped out of the bed. Of course, it was nothing but a dream, but it was a beautiful dream, and the day that followed was one of the most beautiful days of his life. Yet he could hardly wait for the evening, and when he went to bed, he could hardly fall asleep, he was so excited. The dream was even more beautiful now; Etel not only sat down on his bed but put one of her arms under his pillow and wiped her husband's brow with the other. Then she promised him that she would visit him every night. Ferenc took the promise seriously even in the morning and when Etel really showed up on the third night, Ferenc acknowledged the fact that hereafter it would be always like this: he would be a widower during the day and a married man at night, even though he knew that his nocturnal wife was but a dream.

For a while, the thing went on all right and the days did not get mixed up with the nights, although, sometimes, the days bring crazier dreams than do the nights. For instance, five young farmers, all of his age and all veterans of the war, visited him one day, and asked him whether he would like to be their deputy. Ferenc at first thought that that too was but a dream, even though it was less beautiful than the other one. But as the men went on talking and Mátyás showed up too—quite by accident, since he had been promoting Ferenc's candidacy for hardly more than two weeks, both in the Club and in the store—he had to realize that it was not a dream, that these were real men, they even smelled of brandy a little, since before they showed up at Ferenc's they had been with Mátyás, quite by accident. Then he told them that he would not think of accepting it at all, he knew something about the farms but knew nothing about the ways and worries of the country, that needed wiser men than he was, and the present deputy, the Baron, who was the godfather of his son, was better fitted for the job.

But Mátyás was not the kind of a man who would swallow his own words for no reason at all, especially when he had set his heart on something. So he held regular campaign sessions in his big barn which he had turned into a distillery since he had obtained the permit to brew brandy, when Gyurka Messzi, his spy, reported to him that the elder farmers were hard at work on the Baron's wine in the steward's house. Of course, Gyurka Messzi did not tell him that he had collected his regular espionage fees from the steward too, but he did tell them what dirty things the folks over at the steward's had said about the honorable company present.

"Out with it!" Mátyás encouraged the spy and gave him a good-sized drink of his best brandy. There was not one drop of "copper water" in it, as they call the some-

what vile fluid that comes out of the still first and which
tastes a little of copper.

"Well, they said that what the hell do these young
sucklings, that is to say the honorable young generation
present, want with that upstart fool, that is to say, with
Ferenc."

Whereupon the young generation present declared that
one could easily recognize an old ass by its bray, and by
the time Spring arrived their patriotic enthusiasm knew no
limits. It was not so much the enthusiasm itself as the
incentive used; for the steward had wasted eight barrels
of wine and Mátyás's two kegs of brandy, one-third of it
"copper water." Perhaps that was the reason why the two
kegs proved to be more powerful than the eight barrels, so
much so that the Baron suddenly found it advisable to
visit his godson whom he had never seen before. He
brought him a present too, a good-looking toy monkey.
Mátyás bought that from his namesake for a bird trap the
following day and hung it up in the distillery as the
Baron's likeness. The Baron also asked Ferenc whether
he would not like to become something, say an Agricultural
Counsellor?

"God knows," Ferenc smiled, "what do I need that for
now?"

But he did not smile at the Baron when he said that;
he smiled at somebody behind his back, although there
was nobody there. From this the Baron deduced that
Ferenc liked the idea, but merely did not want to show it.

Of course, the Baron couldn't have known that Etel
was standing behind her dear husband's back, and that
her dear husband said nothing but what she had told him
last night.

The midnight visits still went on and Ferenc had not
talked so much with Etel during their entire married
life as he did during the dreamful nights of these past

weeks. He told her about everything, about all his troubles and worries, he told her how quick-witted Marika was, how she could fry doughnuts already, and how clever Matyika was, how he could already drive a team of horses down to the lake, he even told her about Mátyás's ideas and plans for him and it was then that Etel asked him why he needed that for now, since the Virgin had intended to give him a much greater position.

"Me?" Ferenc asked amazed.

"Yes. I'll whisper it in your ears," Etel said and looked around that no one should hear it. "You'll be the scarecrow in the heavenly wheatfields."

It was this that made Ferenc smile when the Baron asked him about the counsellorship—what funny things one dreams about!—and he turned around because it seemed to him as if Etel had been standing behind him, with that secretive look on her face. But, of course, no one stood there, since it was day and the sun shone. That night, Etel came in pouting and she reproached him as she cuddled against her husband's chest.

"You laughed at me today."

"How do you know?" Ferenc was greatly surprised.

"Why, I was standing right in back of you."

"I thought so too. I turned around but I couldn't see you."

"You can't until the Blessed Virgin permits you to. Because I'm still Her servant."

From then on, Ferenc took care to look behind his back as often as possible, but he never saw anybody. On the other hand, if a dream was a dream, why did he always hear the rustle of a gown behind his back, and why did he smell the scent of lilies even when he was awake?

One night Etel told him:

"You've told me everything except one thing."

"That's true," said Ferenc. "I asked the director to write

to Rokus."

"I know it."

"I didn't tell you about it because I don't like to speak about him."

"I know why."

"If you know about it, tell me: whose wife are you?"

"Whoever asks for my hand first from the Blessed Virgin. Then I'll belong to him forever and ever."

Frenc became sad.

"Where can I find the Blessed Virgin? She's moved away from this neighborhood."

Etel pressed his head with both of her arms to her breast.

"Look for Her, dear, look for Her. And when you find Her, you'll find me too, and when you find me, you'll find Her too, because the two of us are one and the same, dear."

Ferenc could not understand this, either in his dream, or during the day, awake, although the rustling was now twice as loud and the scent of the lilies twice as strong. He could hardly wait for the night. But he waited in vain. He fell asleep at once, but Etel did not appear that night.

The next day it took him a long time to fall asleep and in his dream he was walking on a far-away, wide green lawn, one could not even see the end of it. Squares of white linen were spread on the grass, each as large as a tent flap, but they were snow white, and when he got nearer he saw that they were women's shirts. A bald old man sat on the grass, he was clad in the garb of a monk and was playing a flute. Ferenc asked him what he was doing.

"Can't you see it? Watching lambs on the pasture."

And, lo, the shirts had turned into lambs.

"Then I'm in the right place," Ferenc said to the bald monk. "Aren't these the Virgin's lambs?"

"No, these are the Virgin's wheatfields."

Ferenc looked around. There were no lambs there now, nor monk, nor lawn, but a wheatfield as large as the sky, and the golden ears of wheat were all ripe, ready for harvest. Ferenc ran his hand through them and now he noticed that they had no ears, but hair. Etel-like hair. That reminded him what he was looking for and he began to shout at the top of his voice:

"Etel! Etel! Come, get dressed. We're going to church. Have you forgotten it's Lady Day?"

He woke with a start, hearing his own voice, and looked around bewildered in the dark. Where was he? Where did the draft come from? The door was open, he heard the cat run out—Matyika must have forgotten to latch the door properly.

He rose, locked the door, and, smothering a yawn, stepped to the window. It was dawning already, his eyes grew slowly accustomed to the half light. Who was that standing beneath the budding war-pear tree? A skirt fluttered! It could not be Marika, she was sleeping here on the sofa! He tottered and pressed his head against the cool window pane. The skirt fluttered again, he could see the red polka dots—Lord Almighty, it was Etel! Etel!

The vision did not disappear when he rushed out into the garden. It waited until he got near it, then it began to rise, as if something had been pulling it upwards, higher and higher, up among the flower-laden branches, and then still higher, still higher—it was already in the top of the tree, the head was visible above the blossoms, it had a wreath of silver stars on its head, it was the Virgin, no, no, it was not Her, it was Etel, yes, Etel with the same Virgin-like face he had last seen down at the cattle well! But now she did not stare vacantly into nothingness, now she winked at Ferenc and smiled.

"Dear——"

Supremely happy weeks followed for Ferenc. He had

never yet seen a spring like that. Not one single tree lost
its blossoms ahead of time, the sprouts came out of the
soil as if they had been pushed out, the shoots seemed to
race upward, the grapes promised a gorgeous vintage—
everybody was happy, even Mátyás.

"Well, namesake, I'll make a deputy out of your daddy
by Whitsuntide," he said to the boy, patting his head.

Ferenc, who rarely went among people these days, and
if he could not avoid them, kept silent, smiled quietly:

"God knows what may happen before Whitsuntide."

He really did not know it, because he could not tell
what plans the vision had for him. For he had to believe
in it now, he had seen it with his own two eyes. True, only
once, on the morning of Lady Day, and Etel had not appeared in his dreams since. But this did not sadden Ferenc,
he was waiting patiently, because he knew that it was
not over yet. He looked out into the garden at every dawn,
glanced at the pear tree, and on the afternoon of Easter
Monday, he made a latticed fence around the tree so that
the fowl should not dirty the spot where Etel had trodden.

"What's that for?" Mátyás asked him. "Why do you
want to put this damn pear into a cage?"

"I had time on my hand, didn't know what to do," answered Ferenc curtly.

Mátyás thought it would have been wiser if he had
showed himself in the Club if he had time on his hand,
although the way things looked he would be elected anyway, perhaps even more surely this way than if he had
flattered them.

The big meeting to nominate Ferenc was scheduled to
take place the second Sunday in May. Mátyás showed up
early in the morning; he wanted to greet everybody personally. He was talking to the Jewess when Matyika suddenly rushed in, flaming red in the face.

"Granddaddy, Marika sent me to come in a hurry because daddy climbed the pear tree."

"Well, if he climbed it, he'll come down," Mátyás said, taking the boy's hand into his. "Why are you so frightened?"

Matyika excitedly defended his contention.

"No, he won't come down, because he tied himself to the tree with a rope. Marika tried to pull him down but he won't come. Now she is crying."

"Jesus Christ!" the Jewess exclaimed, clapping her hands, and ran over to the storekeeper at once. By the time Mátyás got home with the child—true, it was a long way for the old legs that almost doubled up at every other step—there was a whole flock of old women gazing at the strange fruit of the war-pear tree.

"Like a scarecrow," said one of them.

"No, it isn't that," said another. "You know, I saw some years ago how they pulled up a limping Communist soldier on our mulberry tree, and you know, he got as black as the devil himself, you couldn't even look at him. Now, this one here, well, you could almost say he's got handsomer."

"He looks like he was smiling," said a third old woman, "especially if you look at him sideways."

"He always smiled anyway," a fourth one explained. "But why did he do it?"

They all looked at Marika now, but Marika was sniffling and wiping her nose and they could hardly drag anything out of her. She did not know anything, daddy wasn't complaining of anything, last night he was just like he always was, so sad, but he was not angry. She woke up twice last night because she heard him talk in his sleep, though he used to do that always, but now he laughed too. She heard him going out of the room towards dawn, but then she fell asleep, and in the morning she wasn't even looking for him. She swept the room, and made the beds, and built a fire, and she noticed only then that something like a man was hanging on the tree. And she noticed that only because the other trees were full of crows and they were screeching loudly.

One of the women said that he must have suddenly lost his wits, another one suggested that he was drunk, but most of them agreed with a fat widow who blamed the new-fangled bad morals for everything. None of them thought of Etel.

# XXIII

WHEELS are always turning round—Mátyás knew that, he used to say so himself while the peasants were in vogue, but he never expected that they would have to get off the high horse so soon. But they had to, just the same. There was no more fraternization with the gentlemen, they could no longer sell their vinegar, sour wine, even the stills were taken away from them—although no one touched the taxes. Mátyás wondered why it had been like that for a while and why was it this way now? Why had even wild weeds passed for cultured wheat for a couple of years and why did they now harvest wild weeds instead of wheat, even those who had sowed cultured wheat? Why had they been flooded with banknotes for a year or two and why were they now forced to sell even their horses and cattle to be able to pay the taxes? The men were still the same men, even though they worked harder than ever before. There was no answer to all these questions, and Mátyás, if they occurred to him at all, pondered little over them. He had no time for them, there was enough burden on his lonely old shoulders without them. He had become a silent man since he had been left alone with Marika and the little namesake. For the namesake did not count yet, and the girl, although she grew fast and was quite a handsome creature as girls went, knew little if anything of social problems, like most members of her sex, consequently, Mátyás could not tell anybody that he had reestablished the *status quo* as regards his theories concerning state and government. For he went back once more to his original thesis that it was silly of the Lord to have created government—if inded He had created it at all, because there was not a word about it in the Bible. All the Bible said was that God had created Man and that man had become husbandman and shepherd, but where the revenue agent had sprung from, and the gendarme, and the tax-collector—why, the Bible did not say so much as one word about them!

And then there were all the banks and the contractors and the attorneys, and they all demanded money, even the Jewess showed up, because she remembered that Ferenc had never returned the spade he had taken from her stable when he had cut through the Baron's dam, nor had he ever paid for it. Mátyás stood bewildered among all these blackmailers and asked the Baron to help him. The Baron, no longer afraid of his competitor, directed his steward to look after his godson's inheritance. And so they had to sell Ferenc's lands, his cattle; the farm with the artesian well and the half-built mill all of which had been mortgaged. The Baron's intervention helped a little nevertheless, for they did rescue a million or two for the orphans, which was deposited with the Public Guardian.

Thus it was no wonder that the caretaking of Ferenc's grave was left wholly to the Lord, because Mátyás had no time to grow ivy on it. On the other hand, it mattered little what one used as a quilt on his grave. Mátyás had already heard of dead who came back from their graves complaining that they couldn't rest because their relatives cried so much their shrouds got all wet—but he had never heard of one who came back to complain because he had no ivy on his grave.

Nor did Mátyás worry much when a letter, addressed to Ferenc, was delivered to him. He opened it and saw that it was either in Jewish or in English, so he just pushed it back into its envelope and put it on the window sill. He did not mind if it got lost; most probably it was from another blackmailer who wanted money.

But the letter did not get lost. It was thrown about for a couple of weeks, then Mátyás made up his mind to show it to the director; he most probably knew English too, let him take a look at it. Who knew what was in it; someone might be wanting his farm, and then he would be left out in the cold for his old days.

The director was not in the Museum. The doorkeeper told Mátyás that the director had gone abroad to get cured of his cough.

"I can't go that far after him," Mátyás declared sadly; but when he told the doorkeeper what he wanted and showed him the letter, the doorkeeper discovered that it was in Russian. And that was good, for right around the corner lived a good friend of the director's, an attorney, he spoke Russian too, he could translate it for him. The doorkeeper called him up right away.

"He'll do it for the director's sake out of friendship."

The attorney telephoned back that he would do it if the old fellow hurried over to him right away, because he had to go to court.

The old fellow hurried, he even took two steps instead of one at every pace. His boots no longer shambled, they pounded the city-pavement loudly, and—he himself did not know why—there rose in his heart a peculiar feeling of excitement. But when he got to the attorney's office he managed to control himself. He handed over the blue envelope with one of his customary jokes:

"Find out, sir, whether it'll rain or not?"

The attorney pulled the letter out of the envelope and as he did so, a small photograph fell out. He did not even glance at it, just pushed it aside. Mátyás did not care very much for it either, all he saw was that there were some people on it. He watched the attorney, and although the

feeling of excitement still clutched at his throat, he reflected that they could easily slice three lean tax-collectors
out of this one fat attorney, though, come to think of it, it
would be better to make one attorney out of three tax-
collectors, especially such a friendly one as this one here.

"Well, my friend," said the attorney when he got to the
end of the letter, "do you know a man by the name of
Pavel Antonovitch who lives in the city of Kazan in
Russia?"

Mátyás told him that he did not.

"Now, this Pavel Antonovitch writes here that he has
been thinking a lot of Uncle Mátyás, and Aunt Roza, and
Etel, and of little Peter——"

"Peter?" Mátyás began to remember. "Why, this must
be Spirituto, though it seems he's changed his name."

"Who is Spirituto?"

"He is a Russky and he used to be a prisoner of war
on our farm, that is to say, not on ours, but on Ferenc's.
He used to be Piros's Russky."

"Then that's the one," the attorney said and picked up
the photograph. "Do you know this man here?"

There were a man and a woman on the picture, holding hands. The man was a long-bearded Russky, but he
had little hair—it was possible, of course, that it was
shorn. There were boots on his legs, and wide pants, but
he had no waistcoat, only a shirt, and the bottom of that
hung out from beneath his belt. The woman was rather
fattish.

"I don't know who they are," Mátyás said, putting down
the picture.

"Just look at it more carefully. At the man. You know
him!"

"Could it be Spirituto?" Mátyás wondered, but he was
very doubtful about it. "I don't think he could ever become such a grown-up man. No, sir, it couldn't be him."

"Of course not. Too bad your wife isn't here, she would recognize him at once."

Mátyás began to blink. He held out the picture at arm's length and examined it carefully.

"Sir—if you please, sir——"

He glanced at the attorney, then looked at the picture again. The attorney smiled and nodded:

"That's him! Say it."

"Rokus! My Rokus!" Mátyás had not yelled so loudly for years. "Why, you could even see the scar on his forehead where the horse kicked him when he was a child. God bless him, that's Rokus! Lord, it's too bad Roza can't see it. And who is this woman? It looks to me as if she had been kicked by a horse too, on her nose. Guess she was Rokus's Russian wife, am I right?"

"Was?" the attorney laughed. "She is! They are both alive and well, both of them."

Mátyás leaned against the desk and held fast to its edge. He opened and closed his mouth but no sound came forth. He stammered even when he regained his voice.

"What? You mean—alive—Ro—Rokus? Alive? He? God Almighty!"

The attorney made him sit down and offered him a cigarette. Mátyás began to pull himself together. He thanked him for his kindness, but he did not smoke cigarettes. Rather a pipe. He pulled it out of his pocket, lighted it three times, but the pipe would not work. He did not notice that he put the match next to the pipe and not above it. But the attorney noticed it and lighted the fourth match himself. The pipe began to smoke and Mátyás began to find the floor beneath him a little firmer.

"So my son is alive? Is it in the letter? In this one?"

"Yes, in that one," the attorney answered and began to read the letter to him. It was a very long one. Mátyás listened to it carefully and when the attorney asked him whether he understood it, he said:

"Yes, sir, I did. Rokus is found, God's given him back to us."

The attorney scratched his ear and looked at his watch.

"And the money?"

Of course, Mátyás did not want this great joy for nothing. He took out his purse.

"How much do I pay you for your kindness?"

The attorney laughed irritatedly.

"It isn't that, my friend. Put that purse away now, you'll have to open it wider. Now the question is, what's going to happen to the fifty millions?"

Mátyás bent forward.

"What fifty millions, sir?"

"Now listen to me carefully; I'll sum up what's in the letter," and he began to walk up and down in the room.

"Ferenc, it seems, asked Spirituto to find out all about Rokus. The Russky did so. He writes here that Rokus is living in the city of Minsk, in this and this street, the address is in the letter. It seems that woodcutters found Rokus in the Siberian woods, beneath some dried leaves, and they took him to their house. Rokus recovered, but he was afraid to continue the journey alone, so he turned back to Russia. He had some Tartar innkeeper there, so he went back to her. They lived peacefully together until Rokus got tired of her and begged her to let him go home to his family. The Tartar woman told him that he could go if he paid her for the room and board she had given him these past years. Otherwise she would not give him one copper for the trip. Rokus doesn't want to start off afoot because it is too far away. Now the ransom, according to the woman's figures, is fifty million Hungarian korona, but this sum includes the expenses for the four months from the mailing of this letter to the time your money will get there. But she will not wait one more minute, she will go back to her country at the end of the four months, and if the money does not get there in time, she will take Rokus with her, either as her husband or as her helper, that depends entirely on Rokus. But one thing is sure: if she takes him with her she'll never let him go again. Since Rokus doesn't want to be a camel-herd and since he doesn't want the woman either, he asks you to redeem him from his sad prison, even if you have to sell the farm to do it, after all, he says, he will get it some day anyway. Send the money at once, because the money must be there at such and such a date. He can get a passport from the Polish consul the minute the money gets there. But if the money doesn't get there in time, you'll never see Rokus again in this life. Do you understand it now?"

"Yes," Mátyás answered in a very low voice.

"Now look here, I underline the address in the letter with red ink. You'll have to send the money to this address. Any bank will do it for you. But take care of the letter, because if you lose it, you'll never see your son again. Now let's see, how much time have you? Four weeks, eight weeks, nine weeks—you still have four weeks to send off the money. Look, I'll put down the last date in the corner of the letter. But take care of it!"

Mátyás put the letter into his purse, the purse into his inner pocket, above his heart, and pressed his hand against it. He did not take his hand off until he reached the inn where his wagon was waiting for him, and there he took it off only to take the whip out of the driver's seat. He cracked it, then went to the tailboard to untie the horse and hitch him up. Mátyás went, and went, until a woman shouted at him:

"Uncle, you've lost our whip."

Mátyás looked around. It was a young woman who shouted at him, God bless her for her kindness. He was on the highway, near the bald mulberry trees. Yes, the whip had slid from his hands, there it was, on the highway, in the dust—but where was the wagon, and the horse, damn it! They had been left in the yard of the inn and he had started off like a fool afoot. He had already covered almost half of the distance without having noticed it.

Yes, like a fool—Mátyás knew that, and he sat down in the ditch, in the shade, to fill up his pipe. So it would cost fifty million to get Rokus back? But where would he get the fifty million? Let's see, how much was that? How much was fifty million in old money? The bank had taken over Ferenc's land for forty-two million. True, the prices had gone down since, but lately they'd begun to climb again, now that they were building the railroad. Fifty million, fifty million. . . . Well, if he were to sell his land together with the house. . . . Mátyás cracked the whip and rose and went back to the inn, for the horse.

And while the horse was slowly trudging along on the road homeward bound, Mátyás was seeing all sorts of beautiful things in the smoke of his pipe and the dust of the road. So God was merciful and good after all, to have kept for him his only son, to have kept his being alive a secret until Roza had gone and Etel had gone and Ferenc had gone, to give him back now, so that he should not be all alone for the twilight of his days, so that there should be somebody to take out of his hands the hoe and the scythe. The children would be happy too, they would have a daddy again, although he was only Marika's father by blood. But then he could not very well belittle the other child either; after all, his wife had born the boy too, though not by him, but then he was not at home then. Marika was not Ferenc's daughter, yet he had treated her as if she had been his own. So it would be Rokus's duty to take on Matyika, and then all three of them could have a caretaker. But, how could Rokus take care of them if they would have to sell the land in order to get him home?

How could a beggar take care of three other beggars?

The wagon was already in the sand and Mátyás noticed the sweep of his well. He rose a little in the driver's seat, and he saw the bluish-green grapevines, the rich apple trees, the blond rye waving gently in the tender breeze, the land which had borne bread for his father, his grandfather, his great-grandfather, his great-great-grandfather, whose every mound and hummock had been soaked in the sweat of his brow, whose every lump he knew, by color, by smell, by the feel of it. Too bad that this was all that was left—and now he should sell this too in order to redeem his son? In order that, for his old days, and together with his son, he should become a hired hand, a helper, a farmhand, some one else's servant? Why, then he would not be buried from this old house! From this old house, from which his father, his mother, his wife had been buried? No, not even the Lord Almighty Himself could demand that of him!

Mátyás stopped the wagon when he reached the shore of the lake and got out of it. He decided to do it at once. He took the purse out of his pocket and hurled the blue envelope as far as his old arms could hurl it, into the water. He looked back only when he had got into his seat again. Then he noticed that the blue envelope was on the shore again, caught by some grass; the waves had sent it back.

"That's right, I forgot the picture."

He got off again, pulled the picture out of the wet envelope, put it into his purse, and threw the envelope back into the water. But now he waited; he wanted to see it sink. The letter floated for a while in the center of the ripples, then slowly swam ashore. The lake that had killed Peter and taken Etel was tired of further sacrifices; it did not want to take the old man's son from him.

He fished the envelope out of the water with the handle of the whip and looked around. He saw an ancient stone-axe lying in the sand, a ten thousand year old inheritance from the ancient Mátyáses. He picked it up, stuck it into the envelope, twisted the paper at its end, then flung it into the water once more. There was a splash, and the lake had one more secret to guard. The sad prisoner was going to Fergana to milk camels, and Mátyás went back to the market place because he remembered that he had to look for a helper, the rye would be ready to be mowed by next week.

A month later, after the harvest, when he had already got some money for the new wheat too, Mátyás went up to the Reverend and asked him if he could have a requiem mass celebrated in memory of a living person.

"No, you can't do that," smiled the Reverend, "but you can have a high mass celebrated and you can dedicate it to a proper, godly purpose expressed by that certain person."

"Why, that's just what I want," Mátyás said and paid the fee with relieved heart. The Reverend did not ask any more questions, did not ask what the saintly purpose would be, he just put down the date in his calendar, and was happy that this stubborn old man had such pious intentions.

The stubborn old man turned back from the door.

"Pard' me, Reverend, could you show me the country of the Tartars on the map?"

"Why, certainly," said the Reverend, but now he asked him why he wanted to see it.

"I've just been thinking about a lot of things, and I've thought of that too."

The Reverend opened the encyclopedia and showed Mátyás a map. That was it.

"Well, it isn't exactly a big piece of land," Mátyás said, after a close examination, "but nice grass must be growing there, judging by the drawing here. Now, do you know where that county is that's called—wait a minute—Ferka—

Terka—I don't know what it's called."

No, the Reverend did not know that. But when Mátyás asked him whether it was true that the Tartars were dog-headed, he laughed.

"Oh, no, of course not. They look almost like we do."

And he searched back and forth in the encyclopedia book until he found a picture under which it was written that this was a Tartar woman. Mátyás looked at it and saw that her nose was just like the nose of the woman who held Rokus's hand in the picture above his heart, in the purse; hers must have also been kicked by a horse. And Mátyás was very glad to have seen this, because now he knew that the Reverend was telling the truth.

And in the autumn, after vintage, while listening all night long to the bubbling of the fermenting must, he re-membered Gyurka Messzi, who occasionally did tell a cock-and-bull story, but, on the whole, knew a lot of things and had travelled much in the world. So the next day he called him in as he was passing by his farm and asked him whether it was true that he had become a Nazarene?

"It's true all right," said Gyurka a bit melancholily. "After all, one has to look after one's redemption some day."

"True, true," Mátyás said, "but it isn't the right religion for a watchman."

"Why, that's just the nice part of it, you can't tell lies and can't steal."

"And you can drink? Say, wine?"

The watchman confessed that as regards wine he had reformed the Nazarene religion. He drank the wine, but said no toasts.

Thus, there having been no theological objections to it, Mátyás brought out a bottle of new wine and they be-gan to talk over the problems of the world.

Mátyás asked Gyurka whether he knew anything at all

about Tartary?

"Well, not much, except that I wouldn't like to be a watchman there."

"Why not?"

"Well, because I'd have to walk around there on stilts. Otherwise my head wouldn't show above the wheat."

"Is the soil so good there?"

"It's very good, but that's about all I know of it."

That was enough for Mátyás. Where the soil was good one did not have to worry for the men.

They lighted their pipes and, for a few seconds, they kept silent. Then Gyurka broke the silence.

"Well, the war's done a lot of harm, you know."

"Well, yes," Mátyás said, and lighted another match in the security of his cupped palm because his pipe wouldn't draw properly. Then he shrugged his shoulders. "It's over now and the plough covers up everything."

"That's true," said Gyurka. "But it was a pity for Ferenc and Etel to go like that. They could have lived for a while yet, that's what they were created for. My Lord, it seems like yesterday that I toasted them at their wedding."

Mátyás kicked up an ancient vertebra with the toe of his boot. The breeze turned the decayed bone into dust in a minute.

"Look at that. The director told me some years ago that this might have been a king in the old days. Now what's become of him? The earth's eaten him up, because the earth is the strongest of us all. It ate up my father, and his father, too. And it'll eat me up, and you, too. The earth eats up everybody. But others come in our place and the earth is left to them."

And he blew out a big cloud of smoke.

This book was set in 11 point Granjon on the linotype, printed and bound by J. J. Little & Ives Co. New York, U. S. A.